In Search of Beef Stroganoff

A Novel

by

Robin Coyle

This is a work of fiction. Names, characters, places, and incidents are either the product of the author's imagination or are used fictitiously, and any resemblance to actual persons, living or dead, businesses, companies, events or locales is entirely coincidental.

Cover Design: Paige Coyle
Cover Photography: D. J. Ramirez

First Printing, 2018

ISBN: 978-0692099766

CreateSpace
www.createspace.com

For Richard, Amanda, Jill, and Paige . . . with love.

You encouraged me to do this.

And you believed I could.

And that was a wonderful gift.

Table of Contents

Part I: My Story

Chapter 1: Regrets

If only. Those must be the two saddest words in the world.

— Mercedes Lackey

If only . . . if only what?

My answer to that question is steeped in regret.

Much to my mother's chagrin, cooking didn't interest me when she was alive. If Mom wasn't at work in the garden or on the porch with a book in her lap, she was in the kitchen. Cooking and food were the fabric of her soul. She was happiest when the cookie jar was full, when a casserole was ready to deliver to a neighbor, or when a pot of soup on the stove filled the house with the warm scent of comfort. She offered to teach me to cook, but cooking felt like a burden to me, not a pleasure. She even begged me to join her for a bonding moment over making pesto sauce. I dodged her attempts to lure me into the kitchen with the aroma of toasted pine nuts and the purr of the food processor as it swirled fresh basil leaves and olive oil.

Now, mind you, I love to eat delicious food, but the dicing, measuring, and stirring required to put food on the table bored me. That was the case, at least, until I reached my late twenties and a latent gene inherited from my mother stirred in me. Creating beautiful meals now brings me great pleasure. But my passion for cooking happened too late for my mother to witness. She died eight years ago.

Mom never saw me dusted with flour as I pulled a cake from the oven, or with my brow dewy from the steam rising from piquant sauces bubbling on the stove. If I had enjoyed cooking when she was alive, the time we would have spent together in the kitchen would be a cherished memory. Also, I would know how to make her beef stroganoff.

At every holiday, death, birthday, and straight-A report card, Mom's beef stroganoff was the centerpiece. In my mind it signaled celebration, comfort, and love. I longed for the embrace of Mom's soothing stroganoff and wanted to feel close to her through the meal that always said, "I'm here for you." Mom called her stroganoff "a hug on a plate," and I needed one. I searched for her beef stroganoff recipe for months after she died. My greatest sadness, however, stems from knowing I took her for granted. I am left with an aching shame in my heart.

My memory of Mom's beef stroganoff is imprecise and vague, yet has a strange clarity. The exact ingredients, the cut of beef she used, and the seasonings she employed to make the velvety sauce remain a mystery to me. Did she serve her stroganoff over wide egg noodles, or on slim ribbons of fettuccine? Did her recipe call for mushrooms? Did she use pearl onions, or did she dice a sweet onion that left its scent on the cutting board for days? Those details escape me, no matter how hard I try to recall them. However, I know if I tasted her recipe today I would recognize it in an instant.

My dad died a month after I was born. He had a life insurance policy, but Mom still had to find work to support us. Money was tight, yet I never felt anything but bounty during my childhood. Mom took a job as a cake decorator in a bakery, thus finding her place in the working world. She would come home from work on a wave scented with vanilla and chocolate.

Her wedding cakes became legendary within a 100-mile radius of the bakery. It was rumored that people turned down invitations to weddings if the cake wasn't going to be one of my mom's creations. Until Mom started making cakes in our town, the centerpiece of most wedding receptions was a ghastly tower of white cake staggering under a mountain of lard-based pink rosettes. Mom often adorned her cakes with fondant, which at the time was unknown to the Midwestern palate. The smooth, finished cake would dance on the table with a ring of fresh flowers at its base or Tiffany-blue ribbons of frosting cascading down every layer. Or, she would use silver beads made of sugar to create intricate scrolls on the sides. One bride told her to do whatever she fancied, so Mom made a multi-layer wedding cake of strawberry shortcake. The bride was ecstatic, but the mother-in-law was less than pleased until she heard the mayor's wife call the cake "a triumph." Mom always cleverly hid the bride and groom's initials somewhere on the cake. The talk about town after each wedding was not about the bride's dress or the flowers, but about who had found the hidden initials on the cake.

Since I didn't know anything different, having a working mom and being a fatherless child didn't bother me. However, when I entered kindergarten, I was the only kid in my class with a single mother. My uniqueness gave a handful of my classmates the opening to be cruel. In tears, I ran to the teacher when a snot-nosed boy asked if my dad had run away because I was so ugly. The rest of his buddies joined the attack.

What I didn't understand is that, by reacting to their teasing, I brought on more. Had I laughed off their biting words, they would have soon been bored with the game and found another victim to needle. When they were old enough to know the words, they called me a "bastard" and asked if my mom was a "whore." Rather than turning my hostilities on the kids who taunted me, I fired my anger at my mom. I blamed her for my father's death. The sweet relationship with my mom soured, because it was safer to be angry with her than standing up to rotten three-foot-tall bullies.

To protect my fragile soul from my schoolmates' teasing, I developed a tough exterior and kept people at bay. If I didn't let people get close to me, they couldn't hurt me. Caring about other people took too much time away from my self-interests so I made selfishness a full-time job. As a result, I had few friends. People viewed me as a stiff, humorless child harboring a grudge. What the world didn't know, and what I didn't acknowledge, was that I was a frightened, sad little girl hiding behind an aloof exterior.

My mother was a saint. Well, she had a few flaws like all humans, but not when it came to my well-being. She endured my indifference and selfish behavior without a word of complaint. I came and went at my bidding without a "please," "thank you" or "may I" to be found. Perhaps her biggest fault as a mother was that she allowed me to treat her like shit. Self-indulgent, I turned to her only when I wanted something. I wasn't cruel, but I was removed and uncaring. While she was devoted to me, I was devoted to myself. My behavior was inexcusable. If I were my mom, I would have hated me.

But then I changed. A series of events during and after college altered how I viewed my place in the world. I forced myself to quit acting as if the sun and the moon revolved around me when I realized life wasn't going to be handed to me wrapped in pretty paper with a satin bow. I wanted to become a better person. Each event alone was not a big deal, but, when bundled in a package, they served a mighty blow.

Chapter 2: Bony Elbows and Knees

You don't have to suffer to be a poet;
adolescence is enough suffering for anyone.
— John Ciardi

Junior high was hell. There, I said it. Hell. The tweenage years are cruel. Rather than incarcerating our nation's criminals, we should send them to junior high school. That would teach them a lesson. Junior high-aged girls know how to spot an exposed nerve and pierce it with venom. Every girl in my school, except me, had breasts, pink lip-gloss, a boyfriend, and confidence. I watched with envy as the cool girls walked around the campus holding hands with the popular boys. I wanted a boyfriend, but I was skittish around boys and was also acutely aware of the angry pimples popping up around my nose. The boys had the same acne issues, but I somehow overlooked that. I carried dreamy schoolgirl crushes in my heart while I was in that strange preteen stage of taking an interest in boys but still secretly playing with Barbie dolls. My mom said it was my "boney elbows and knees phase."

By the time I was in junior high, many of my fellow classmates' parents were divorced, so I was no longer the only skinny kid with no father around. However, I was the only one with a dead father. That made me an anomaly. A freak. I hated seeing fathers drop off their children at school, painting sets for the drama club's play, and cheering for their kids at track meets. It wasn't fair. My mom attended every school function, but it always felt as if she had left my dad at home. I was sure she was responsible for my dad dying so young. Her explanation of his fatal reaction to an allergy medication seemed implausible. Even though the anger about my father's death was unfairly redirected at my mom, she worked hard to retrieve my love from the bottom of my unforgiving soul. She made a good effort, but I was stubborn.

Sandra was my best friend in junior high, but she started out as my mortal enemy. She disliked me from the moment I walked into the classroom. Our lockers were assigned in alphabetical order, which meant her locker was above mine. Like a two-hundred-pound linebacker, she blocked access to my locker until seconds before the bell rang to signal the end of the five-minute passing period. She was a wisp of a thing—and a nerd, too—but she could have prevented a star football player from fetching his math book before class. Because of Sandra's strong-arm maneuvers, I did many stints in the principal's office for chronic tardiness. During a dozen rounds of detention, I picked up schoolyard trash with the kids who were caught smoking in the parking lot or penalized for tormenting their teacher. There was mousy me, with acne, braces, and unbecoming eyeglasses alongside scrawny ruffians as we picked up greasy cupcake wrappers and half-eaten apples.

My mom was upset with me for being sent to the principal's office, but it mostly saddened her that I wouldn't explain the reason I was often late to class. One night at dinner, she let out a pained, ragged sigh while reading a note from the principal. I gave in and told her about Sandra, The Bully. Mom dried my tears and offered to beat up Sandra. She also gave me some tips on throwing left jabs to get the girl away from my locker. The twinkle in her eye and the goofy pantomime of a heavyweight boxer deflated my frustration and indignation over Sandra's mean behavior and made me giggle. Then Mom said, “Instead of doing time in juvenile hall for assault, I suggest that tomorrow you get to your locker first. Stand aside, smile at Sandra, and say, ‘After you.’ She won’t know what to think.” The next day I took Mom’s advice and ad-libbed a bobbed curtsy in front of our lockers. Sandra blinked at me. She didn’t block my locker again after that day, but she still hated me.

Our teacher, poor Mr. Silva, was shaped like a penguin, and walked like one too. His students liked to waddle behind him down the hallway and flap their bent elbow wings. The one time I dared to join in on the mocking, he turned and caught me mid-flap. My punishment was an hour-long sentence scraping chewing gum from the undersides of the desks in his classroom.

Mr. Silva paired up the students to work on a report about a South American country, and I had the bad luck of being teamed with Sandra. We pushed our gum-free pink plastic and grey metal desks together and argued about the format for our report. She scoffed at my ideas until I suggested we make a chart of the country’s export commodities with hand-drawn cutouts to represent each product. The idea appealed to Sandra’s creative sensibilities, and she finally warmed to me. Learning that I, too, was crazy about horses, she adopted me as her best friend.

I suspect Sandra had bullied me because I was the only girl in school who was lower on the totem pole than she was. As friends, we were a goofy-looking pair with our chicken legs, feet that looked as though God had bent off too much at the bottom, and freakishly big ears. We were more bobble-heads than beauty-queens. Why is it that, at that awkward age, eye doctors feel the need to prescribe glasses and dentists insist on braces? Isn’t junior high punishment enough?

In Search of Beef Stroganoff

As with many eleven-year-old girls, Sandra and I were relentless in our desire to own a horse. I launched a valiant campaign to convince my mom to buy a horse for me. My three-page letter to her outlined why I deserved a horse and described how unreasonable she was for not granting my wish. This is not a good tactic if you want to win your case. My mom's refusal to buy me a horse because she couldn't afford it was yet another injustice waged against my happiness. Sandra had no luck with her parents, either. The closest we came to being horse owners was six riding lessons that summer.

Mom started her own wedding cake business, but the income was modest, and a horse still wasn't in the budget. She named her business after me: "Meredith Makes Marry." I didn't understand her play on words until I was in high school. Mom paid me to help her set up the blasted cakes, and my Saturdays were spent in wedding reception halls, musty church basements, or at the country club. I complained and sighed every time my mom was in earshot, but I did love seeing the wedding gowns and flowers, and especially checking out the cute groomsmen.

Mom quietly tried to make it up to me for not buying a horse. She gave me horse figurines for every occasion and teased me about my extensive collection. "Be careful," she said. "If you snore in the middle of the night, you might start a stampede." I never asked her to, but she would bring home an armload of horse-y books for me from the library every week. Given the popularity of the topic for my age bracket, I imagine she had to wait by the depository for other moms to return books I had not yet read. Mom also gave me a subscription to a horse aficionado magazine. I cut out photos from the magazines and plastered them all over my closet door.

Chapter 2: Bony Elbows and Knees

My fascination with horses eventually waned, and I moved on to teen idols. It took Mom a day to scrape the pop star photos I cut out from *Tiger Beat* magazine off the closet door when she painted my room. She never said anything, but I imagined she cursed me under her breath.

It was a momentous event when an out-of-state developer built an indoor mall and multiplex movie theater in my nondescript Midwest hometown in Nebraska. The town turned out for the grand opening, as if the President of the United States was slated to do the ribbon cutting instead of the Corn Belt Princess from the State Fair. Because it was the 1980s, the crowd of girls at the opening had teased their bangs and sprayed their hair with half a can of hairspray. We had to be careful around an open flame. I wasn't the only preteen dressed in legwarmers over jeans and a sweater with shoulder pads bigger than a linebacker's.

I insisted my mom drop Sandra and me off a block from the mall so we wouldn't be seen with her. In a brazen moment of criminal behavior on the walk to the mall, I stole a compact of neon-blue eye shadow from the dime store. Our giggles while we put it on in the mall bathroom brought stares from two elderly ladies, so we tossed our hair and waltzed out. We felt sophisticated and worldly, but more likely the blue glow over our eyes made us look like prepubescent drag-queens. Guilt over my petty theft haunted me for a week, so I left four dollars on the dime store's counter.

Another big event that year was spending five days at sixth-grade Outdoor Education Camp. It meant hiking, classes held in mountain meadows, and not getting any sleep in dormitory cabins because we would play games and gossip all night. I couldn't wait. The school secretary sent home a sheaf of papers about the camp, including a chaperone volunteer form, a packing list, and the rules and regulations. Before my mom could see it, I threw away the volunteer form. The rules dealt primarily with forbidding any interaction between campers of the opposite sex. The letter from the principal, which I couldn't throw away because it included the packing list, read, "Here is Camp Minihehe's mailing address, in case you parents want to send your 'little scampers' a letter." Checking my duffle bag against the packing list twenty times, I then hid the letter with the camp's address in a book in the living room. I wanted to be doubly sure the kids couldn't tease me about getting a letter from my mommy.

Adrenaline made it impossible to sit still as the bus pulled out of the school parking lot and headed to Camp Minihehe. Sandra and I were assigned to a cabin with four of the most popular girls at school. This was our chance to impress them. They would be forced to speak to us, because we would be sharing a cabin with them for a week. And when they saw my super-cool down parka, they would beg me to be their friend. My class unloaded off the bus, and the four popular girls got into a heated conversation with Mr. Silva. I later found out they were protesting their assignment to a cabin with Sandra and me. He didn't budge, but I wish he had.

Nights in the cabin were miserable. My cabin mates played "Light as a Feather, Stiff as a Board," told ghost stories, and braided each other's hair. Sandra and I weren't invited to join them, so we had to pretend to have fun playing the card game "War" until it wasn't fun pretending anymore. We crawled into our bunks, and while I counted the knotholes in the ceiling, Sandra counted the stains on the bottom of my mattress. Mornings couldn't come fast enough.

Chapter 2: Bony Elbows and Knees

I wore my down parka every day, because it was the only thing I had packed that had any potential of impressing my classmates. But it didn't work. Wearing the parka was ridiculous, because the weather turned unseasonably warm, and all of the other girls were frolicking on the hiking trails in tank-tops and shorts. The old woman in me wondered why there wasn't a dress code forbidding that much exposed skin.

We had mail call after breakfast on the third day of "Camp Mini-Hell," as I called the miserable place. I was the only one who didn't get to strut to the front of the dining hall to collect a letter from home. Some campers received multiple letters. Grandma, their younger sister, and the boy next door saw fit to write letters. How could my mom embarrass me this way? I know, I had barred Mom from writing to me, but how did she not know that every scamper but me would get mail?

My mom's smile was a welcome sight when the bus pulled into the school parking lot after five days of hell at camp. I hadn't slept, my poison oak rash was weeping, and I was no closer to being one of the popular girls than before camp started. Sadly, the camp experience confirmed to me that popular status would never be mine.

At home, I dropped my duffle bag on my bedroom floor and peeled off my down parka. The jacket smelled rank. On my dresser were a stack of envelopes and a note from my mom that read, "You didn't want me to write you while you were at camp, but I did it anyway. I didn't want to be an embarrassment to you, so I didn't mail the letters." There was one letter for every day I was away at camp.

I survived junior high, but not without hopeless bouts of tears, visits to the dermatologist, and an embarrassing moment when a boy lifted up my skirt when we had to learn how to square dance in stupid P.E class. There were countless other moments when I was mortified at school, like the time I told the teacher I didn't feel well and she refused to excuse me to the nurse's office. Throwing up on your desk during math is the world's most horrible thing to have happen while you are in school. But I, with my boney elbows and knees, endured junior high to the end of what seemed like eternity.

Life eased a little during high school. My braces came off, I tortured my mom until she let me get contacts, and I sprouted breasts overnight. My body finally grew into the size of my feet, and my boney angles softened into curves. But my classmates still thought of me as the fatherless geek from grammar school and junior high. I longed to be part of the beautiful people who ate lunch in the quad, but I wasn't welcome. I tried eating my lunch in the girls' locker room so I could hide, but the rank smell of sweaty socks and moldy shower stalls ruined my appetite. Eating lunch in the cafeteria with the band-freaks and the chemistry-brains was my only other option.

I found a safe place in the school's music department when I signed up for the girls' glee club with my fellow outcasts and non-cheerleaders. Mom always had music playing at home. Her tastes ranged from classical to show tunes to hillbilly rock. The others in glee groaned when the choir director selected "The Way You Look Tonight," and I pretended I didn't know every word. After two years in glee club, I auditioned for a coveted spot in the choir. It was a place for the elite-among-the-geeks, and I qualified. Mom was overjoyed that I had made the choir and treated me to dinner at my favorite restaurant to celebrate. She didn't complain that my favorite restaurant of the moment was a roadside hamburger stand. In a rare moment of solidarity over dinner, we called out our favorite songs and challenged each other to remember the lyrics.

For once, I didn't protest when Mom offered to volunteer at my school. She was the sheet music librarian and ironed our choir robes before performances. My heart swelled when the other choir kids called her Choir Mom. I suspected that some of the tenors had a crush on her, including the music director. He always found reasons to be in the music closet when Mom was filing.

Never cool enough to be a cheerleader or a homecoming princess, I decided to try out for school mascot, the Fighting Pirate, during my senior year. I didn't really like football or even understand the rules, but I had a crush on the defensive right end. I figured the only way he would ever notice me was if I made an ass of myself on the sidelines. No one at the school had self-esteem low enough to try out for mascot, so I figured my odds of landing the position were pretty good. However, I was still leery of putting myself out there. The ever-perky spirit commissioner gave me the nudge I needed to try out when she made the mascot a two-person job. If I could persuade Sandra to try out with me, we could be the Dueling Pirates, or, as the tryout flyer read, the "Dualing Pirates." *Oh brother,* I thought. *Did she mean the Dualing Pirates, as in two pirates?*

Sandra and I worked up a tryout routine to perform in front of the school student body. It wasn't good, but not bad. At least it wasn't as bad as the other dual mascot hopefuls. The votes were counted, and there was a problem with the results. The ballot for mascot allowed you to vote for individuals rather than the team. Sandra won, and I didn't. In a political maneuver worthy of study by historians on the art of détente, the spirit commissioner found a way to recount the ballots so that Sandra and I won as a team.

In Search of Beef Stroganoff

I loved being mascot with Sandra. Unspoken protocol required that the real cheerleaders fraternize with us on the football sidelines. Before each game, the cheerleaders gathered around me as if I were a beloved member of their clique. I was flattered until I realized they did so because my mom always packed a box of homemade cookies in my gym bag for me to share with the cheerleaders. I didn't mind. Mom's cookies helped me feel like a part of the group.

The cute defensive end didn't know I existed, not even after he plowed into me when he sacked the opposing team's quarterback near the sidelines. My papier-mâché head came off, my knees were caked with mud, and I was in heaven because he touched me. I also had a strained back and had to take muscle relaxants for a week to help with the pain. After football season, a spiked basketball gave me a black eye, a member of the baseball team mooned me, and the golf course banned me from cheering for the golf team. The novelty of being a team mascot wore thin.

The last semester of my senior year, I was stuck taking home economics, because it was the only elective that had space. Mom was delighted, however, and offered to help me when we were assigned planning a menu for a themed dinner party using an imaginary budget. I let Mom help me, because I had no idea where to begin. The assignment brought us together, and it was the first time in a long time I voluntarily did anything in the kitchen. Mom acted as though I was a celebrity granting her an audience. I was a little embarrassed for her.

The teacher selected one of the menus, and at the end of the school year the class prepared each course of the menu for a party for the parents. I didn't tell Mom about the invitation. After school on the day of the party, Mom's eyes were rimmed with red, but I didn't have to ask why. I overheard her on the phone telling her friend I hadn't invited her to the home economics class party. How did she find out? A pang of remorse pierced my teenage armor. I invited Mom to go to a movie with me that night, but she declined. I don't blame her for that.

Sandra was a star student without the need to study. She absorbed the information by simply carrying her books around. I, however, was passive about school and earned average grades. Sandra took chemistry, calculus, and Brain Surgery 101 while I relaxed in typing class, choir, and Daydreaming 101. I learned a little of the subject matter and bullshitted my way through the rest. Sandra got into world-class universities and received academic scholarships, whereas I was lucky to find a college with standards low enough to accept me.

Like most high school seniors, I longed for the freedom and independence college would offer. I wanted to stay out all night, set my own schedule, and become an actualized adult. In college I hoped to grow wings and show the world what I had to offer. I felt strangled by my mom's apron strings. (Who am I fooling? What I wanted to do was drink beer at frat parties.)

Chapter 3: Freedom, in the Form of College

College is like a fountain of knowledge—
and the students are there to drink.

— Author Unknown

Like a miser, I had saved the money I had earned setting up Mom's wedding cakes and babysitting, and I bought a car for college. I was a ruthless negotiator at the used-car lot. In the heat of the battle, the salesman became so infuriated he felt the uncontrollable need to call me stupid. He then hurried after me and blubbered his apologies as I stormed out. The filibuster strategy worked to my advantage, because he ended up giving me a great deal. The car's mileage was low, but it looked as if someone had attacked the car with a ball peen hammer or had parked it in the middle of a golf course driving range. The dents on the car didn't matter to me, because she was mine. I named her Athena, after the goddess of wisdom, courage, strength, and war.

The notion of a tiny dorm room didn't stop me from filling Athena to the sunvisors with my bedding, clothes, small appliances, and every pair of shoes I owned. Mom squeezed into the front seat and rode the 200 miles to my school with my makeup box on her lap and her feet on a microwave. I turned up the radio to drown out Mom's sniffles and sighs. Mom unloaded my crap from the car while I waited in line to check into the dorm and pick up my key to freedom. I parked Athena in the student garage and left Mom to haul my boxes up to my room. Driving through the garage was like browsing a luxury used-car lot. Athena sputtered when she saw her new high-end neighbors and acted as though she were Sadie Hawkins at a debutante ball. I patted the dashboard to reassure her I still loved her. But I lied; I coveted the racy red convertible we parked next to.

Mom unpacked my clothes, shoes and blow dryer while I pretended to help, which consisted of rearranging where she put my school supplies and visiting with my neighbors. My room was set up, thanks to Mom, and she offered to treat me to a goodbye dinner. I declined the invitation, because I wanted to eat in the dining hall and make new friends. I drove her to the bus station, where we exchanged an awkward farewell. Anxious to return to the dorm, I ignored the reappearance of her tears. Her bus pulled away from the depot, and I ran two red lights in my hurry to get back to campus.

The dining hall was still closed, and with nowhere to go I went to my dorm. My roommate, Candi, had dumped her belongings in the middle of the room and left for parts unknown. Sitting on the corner of my bed, I said aloud to nobody, “Now what?” Tears left trails of mascara down my cheeks. The independence I once craved now echoed with loneliness, fear, and dread. I got what I wanted, but did I really want it?

I discovered I wasn’t the center of the college universe during the first few weeks of school. Grappling with getting into the classes I wanted was no less of a hassle than mastering the subject matter afterwards. Pompous professors doled out reading assignments as though their classes were the only ones the students were taking, and they delegated the menial task of grading exams and essays to graduate-level teaching assistants. My papers earned mediocre grades, and I was lucky if a TA took the time to scribble a terse comment. Gold stars and smiley faces were nowhere to be found. I was sure the grad students had something against me. Even the academic counselors had the audacity to not drop what they were doing when I called for an appointment. College was an enormous pond, and I was a big nobody.

Until college, I earned average grades, and I assumed college would be the same way. All I would need to do was to jot notes in lectures, skim the readings, write a few essays, and go to parties. Projects and papers were an annoyance, and I started them at the last minute. Procrastination and I were best friends.

My first set of grades came in the mail, and I was dumbfounded. The abysmal GPA sobered me up. My easiest college class was harder than my most rigorous class in high school. I shouldn't have partied all night, dozed through lectures, created a dozen flashcards, and called it a day. That was when I understood that college required hard work. Serious hard work. Just because you *can* party all night doesn't mean you *should* party all night. From then on, I studied my butt off.

Life as an only child is solitary, and the prospect of a college roommate had excited me, even though at heart I was a loner. I was sure we would become best pals and share our most intimate secrets. We would stay up late and paint each other's nails, do homework together, and be a shoulder to cry on over a heart broken by some jerk. Her parents would adore me, because I am charming, or so I thought. Her family would invite me on winter break ski trips and insist on paying my way. They might even name me in their will.

Boy, was I wrong about the whole roommate situation.

Candi, my roommate, was obnoxious. First of all, she dotted the "i" in her name with a heart. That annoyed me.

What was she, twelve? Then there was her hair. Curly brown strands were everywhere . . . the sink, the floor, stuck to my socks, and on every article of clothing I owned. She shed like a dog in summer. I whined, complained, and pleaded that she vacuum, sweep, or shave her head. My pleas were to no avail, not even after I scraped copious amounts of hair from around the room and deposited a wad of the nasty mess with great fanfare on her pillow. It looked as though a cat had hacked up a hairball. I anticipated retaliation, but for days I got nothing—that is, until I fell into bed after a party without turning on the light. In the morning, I stumbled to the bathroom and saw in the mirror that a snarl of hair was plastered to my forehead, the same one I had placed on Candi's (with a heart-shaped "i") pillow. Ugh! She had exacted her hairy revenge.

The hair was annoying, but my biggest complaint about Candi was her sex life. With a voracious appetite for men, she ran through seven different guys each week like a New Orleans prostitute. She dropped everything, including her panties, whenever a boy crooked his finger at her. My roommate's early-morning walks of shame from fraternity row to our dorm room beat down a path as wide as an interstate highway, complete with rest stops, where she vomited up the tequila shots from the night before.

Bursting into my room one afternoon after class, the sight before me made me skid to a stop. Candi was on her knees in the center of the room. Her humongous breasts bobbed in rhythm to the beat of some guy's pleasure. She looked like a sword-swallower inhaling a zucchini. Seeing my naked roommate was bad enough, but I gagged when the massive football player with his pants puddled around his ankles gave me a thumbs-up. I did a U-turn and yelled through the closed door, "Put up a bloody sign!"

In Search of Beef Stroganoff

My neighbor stopped me as I flew down the hall and asked where I was headed in such a hurry. With plenty of colorful expletives about my lovely roommate, I described the orgy I had just witnessed. She invited me to hang out in her room until the passion subsided in mine. We entered her room and stopped dead in our tracks. Her bimbo roommate and some jock were dancing between the sheets.

I'm not a prude, and I didn't care how many sexually transmitted diseases were coursing through Candi's body. I just didn't want to be a witness to her exuberant libido. Nor did I want to hear about her frequent exchange of bodily fluids with randy boys. I stupidly assumed college would be about classes, parties and football games, not watching sex jam sessions.

Another one of Candi's glorious sexual exploits happened while I slept in my bed next to hers. To be clear, I wasn't asleep the whole time. My room was blissfully quiet and unoccupied when I crashed into bed in a party-induced, beer-buzzed state. Candi and her latest male conquest had slipped into the room during the night, hopped in bed and proceeded to enjoy each other's company, if you know what I mean. Either they had assumed I was passed out or they had thought they were being quiet, but their sex rattled the windows. With my pillow smothered over my face I thought happy thoughts to blot out their grunting. Where could I go at three in the morning?

Two hours later, they were at it again. The guy had stamina. I couldn't take it. Lights came on across the campus when I yelled, "Knock it off!" The headboard stopped banging against the wall. The other type of banging stopped, too.

My peaceful cocoon at home seemed hundreds of miles and a thousand memories away. In my room at home, I would snuggle in bed in the morning and listen to my mom rustling in the kitchen while she made breakfast. The aroma of pungent coffee and sizzling bacon wandered into my room. The comfort of home was the complete opposite of listening to your roommate boink a guy a mere three feet away from your head in a cramped dorm room. Did I appreciate home when I lived there? Nope, not a lick. If my doting mom made a ham-and-cheese sandwich for my school sack lunch instead of my favorite turkey and avocado on rye, I had the nerve to grumble. If Mom didn't put away my laundry, I pouted. The sound of her footsteps in the hall when she made her way to bed irritated me. Lord, I was a spoiled brat.

Candi and I reached an international peace accord over our living situation. The terms I negotiated were that she had to move out . . . or I would hurt her. Thank God she used her head for once—instead of her crotch—and found a new place to live. The university housing department found a replacement roommate for me. The clerk explained that the new girl wanted to move because her roommate did nothing but party and their lifestyles were not compatible. I took it as a good sign.

The new roommate, with the unfortunate name of Penelope, wasn't better, but she was a different brand of bad. She never left the room. Well, she attended classes and had a part-time job at the library, but she didn't stay out late at parties, eat in the dining hall, or visit home. Nothing. Her social life consisted of being hunched over her textbooks for hours. Beige wallpaper was more exciting. Penelope's diet was ramen noodles, saltine crackers, and instant coffee. How she wasn't more anemic than a kid from Ethiopia, I'll never know.

In Search of Beef Stroganoff

As an only child, my own space was not a luxury but a given. College was different. Classes are held in lecture halls that seat over a hundred, and an intimate meal means eating in the dining hall with five hundred of your closest friends. A visit to the library includes an unsuccessful search for a secluded study carrel. Parties were a crush of inebriated students in every room, including the hallway to the bathroom. Because Penelope planted herself in our room, the only time I was alone was when I locked myself in the bathroom. The masses of students didn't bother me until I lost the sanctuary of moments of privacy in my room. Like a bad haircut until it grows out, Penelope was always there. How would I last until the end of the school year?

I figured she was an orphan, because she never mentioned her family. She didn't receive calls from home, care packages didn't arrive, and she didn't scramble to book flights home for the holidays. Weird. If I weren't caught up in caring only about how she annoyed me by staying in the room all the time, I would have found her pathetic life sad. Instead, she imposed on my world that revolved around me, and me alone.

Candi won the prize for wretched roommates, but in hindsight, I know I was a terrible roommate as well. Poor Penelope. I sulked, slammed doors, and threw my dirty clothes on her side of the room. She didn't complain when I used her shampoo, stole her school supplies, and acted like an all-around bitch. If I cared one whit about anyone other than myself, I would have seen that she was a lovely, yet lonely person. If I had extended my friendship, walked with her to class, invited her to a party . . . anything . . . she might not have ended her life.

I learned about Penelope's gentle character from the letter she left on my bed. A small inheritance from her parents paid for her tuition and housing. With an apology, she said the reason she never went out was she sent the money from her job at the library to help support her aging grandmother. You see, her grandmother had raised Penelope and given her every ounce of her heart. The state-run senior facility where she lived provided the barest of essentials. Whenever she could, Penelope sent money to the nursing home social worker to supplement her grandmother's meager existence. The social worker bought her a fuzzy robe, chocolates, books and flowers to make her grandmother's life more tolerable in the featureless institution. My roommate sacrificed the carefree life of a college student for her grandmother. When her grandmother died before Christmas, devoted and depressed Penelope couldn't bear to go on. The last line of her letter to me made my guilt acute. It read, *"Meredith, thank you for being my friend."* Some friend I was.

Penelope's cousin made the funeral arrangements yet didn't bother to attend. The funeral was a sad gathering, only in part because Penelope had hanged herself with a sheet in the communal bathroom. The other reason the service was heartbreaking was that the meager assemblage was made up of me in a scratchy wool skirt, her grandmother's social worker, the priest, and the funeral director. That was it. The empty church echoed with my guilt about her suicide. The damn wool skirt was my version of St. John the Baptist's hair-shirt. I realized that my motivation in life was to please myself, and I wasn't concerned about others. I couldn't look in the mirror for a long time.

The university took pity on me after Penelope's suicide and moved me to a larger room with two roommates. Once again, the housing gods frowned on me. My two new roommates slept until noon, then snorted a line of coke and fired up the blender for the day's first round of frozen margaritas. *Good grief, how does anyone graduate from college?* I didn't ask for a new roommate, because, with my luck, the next housing assignment would be with an axe murderer, habitual gambler or heroin addict.

Holden Caulfield's angst paled in comparison to mine while I decided on a major. What if I picked a major and discovered after graduation I hated the field? Would I need to start college over in a new major? What if I hated that one, too? The decision paralyzed me. The academic counseling department grew tired of my whining. One exasperated advisor said, "For crying out loud, pick a major, and be done with it!"

I considered myself artistic and creative, but majoring in art would condemn me to a life of living on food stamps and coffee. I pondered majoring in English, but what does one do with it after graduation? Write books? Enter the world of print journalism? Math and I aren't on speaking terms, and science baffles me. Since I can't comprehend how electricity works, I crossed engineering off the list, too. Because I like kids, I thought about becoming a teacher, but I dismissed the notion in a hurry when I remembered I didn't care for the parents that were annoyingly attached to their children. I researched every major offered and, for one reason or another, rejected each one.

After sleepless nights, medications for an acid stomach, and chewed fingernails, I settled on majoring in business. I couldn't go wrong with that, right? However, the decision niggled in the back of my mind; a major in business seemed vanilla and didn't represent the core of my self-described complex being. But I vowed that, if I were to be a business major, I would be the best darn business major on the planet.

I convinced my mom to let me live off campus the following year. For safety's sake, she wanted me to find a roommate, but after what I had been through I couldn't swallow the thought of living with someone. Mom balked until I started telling her stories about Candi. She cut me short when I got to the sexually explicit parts and agreed that I could live alone. For once, Candi's sex life was useful to me.

A rundown yet charming Victorian house near campus had been converted to five furnished apartments and catered to college students. The battered hodgepodge of furniture suited me just fine. I didn't worry if I left one more water ring on the table or knife mark in the kitchen counter. The landlord wouldn't be able to tell my damage from that done by the previous tenants. Plus, given my housekeeping abilities, it didn't matter what the furniture looked like. Every surface was covered with schoolbooks, random articles of clothing, and general clutter.

My mom came to visit me once a year. As much as she loved me, she wouldn't stay with me in my apartment. At first I was insulted, but then I gave my apartment a good hard look. I didn't blame her for wanting to stay someplace where they washed the sheets and cleaned the bathroom. She timed her visits so we could go to the annual flower show put on by the town's botanical garden. The whole affair bored me, and I was by far the youngest person in the hall of flowers, but I went along anyway, because I knew there was the promise of lunch afterwards in the garden café. Unless you count heating up a frozen dinner, I didn't cook much in my apartment. I couldn't afford to eat out, either, so I longed for real food. My mom would spend all day in the kitchen before she visited me and made meals to tuck in my freezer. What a treat it was to come home after a day in class and warm up a home-cooked meal.

My collegiate experience fell short of my expectations. Not one single roommate became my best friend. The professors didn't consider me brilliant. A handful of classmates were friends, but you wouldn't call me popular. My fellow students didn't warm up to me much, or maybe I didn't warm up to them. I overheard a sorority girl call me "standoffish." I did, however, frequently exploit the freedom to party and stay out all night. One of those occasions led to a regrettable drunken hook-up with a guy who didn't even know my name. The football team and fraternity crowd liked me because I drank beer like an Irishman. With a slap on my back, one intoxicated guy said he liked how I held my liquor. He meant it as a sincere compliment.

Chapter 4: A College Graduate

You cannot be lonely if you like the person you're alone with.

— Wayne Dyer

A college diploma was finally in my hand despite so-so grades, three flunked classes, and countless nasty hangovers. It was only by dumb luck that I passed my Spanish class. If I hadn't passed, I wouldn't have been able to graduate. A nasty roommate, a tragic roommate, alcoholic roommates, and asshole professors were in my rearview mirror. My mom's graduation gift was $10,000 she had set aside from my dad's life insurance policy.

I grew up in a small town and went to college in a medium-sized town, so I longed to live the life of a city girl. One of my favorite movies is Hitchcock's *Vertigo,* which is set in San Francisco. Aside from being a suspenseful masterpiece, it is a travelogue of iconic San Francisco locations. I fell more in love with Jimmy Stewart and San Francisco every time I watched the movie. Something about The City by the Bay made my heart ache, and I knew I wanted to live there.

Once again, I packed Athena to the gills with my possessions. I left my college town in the middle of a summer heat wave and drove to fog-engulfed San Francisco. I didn't know it at the time, but, as Mark Twain is incorrectly credited for saying, "The coldest winter I ever spent was a summer in San Francisco." The day I arrived in San Francisco was damp, cold, and gloomy. I wondered if I had made a mistake moving there. The shroud of thick fog didn't look nearly as glamorous and romantic as it did in *Vertigo*. A wave of panic induced vertigo of my own.

My studio apartment in the Mission District was too small to whip a cat around by the tail. The nearly freezing fog on the day I moved in made the whole affair miserable. My winter clothes were buried in the car, so I had to unload my belongings while shivering in a thin tank-top and shorts. My neighbors and the resident homeless people looked at me as if I were crazy. I was beginning to think so, too. The apartment's heating unit did little to warm the air; when I finished unloading the car, my skin was a sickly shade of blue. The monthly fee for a parking spot in a nearby garage was almost as much as my rent. I knew I didn't really need a car in San Francisco, but I couldn't bear to part with Athena. I liked the illusion of freedom the car represented.

The neighborhood was sketchy, but anything better was beyond my budget. The building was run-down inside and out, yet I wanted my apartment's interior to reflect my personality. The 400-square-foot space would be artsy, sophisticated, and comfortable. That bubble burst when I went furniture shopping. The tiny apartment could accommodate a bed, small sofa, and a kitchen table. If I didn't mind losing all my floor space, I could squeeze in a desk and a dresser.

What I didn't know was that buying furniture required access to Fort Knox or a Swiss bank account. Mom's gift of $10,000 wouldn't go very far in San Francisco. The fancy furniture stores were far beyond my means, and the sales clerks intimidated me.

Lowering my expectations, I shopped the cheap places. The furniture looked fine on the outside, but when I opened the drawers I saw that the pieces were assembled with staples and a hot-glue gun. As a last resort I searched the classified ads and frequented thrift stores in the hope of finding castoff treasures. I lowered my expectations even further and drove around on garbage night, picking up a few discarded chairs. Rather than artsy, sophisticated, and comfortable, it looked as though I had hired a homeless person to decorate my apartment.

Even though my apartment looked like the equivalent of a Goodwill store, pride of ownership kicked in. As a kid, I left a path of destruction in my wake. A homework session left the kitchen table looking as though my backpack had thrown up papers and snack-wrappers. My childhood bedroom was in a chronic state of disaster, which infuriated my mom. To get back at me, one day she emptied my closet and drawers and put every piece of clothing I owned on my bed. She stacked the dirty dishes from around my room in a teetering tower on my pillow. I wasn't allowed to leave my room until it was all in order. But in my new apartment, I kept the place tidy and organized. Clutter drove me crazy—I never left dishes in the sink or the mail strewn around. Maybe I became a neatnik because my furnishings were trashy enough on their own.

Through the thin apartment walls I learned everyone's business, whether I wanted to or not. I heard my neighbors having sex, I could tell whose husband was a lazy bum, and, on more than one occasion, I called the police to intervene during a loud domestic dispute. And, in case you didn't know, makeup sex after a blowout fight is raucous.

The building's super scared me. I don't know if it was his dirty wife-beater T-shirt or the way his lecherous eyes followed me. With apartment keys in hand, I didn't linger in the hallway longer than necessary. I hired a handyman to install a deadbolt lock on the door and locks on the windows. It helped me to sleep easier at night, at least when the neighbors weren't at each other's throats or testing the limits of their bedsprings. The can of pepper spray in my purse and the one by the front door also gave me comfort. A single girl in a city must be careful.

I had always been a bit of a hermit and never had a large circle of friends. That didn't bother me—I was used to amusing myself. But, not knowing a soul in San Francisco, my days were lonely and my nights pathetic. My phone rang only when Mom called to check in or it was a wrong number. Watching old movies on television helped fill the void. On a perfectly good Saturday night, instead of bar-hopping, my companions were a movie, popcorn, and a glass of wine. With a box of tissues between my knees, I would lose myself in a Hollywood classic. They knew how to make movies in the 1940s. The murder mysteries were complex, the romance movies sweet and sappy, and the humor in the comedies was smart. My favorites were the musicals. Do you know how many tender ballads are from old musicals? My black-and-white movie exposure on those Saturday nights makes me scoff at the movies they make these days. Now Hollywood relies on overblown high-tech special effects, endless chase scenes, and gratuitous sex and violence.

One benefit of not having friends to go out with was that I didn't spend money. But, even while leading a monastic and hermetic lifestyle, my debt racked up. The tremendous outgo of cash from my bank account was not offset by any income. I needed to find a job, but after four years of college I also needed a break from assignments and deadlines. I didn't want to tax my brain with anything more difficult than deciding what to eat for lunch. A primordial slug took over my body, and I spent my days leaving a slime trail between the refrigerator in the kitchen and my couch. Being a hermit was no way to make friends, but the inertia was delicious.

I met a man at the only non-porn video store in my neighborhood. It sounds cliché, but we bumped into each other, literally. With nothing interesting on television one night, I combed the aisles of the classic movie section. I bent to pick up a video off the bottom shelf and rammed into the man behind me. He laughed off my apology and asked what movie I had picked out. We chatted about old movies and discovered we shared many of the same favorites. He asked for my phone number, but I refused. Being a fan of old movies didn't make him dating material.

We often ran into each other at the video store and had comfortable conversations. He asked for my number at the end of each one. At last I relented, and we made a date. I didn't need to check my calendar. Goodness knows my schedule was free for the next two decades.

We dated a few times before I invited him over to my place. He was cute, seemed normal, and held a job. I didn't feel romantic magic around him, but he was an interesting diversion from my solitude. He didn't make demands of me, nor did I of him. The sex wasn't bad, either. Am I kidding? The sex was fantastic.

Chapter 5: The World of Employment and Unemployment

To profit from your mistakes, you have to get out and make some.

— Anonymous

After two weeks with the activity level of a potato, I needed to face the corporate world and find a job. I was a cocky graduate of an insignificant college with a highfalutin degree. Well, if you consider a degree in business highfalutin, then that's what I had.

I embarked on a search to find an employer who was looking to hire someone as delightful as I thought I was. Searching for jobs was a time vortex. There were few jobs I was qualified for, or even interested in, and I became discouraged. I submitted my resume for six positions with promise and didn't hear anything. Then I sent my resume to a dozen companies I was only slightly interested in. No response. Then I applied for every job available as long as it wasn't manual labor or at a strip club. The corporate world was poised to dodge my attempt to wow it. I checked my message machine hourly to make sure it was working. My mailman eyed me as if I were a creepy stalker, because I would wait at the mailbox for him, hoping for a response from a company. Every day I was disappointed to see that my mailbox was a black hole, without even a note saying, "No, thank you, Meredith. You don't interest us one bit." Not one company contacted me, and the lack of interest had me flummoxed.

Chapter 5: The World of Employment and Unemployment

At last, a company that imports cheap souvenirs and sells them to Fisherman's Wharf tourist shops invited me for an interview for an entry-level position in their sales department. Dressed in my sole interview suit, I arrived for the appointment far too early. My mom was a stickler for being on time. She awarded me an advanced degree from her school of punctuality. I make a habit to be prompt for appointments, and I get peeved when others keep me waiting. Mom taught me that a person's most valuable possession is their time. Her motto was, "If you are early, you are on time. If you are on time, you are late. If you are late, you are just plain rude." This worked to my disadvantage for this interview; arriving early gave me time to produce gallons of sweat under each armpit.

An ancient secretary showed me to a cluttered, airless office. I introduced myself to the man behind the desk and waited for him to ask me to be seated. (My mother did manage to teach me manners as well as punctuality.) The invitation to be seated never came, so I brushed what looked like cookie crumbs off of his guest chair and sat down. The man's eyes traveled from my crossed legs to my breasts and then loitered at chest-height. He ignored me when I handed my resume to him. Flapping the pages under his nose made him jerk to attention, but then he dropped the paper on his desk without giving it a glance.

Ten minutes into the interview, and this is what he learned about me, my skills, and how I could be of service to his company. Not one thing. I, however, learned he was a bass fisherman, had been divorced for two years, and cleaned his nails with a paper clip while he talked. The lecher asked if I wanted to come along on his weekend trip to Las Vegas. With a loud "Not on your life!" and a curt nod,

I stormed out of his office and slammed the door. Mom would have been proud of me.

Thankfully, another interview came along for a job in an insurance company's sales department. I was tongue-tied during the interview, but, much to my surprise, the sales manager offered me the position. Because of my electrified nerve endings, I made a fatal mistake and didn't ask for clarification about the job responsibilities. All I knew was that the work involved life insurance and phone calls. That couldn't be too hard, or so I told myself.

In the Human Resources department, I spent an hour filling out a mountain of requisite paperwork and was ordered to read the Employee Handbook before my first day on the job. Paperwork completed, the Human Resources manager offered to introduce me to my future coworkers. Good idea. I could impress everyone right away so my charisma wouldn't take my colleagues by surprise on my first day. But, in truth, I was scared to death. I was afraid my new coworkers wouldn't like me and would see right through my confident façade.

We set off on the tour, wound our way through a cubicle maze, and headed toward what I assumed would be my corner office. But no. We stopped short and, with a cheerful twitter, my tour guide said, "Here is your new home away from home, Meredith." A computer, chair, and telephone huddled in the corner of a tiny cubicle. A chicken coop would have afforded more space than my assigned office. I wouldn't be doing million-dollar deals in a corner office. I would be making telemarketing calls from a shoebox. How humiliating. But my rent was due, the gas bill was delinquent, and my bank account was dwindling. I needed the job, no matter how dreary.

Chapter 5: The World of Employment and Unemployment

On my first day, I was determined to make a fantastic second impression. My manager would see my new consignment store Gucci briefcase and Ralph Lauren suit (still expensive even when purchased on consignment) and surely move me to a corner office. I arrived at the office, and, after several wrong turns, I found my cubicle. I would need to leave a trail of breadcrumbs when I left for lunch to find my way back.

My boss dropped a computer printout on my desk with a dull thud. A ream of paper listed the telemarketing calls I needed to make to potential clients. The minimum-wage pay would be supplemented with a bonus for each appointment I managed to schedule. In the corporate world, I was a bottom-feeder—one step up from a debt collector or repo man.

My manager told me to report to the conference room, where I endured a wearisome two-day training session only by drifting into outer space. I suppose the instructor knew his stuff, but with his monotone delivery style I was lulled into daydreaming about the next coffee break. He stressed the need to be engaging on the phone, but he was one to talk. He was as charismatic as a jar of pickles. I tuned out his other boring tips for success, and when the time came for role-playing, I froze. I forgot how he said to move past the gatekeeper to reach the household decision-maker, the difference between term and whole life insurance, and how to close the call by scheduling the appointment.

On the morning of day three on the job, my coworkers swapped stories about their weekend while I sat alone in my cubicle. The conversations came to a screeching halt promptly at nine, as if a starter's gun had gone off. Telephone numbers were punched into phones, and sincere voices touted the benefits of life insurance. A chorus of telemarketing calls echoed in the miniature Grand Canyon of cubicles. Undaunted—well, a little—I picked up the phone and dialed the first number. They hung up on me. I dialed the second number and was hung up on again. After I dialed the fiftieth, my ear began ringing from the phone slamming down on the other end so many times. I wasn't cut out for the job. How did my manager overlook my skills in other areas? I offered more talent than making lame sales spiels, but I plowed on.

My first paycheck was one half of my rent. If I ate stale bread and bologna, my money would last two months. If I bought anything or even took in a movie, my money would be gone by August. I was twenty-two, in a dead-end job, and was staring into the face of impending debt and probable doom.

The company didn't give me any awards for my telemarketing skills, but I eventually made decent money. I paid off my credit card bills and tucked some money in my saving account. My moderate success on the job made me cocky—or, I should say, cocki*er*. Convinced of my inordinate value to the company, I figured my boss wouldn't mind if I bent the rules a tad. I wandered in late for work and indulged in long lunches. Calling in sick on a Monday or Friday became my regular practice. Office supplies mysteriously ended up in my purse. The company owed it to me as their model yet frankly, grossly underpaid employee. That was a mistake; my piss-poor work ethic got me fired after fifteen months on the job. I was expendable.

Needing to pay the bills while I looked for a new job, I signed up with a temp agency and hopped around San Francisco for three months in various secretarial and receptionist positions. The pay was lousy, the work monotonous, my credit card balances were creeping up again, and my savings account was dwindling. I even took a two-week stint as a cleaning lady for Home Sweep Home House Cleaning because the name of the company amused me.

Mom cried when I told her I couldn't afford to come home for Thanksgiving or Christmas. The temp agency kept me busy during the holiday rush, which was a godsend to my bank account. I filled in for people who had normal lives and could be with family. It was depressing. Even the small Christmas tree I bought for the apartment looked forlorn and abandoned.

Something had to change.

Chapter 6: Mom is Gone

If you suppress grief too much, it can well redouble.

— Molière

Things did change. My mom died. I assumed she would live well into old age like her mother. One minute, she was sitting in a planning meeting for the church's January rummage sale; the next minute, she was gone. She shocked her church lady friends by falling face-forward onto the conference table. She was dead before they could react. A brain aneurism had brought down a vibrant woman before she could know her future grandchildren.

I got the call from the priest, and in a trance, I packed my suitcase and set off on the drive for home. But what was home, really, without Mom there? A house where a basketful of laundry waited to be folded? A space where memories and photographs lingered? A place that was home only when she was there? What was I going home to? It was an empty shell that was waiting for Mom's return, and I had to break the news to the walls, garden, and peaceful spirit of the place that she wasn't coming home ever again.

In a daze, I wandered around Mom's house, sifted through unopened mail, and took out the garbage. While I was sitting at her desk making calls to distant family members, a file folder caught my eye. The label read, *"Meredith . . . Just in Case."* Inside the file was a list of bank account and credit card numbers, the deed to the house, her will, and other important papers. She also left me a list of instructions. At the top it read, *"Meredith, when I die, let the church ladies handle the funeral. They know what readings I like and my favorite hymns. You won't need to do a thing to arrange the gathering after the service. The church ladies know how to do it up proper. Lord knows you'll have enough to do to empty this house and settle my estate, what little there is of it. Also, I need you to find someone to walk dogs for me at the ASPCA, now that I am gone."*

Mom died with few assets, because every extra cent she made went toward my college tuition and helping me survive financially once I was out of school. The modest funeral arrangements just about drained her bank account, as well as mine. Unlike Penelope's funeral, Mom's funeral filled the church pews. The altar was banked with flowers, and poster boards on easels had dozens of photos of Mom at the Fourth of July party, the church rummage sale, the ASPCA and the like. I didn't recognize most of the faces in the crowd, but Mom's friends knew who I was. They offered their condolences at the potluck luncheon organized by the church ladies, and I gathered that Mom had talked a lot about me to her friends. They knew about honors won, grammar school soccer feats, and straight-A grades in college (a fabrication on my part). I didn't know she had talked about me to anyone, and I didn't know her bevy of friends had loved her so dearly.

Had I paid attention, I would have known my mom was an active member of the community and a self-appointed professional volunteer. She helped neighbors in their gardens, organized school bake sales, read to shut-ins, and babysat colicky infants. The altar society at her church had honored her at their annual luncheon, which had been a first. As a kid, I had failed to notice her kind heart because I was busy complaining about the fact that she had made me a ham sandwich instead of turkey for lunch. Her friends saw her refreshing spirit and benefited from her giving nature.

After Mom's funeral, shadows lurked in the corners of her house, and I hated the quiet gloom. I reflected on the kind words her friends had said about her and how much I had missed. Too caught up in my own world, I wasted the opportunity to know her. I had invented elaborate excuses to avoid spending time with her. With disdainful arrogance, I had shut her out. Now my mom was gone, and my life was the worse for it. It was too late to atone for how I treated her.

I set about clearing out Mom's house like a professional organizer. I had to. I needed to get back to San Francisco to find a real job. Mom's death had left me numb, and I was glad for its anesthetic embrace while I cleaned out the house. I created three piles: what I would sell, donate, or throw away. I kept a few of her belongings, like her mother's china, but got rid of most of the rest. I couldn't afford to ship what didn't fit in my beat-up Athena.

Because Mom had been an avid reader, sorting through her books took time. I opened the book *A Tree Grows in Brooklyn*, and a note from my mom was written on the first page. *"Keep and read this one, Meredith. Francie reminds me of you. She's a fighter, too."* In most, but not all, of the books, Mom had written notes to me that included mini-reviews or warnings:

"This is a beautiful read, has vivid imagery, and the ending will make you cry. I guarantee it."

"Stick with this book. It starts out slow, but then it is a roller coaster ride with a redemptive ending. You won't be disappointed."

"I paid a lot for this best seller, so I couldn't justify getting rid of it. Don't waste your time. It is rot. The author

manipulates the reader, and with every line you can see how he's trying to jump on the pulp-fiction train to megabucks."

A piece of paper fell out of the next book I opened. As soon as I saw the salmon-colored paper, I knew what it was . . . the address for Camp Minihehe. I unfolded the paper and saw that Mom had written a note under where I had scratched out the camp's address. *"Don't worry, honey. I would never want to embarrass you."* I stopped going through each book, boxed them all up, and lugged them to my car.

My emotions were in check until I reached Mom's bathroom. Prescription bottles and a half-used tube of toothpaste went into the trash, along with old hairbrushes and makeup. When I opened her jar of cold cream and brought it to my nose, a lightning bolt of memories almost knocked me to the floor. It smelled like my mom. She would wash her face and slather on cold cream before tucking me into bed and kissing me goodnight. Her scent would linger in the room and cradle me off to sleep.

The cold cream's scent brought on an unexpected wave of uncontrollable sobs and the overwhelming grief left me weak. When I felt my knees begin to buckle, I sat on the rim of the tub and let the tears come. It felt good to unleash what I didn't know I had been keeping bottled up. When my tears subsided, I blew my nose and tucked the cold cream jar in my purse. I put The Beatles' album *Rubber Soul* on mom's old hi-fi and cleaned the bathroom like a tornado with a sponge.

Her bedroom was the last room to finish clearing out. I had originally put her clothes on the donation pile, because they smelled like her too, but I regretted my rash decision and rummaged through the heap, pulling out Mom's favorite sweater and all of her scarves. As soon as the furniture consignment store and thrift shop picked up her things, I flew out of the house before hysteria could run amok with my emotions any further.

The drive home gave me an agonizingly long opportunity to think. I lost my job, my mom was dead, and my emotions were raw. A sad footnote to my life was that no one volunteered to lend moral support while I tackled the painful job of cleaning out Mom's house, not even my so-called boyfriend. I had no true friends. It was my fault because I had shut the world out, including my mother. The notion caused me to spontaneously combust into tears at fifty-mile intervals.

Aside from her house, which she owned outright, Mom had few assets, and settling her estate was simple. Mom's credit card statement made me sad. The bill's $25 balance was for the sweater she had given me for my birthday, and I had never even bothered to wear it. Selling her house was not a simple matter and took five months. The house itself was in good shape, and I would swear the faint scent of chocolate chip cookies baking in the oven still floated in the air, but the neighborhood had long ago lost its charm.

Chapter 7: Bad Boyfriends, Bad Decisions

Though we adore men individually, we agree that as a group they're rather stupid.

— Mary Poppins

In need of consolation, I turned to the man in my life. As I said before, our relationship worked, because we didn't make demands of each other. That is, I didn't ask anything of him until I needed to be comforted. That was a mistake. He liked me because I didn't make uncomfortable requests of him. The tremendous sense of loss and regret over my mom's death was too much for me to bear. I needed to find comfort in his arms. My heart was filled with sorrow, and I wanted to open it up to him to keep it from bursting. But he just wanted to have sex. My grief made him uneasy.

We stood on a precipice. He hated my tears, and I detested how he treated me like a sniveling idiot. We might have repaired our relationship after my emotional breakdown, but not long after my mom died, he said, "Meredith, we need to talk." *Oh, God.* For a single woman, those are the four most dreaded words to be spoken, as opposed to the four most coveted words . . . "Will you marry me?"

Everything came together in the conversation with him that night, as if someone hit me on the head with a frying pan. The early evening departures from my bed, the unanswered phone calls, and the cash transactions made sense. He had given me excuses about his apartment being a mess or his roommate being home, but I learned the real reason he didn't invite me to his house. My allegedly single boyfriend did, in fact, have a wife and kids. The life he had portrayed to me was a lie. I chastised myself for being naïve. With blindness caused by gullibility, I swallowed his thin alibis. He was a moron and an idiot for lying to me and betraying his wife and family. I kicked him down the hall, and after my fifth glass of wine . . . you know what? I realized that *I* was the moron and idiot, not him.

He came sniffing around my apartment door the next morning and begged me to forgive him. In my semi-hung-over state, I shook off his sorrowful pleas and demanded he never darken my doorstep again. He stayed away, because I'm scary when fired up. As they say, "Hell hath no fury like Meredith scorned." His bloodied nose was evidence of that. I wondered how he explained the blood on his shirt and the black eye to his wife. Mom would say, "Good riddance to bad rubbish."

In time, another bad boyfriend came along. He was decent at first but turned out to be a nightmare. The guy was clean cut, from a modest family, and in love with me. Everything was fine until he became too intense. If I was slow to return his call, the guy came uncorked. Initially, I reveled in his attention but soon realized his behavior was obsessive. The language in his angry phone messages would have offended a truck driver. In short order, instead of thinking, "How sweet, he adores me," I panicked and thought, "Oh, my God, is he stalking me?" I feared for my safety. Where was Mom to step in? She would have shut him down and told him where to get off. Channeling my mom, I screamed, "Get the hell out of my life." He got my point.

I swore off men.

Chapter 8: Next Step on the Corporate Ladder

A sobering thought: What if, at this very moment, I am living up to my full potential?

— Jane Wagner

Not long after Mom died, a one-stop marketing, advertising, graphic design and public relations firm in the Financial District offered me a paid internship. I had given them a vague reason for leaving my previous employer. Lucky for me, the insurance company's reference-check policy was to give only the dates of employment and position held.

The new job was an improvement, but still not in a corner office. Awash in a sea of cubicles and surrounded by talented colleagues, I bluffed my way along. I worked hard to prove to the higher-ups I was worthy of their paycheck and capable of more than my internship's mind-numbing tasks. They promised me the position was a training program for something bigger than filing, setting up the conference room for meetings, and keeping the kitchen tidy. When my supervisor gave me a special project, I was thrilled until she explained that I had to organize the mess the previous intern had made of the client files. Unbeknownst to them, I am an expert at creating order out of a mess, except when it comes to messes in my life.

A position became available in the advertising department, and I was perfect for the job. Apparently, I was the only person who thought so, and I was passed over. My bravado unshaken, I applied for every interesting position that came along. With a fifth rejection added to my vast collection of rejections, my confidence was traumatized. Maybe I wasn't wonderful after all.

At one of the weekly staff meetings, I cowered in my chair at the back of the room. I didn't want to be called on for an update on my client file project, because my report would have lulled the room to sleep, even though I thought I was pure brilliance in realm organizational abilities. The head of the firm's international division, Olivia du Maurier, sat down next to me. Her stature in the company intimidated me, and my voice failed me when she said hello. My fear was unfounded. She complimented my dress before the meeting started, and within minutes we got along like a house on fire.

Olivia took a liking to me and often stopped me in the hallway to chat. I would hope to run into her in the ladies room or by the copy machine, because she somehow managed to bolster my confidence. She embodied who I wanted to be; I worshipped her. Her patrician features, custom suits, and jewelry were reminiscent of Jackie Kennedy Onassis. Olivia exuded an understated elegance, and her grace engendered trust. Rather than schlepping across the room like a mere mortal, she seemed to glide across the floor.

I failed to comprehend what she saw in me, because a coworker had told me my haughty air of superiority was offensive. Olivia cleared up my confusion when she said, "You remind me of myself when I was your age, Meredith—overly self-assured on the exterior, but fragile on the inside."

A position opened in Olivia's department after I had been with the company for a year. I applied for the job and then lost sleep because my confidence was brittle. Certain that dozens of applicants were better suited for the job, I would be left holding my limp resume while standing on the street corner with a cardboard sign that read, *WILL WORK FOR FOOD.*

Olivia interviewed me for the job over lunch at a restaurant with white tablecloths and tranquil lighting. The interview was more like having lunch with a friend than a chance for me to showcase my experience and winning personality. I tried to talk about my skills, but she changed the subject and ordered another appetizer. At the end of the lunch she said, "You passed the test, Meredith. You're hired."

"What test?" I asked.

"I knew you were right for the job, but I wanted to see your table manners. I don't hire people who don't know how to hold their knife, which fork to use, or don't put their napkin in their lap," she said. (Passing Olivia's test was easy. My mom had drilled table manners into me.)

The new job's pay was an improvement, and one of the perks was occasional international travel. The work mostly handcuffed me to my computer while I pulled together media lists and researched demographics. However, because some assignments were on foreign soil, I knew I wasn't destined to sit in a stuffy cubicle for the rest of my life. On occasion, the job handed me the world and the plane tickets so I could explore it.

As my mentor, Olivia would explain how my trifling task fit into the larger project. She coached me on how to speak to clients with self-assurance, but also with humility. She taught me how to polish presentations to help her land new projects. I learned the subtleties of the industry that would have taken me years to learn on my own, if ever. Finally, somebody seemed to recognize my worth.

I asked her how she became successful in the business. She said, "By making an awful professor I had in college my anti-role model. He was an internationally renowned expert in public relations and marketing, and he scared me to death. That is, until his lecture on the art of pitching an idea to a client. This supposedly articulate guru said, 'Never repeat yourself, and don't be redundant.' He *was* redundant when he lectured the class on not being redundant. I thought, 'If that numbskull can be successful, so can I.'"

"My advertising professor told the class to *be* redundant when working with clients," I said, "because they don't internalize what you have said until they hear the message three times."

Olivia replied, "Then don't take on stupid clients."

Chapter 9: Still Lonely

The most terrible poverty is loneliness, and the feeling of being unloved.

— Mother Teresa of Calcutta

A sad soul can kill quicker than a germ.

— John Steinbeck

With my bolstered paycheck, I could now move out of my dumpy apartment to one in a Victorian house converted into apartments in the Marina District. It had a heater that worked and didn't just blow cold air around the room, neighbors who didn't argue at all hours, and a super who didn't tell off-color jokes. My big move up was a mere half step, but the new apartment was a tad larger, and the floors didn't creak . . . as much. Other than that, my living conditions remained humble. Except for my mattress, I left my thrift store and trash bin furniture for the creepy super to deal with. It was sweet revenge, but I regretted the decision after he kept my cleaning deposit because I had left him to deal with my junk.

My budget allowed me to purchase a few pieces of quality furniture. I decided to forgo items like a coffee table until I could afford to buy one I loved. Plus, I rather enjoyed my spartan lifestyle. Half of one of my paychecks was spent on luxurious sheets and down pillows. Since I slept alone, I might as well slumber in style. Another two full paychecks were spent on a dining room table from an antique store.

I refused to spend the proceeds from the sale of my mom's house. The jaws of poverty caused by unemployment crushed me before, and I never wanted to feel the pain of its cruel fangs again. If Olivia fired me—which, given my history, could happen—the money from Mom's house would keep me from starving. Knowing it was there gave me comfort. I was tempted to dip into the savings on occasion, but I let it sit in the bank.

The tiny bedroom in the apartment boasted an impressive view of the wall behind my apartment building. I contemplated painting a mural on the bricks so I could pretend the room afforded a lovely vista. Although the bedroom had a terrible view, the living room faced the street, and the windows let in glorious light—when The City wasn't blanketed in fog, that is. The oak floors were burnished to gold from years of wear. The wood looked soft to the touch. I wished the floor could tell me the stories of the ghosts who walked its planks.

The dining room, a rarity in a small San Francisco apartment, was my favorite space. White wainscoting with burgundy walls made the room inviting, especially when the sun streamed in. I didn't pay attention to the chandelier when I moved in, but late one night while bored to distraction, I decided to clean the dust and cobwebs from its brass curlicues and glass shades. With the layers of city grime removed, the fixture was magnificent. Maybe 'funky' is a better word, but I loved it. Lowering the dimmer switch on the chandelier made the dining room scream for a dinner party.

The most woebegone area of my apartment was the kitchen, which was two square feet larger than a broom closet. The refrigerator was circa 1950s. The darn monster had an annoying habit of making an unnerving screeching noise at night and kept me awake for hours. The bastard kept silent during the day. Any workspace vanished when my purse was on the counter. But the size of the kitchen didn't really matter, because my meal preparation efforts mainly entailed making a tuna sandwich or reheating delivered Chinese food. However, no matter how humble my meal, I set a place at the dining table and pretended to dine with the Astor family.

Still lonely, I wanted to find some friends. Not male friends, mind you, because I was still off men. Making friends at work was unsuccessful, because everyone was already busy with boyfriends, husbands, or family. I joined a gym because I thought it might be a good spot to meet new people. That didn't pan out either, because small talk while running on a treadmill is impossible—at least it was for out-of-shape me. I wormed my way into a casual acquaintance's book group, but I quit because I found the books they chose too heavy for my taste. In a moment of desperation, I considered signing up with those new things called online dating. Sheesh, I was pathetic.

One night when I was coming home from work, a woman about my age named Margo was moving into the building. She was struggling to carry her moving boxes up the stairs. The memory of my recent move and strained back was vivid. Taking pity on her, I offered to change out of my work clothes to help move the rest of her boxes into her apartment. With the rented moving van emptied, Margo opened the box marked *KITCHEN*, dug out two coffee mugs, and filled them with wine. Her fridge was already stocked with wine and beer, and I knew then that we would be great friends. Wine out of a coffee mug is an interesting twist; it's like a wino drinking hooch hidden in a brown paper bag. A coffee mug holds a dangerous quantity of wine, and we polished off two bottles with no trouble.

In Search of Beef Stroganoff

Margo's wicked sense of humor tickled me, and her stories about the modeling she did to help pay her Harvard tuition intrigued me. Adept at conversation, she compelled me to talk about subjects I normally wouldn't share with a new acquaintance. It wasn't that she was a good conversationalist; she could qualify for a job as an FBI interrogator. She riddled me with questions, delved into my secrets, and seemed fascinated by my answers. In a moment of wine-induced weakness, I committed to help unpack her boxes over the weekend. Later that night, I realized I dominated the conversation, but was thrilled I had made a new friend. Maybe she would be like the roommate I hoped for in college.

I forfeited my weekend to help her settle in. Unpacking Margo's belongings was a pleasure, because of her distinctive flair for decorating. Emptying her boxes was like opening a shipment from Gump's. That made sense; she was the manager of Gump's home furnishing department. By Sunday afternoon, her apartment looked ready for a magazine photo shoot.

We became close friends and drank wine together almost every night. She invited me to go shopping and to the movies, we sewed throw pillows, and, yes, we did each other's nails. For the first time in my adult life, I became chummy with another female. When the holidays rolled around, Margo couldn't get time off and I had nowhere to go, so we spent Christmas together. Finding a Christmas gift for her was a challenge. She had all of Gump's at her disposal, and I couldn't think of a thing she might need or want. During my search for the perfect gift for her, I found a delicate inlaid music box in an antique store. It was more than I wanted to spend, but I loved it. I knew she would too.

Chapter 9: Still Lonely

Neither of us knew how to cook, so we ordered in Italian food for Christmas dinner and drank several bottles of red wine. We celebrated in her apartment, which looked as if Santa himself had decorated it. Every surface had been cleared of knickknacks to make way for a miniature snowy village, a team of glittery angels, and fake Christmas presents wrapped in jewel-toned moiré silk. Santa had even removed all the artwork and replaced it with Christmas-themed Americana. A little tipsy, we sat by her Christmas tree after dinner to open presents. Margo gave me a cashmere scarf so soft it felt like vapor. She seemed to like the music box, but I never saw it in her apartment again after that. I would have loved to take it back.

The more time we spent together, the more my view of our friendship changed. Margo handed out compliments that were thinly veiled insults. For instance, I wore a baseball cap on one of our trips shopping, and she said, "Gosh, Meredith. I wish *I* looked good in hats on *my* bad hair days." Another time, I wore a floral spring dress with a slimming bodice and flowing skirt, like a wearable garden party, and she said, "How cute. You look like the Easter Bunny." Her message was clear. She thought my dress was ridiculous. I pulled back from her when she said, "I wish I could wear bold prints like you. My frame is much too small. It would look like that dress you have on was wearing petite little ol' me."

At first I wasn't bothered, but after being stung by one too many of Margo's barbs, I noticed how often she did it. She made innocuous comments, but under the surface her words were judgmental and mean-spirited. Her catty comments were coated with syrupy Southern-belle charm. She knew how to subtly take me down a peg with a winning smile. When we first met, her attentiveness bolstered my ego, but her backdoor insults soon chipped away at my self-confidence. But perhaps I had thin skin and vilified her unfairly. I decided to write down her barbs as she dished them out. Two months into our friendship, the list of her snipes—or, as I called them, Margo-isms—filled three pages. I stopped returning her calls. She saw me in the hall one afternoon and invited me to dinner. Pleading a headache, I turned down her invitation. She realized I was avoiding her when she caught me standing in line for a movie that same evening. She didn't call me again.

Stepping away from Margo's passive-aggressiveness, I realized she was the one who was insecure. She created a false swagger by surrounding herself with luxury to give off an air of grandeur and self-confidence. Her looked-like-it-was-designed-by-a-decorator apartment was her way of showing the world she was better than the rest of us peons. She over-bleached her teeth to an eerie shade of blue-white and spent hundreds of dollars at the salon to lighten her dark roots. She once made a mean crack about my natural yet dirty-blonde hair. I would hide my hands when I was around her, because I was afraid she would make a comment about my jagged cuticles and unpainted nails. By tearing me down, she used me as a step stool to build up her self-worth. I was done with her. She needed to find another victim to suck the life out of, like Dracula searching for a pale, vulnerable neck to nourish his ego.

With yet another failed relationship behind me, that time with a female, I returned to leftover Chinese from the fridge and nights watching old movies. With my need for companionship taunting me, and three glasses of wine making me morose, I picked up the phone to call Margo. I decided to offer an apology and beg her to be my friend again. But then I glanced down at my chipped toenail polish and slammed down the phone before she answered.

In the hopes of running into another candidate for a friend, I lingered at the apartment mailboxes. Two couples about my age lived in my building, and I took my time wooing them, because I didn't want to scare them off. Two months of courtship by the front door of the building gave me the nerve to invite both couples over for dinner. Ah, but that posed a problem, because my culinary efforts thus far included grilled cheese sandwiches and canned soup. Lunch-counter food wouldn't do much to impress my new friends. But I reasoned that if you can read, you can cook . . . right?

Chapter 10: Poisoning My Neighbors

I seem to you cruel and too much addicted to gluttony, when I beat my cook for sending up a bad dinner. If that seems to you too trifling a cause, pray tell for what cause you would have a cook flogged?

— Marcus Valerius Martialis,
Roman poet, 1st century B.C.

Complaints to the cook can be hazardous to your health.

— Sign in a truck stop diner

Desperate times call for desperate shopping. The first thing I needed was a cookbook. After that, I hit thrift stores to supplement my meager collection of pots and pans. They were nothing fancy, but serviceable. At the bookstore, I reeled when I saw the number of cookbooks lining the shelves. Two hours hunched over cookbook after cookbook brought me to one that was all-purpose and suitable for a fledgling chef like me.

Back at home with a glass of wine by my side, I curled up on the couch with the cookbook to decide what to serve. I became absorbed reading the recipes and drooled over the photographs. The cookbook entranced me like a page-turner from *The New York Times* Best Seller list. Poring over the book, I hit on what to serve and slammed the book shut. *Beef stroganoff was my mom's specialty. Why couldn't it be mine, too?* I would be known around town for my beef stroganoff, as well as for my extraordinary skills as a hostess.

Chapter 10: Poisoning My Neighbors

The next day I made my grocery list with care and combed the store aisles for the freshest ingredients. I took great pains in setting the table that night. My mom had taught me the trick. "The first thing you need to do when you invite company over for dinner is set the table. That way, if your guests arrive early, you look prepared to welcome them into your home." I dug out my grandmother's china, crystal and silver, and ignored the minor detail that a red wine stain scarred the center of her yellowed linen tablecloth. I arranged roses for the centerpiece, tied a French ribbon around the vase, and positioned the vase to hide the ugly stain. With the candles lit and the lights dimmed, the scene would have made Martha Stewart jealous—either Martha, or a grandmother, because it appeared that an 80-year-old woman had set my table.

I spent the afternoon of the dinner party in the kitchen, where I dirtied every pot, pan, bowl and utensil I owned, and I found I enjoyed myself. The aromas emanating from the stroganoff made my mouth water, but I resisted the temptation to taste the sauce so I wouldn't ruin my appetite for dinner. I noticed my reflection in the microwave's glass door, and I looked a fright. My hair looked as if it had never met a comb, my face was smudged with who knows what, and sweat beaded my upper lip. In five minutes, I semi-pulled myself together while the sauce simmered and the wine chilled.

I turned on appetite-inducing music and swung the door open before my guests finished knocking. Nervous, I gushed over the small hostess gifts they brought, but then censured myself for coming off as too eager. I had made it sound as though they had given me the crown jewels instead of a bottle of wine and three votive candles. We lingered over a glass or two of wine while I made captivating small talk and then announced that dinner was ready.

I served up a heap of beef stroganoff on each plate and leaned back in my chair, waiting for my guests' praise. With their first bite, they shot each other furtive looks. Maybe they were too stunned to speak because I had created such a wonderful meal. No one said a word. The sidelong glances toward the door were disconcerting. I noticed that my guests gulped wine with each bite, so I raced to the kitchen for another bottle.

Tired of waiting for the shouts of bravo, I dug into my meal. It was ghastly. No, it was beyond that. Repugnant is a better description. The meat was shoe-leather, and the sauce was a coagulated mess of grease. I served undercooked noodles and a clump of decimated seaweed that in its original form was broccoli. The salad was overdressed. If cherry tomatoes knew how to swim, they could have done the backstroke. Not knowing what to say, I kept my mouth shut. Everyone, including me, pushed the food around on our plates like children forced to eat spinach. I cleared the table, which I'm sure was much to my guests' relief.

We continued to exchange pleasantries, and I served more wine. They probably thanked the heavens I didn't poison them with my efforts at a dessert course. During a pause in the conversation, one of the couples begged off for the night by saying they had an early morning at the office the following day. Seeing an easy way out, the other neighbors jumped to their feet, too. They ran for the door while I protested by saying the night was still early. I closed the door behind them, and it hit me. It was Saturday night. The declaration of an early morning at the office . . . on a Sunday . . . was unbelievable. That was clear to me, as my neighbor worked for the government and wouldn't be caught dead putting in extra hours on a regular workday, let alone working on a weekend.

I wept while I washed the dishes and scrubbed out the pans. *Where did I go wrong?* I followed the recipe faithfully; at least I thought I did. Mom made it look easy when she had friends and neighborhood strays over for dinner. How did I fail as the hostess of my first dinner party? Blowing out the candles and turning up the chandelier's dimmer, I saw I hadn't created a quaint, quirky vintage tablescape. Instead, I had made a sorry attempt at putting on airs.

I curled up on the couch again to reread the recipe and found I had mistakenly doubled some ingredients, left out others, and cooked the meat for a fraction of the time the cheap cut of beef needed. I once thought that if you can read you can cook, but my reasoning was faulty. False confidence made me think that, because my mother was an exceptional cook, I could be one, too. But I was lousy in the kitchen.

Chapter 11: Hard Realities

The reality of life is that your perceptions—right or wrong —influence everything else you do. When you get a proper perspective of your perceptions, you may be surprised how many other things fall into place.

— Roger Birkman

When they discover the center of the universe, a lot of people will be disappointed to discover they are not it.

— Bernard Bailey

My history of bad behavior and poor decisions converged as one that night. My falsely inflated ego and selfish behavior cost me dearly. I believed I could excel at whatever I did. In reality, that was false bravado. That nonsense caused me embarrassment, got me fired, and nearly poisoned my neighbors. My conceit was unattractive and needed to go. I realized that night that my shit does, in fact, stink.

I remembered Mom's funeral and her friends' outpouring of love. Would that be the case at my funeral? To answer that question, I had a frank conversation with myself. The answer was a flat no. No tears would be shed at my funeral. Especially since no one would be at my funeral except me. I made three promises to my mom and myself that night.

The first one was that I wouldn't host another disastrous dinner party. Mom knew how to make her guests feel loved and comforted by her welcoming meals. I would learn how to create that same warm atmosphere.

The second promise was that I would find a way to duplicate my mother's beef stroganoff, even if I needed to search the world for the recipe. I needed her recipe to feel close to her.

The last, and most important promise I made to myself was that I would behave in a way that would have made my mom proud. My life needed to have value, meaning, and friendship. That night, I cast off my heavy coat of pomposity and put on a more comfortable one. It was made of humility and lined with humanity.

Chapter 12: Promises, Promises, and the Search Begins

A good cook dispenses happiness like a sorceress.

— Elsa Schiaparelli

Arranging a bowl of flowers in the morning can give a sense of quiet in a crowded day – like writing a poem, or saying a prayer.

— Anne Morrow Lindbergh

In pursuit of the first promise I had made to myself, I cooked like a fiend. I experimented with techniques and read cookbooks as though they were novels. Although cooking classes were an option, I wanted to be self-taught.

At first, my cooking was pathetic. I over- or under-cooked food, got the seasonings all wrong, misread recipes, and made meals I wouldn't feed to a cat—and I detest cats. More than once I wished I had spent time in the kitchen with my mom to jump-start the learning process.

The local public television station reran episodes of Julia Child's *The French Chef* and Graham Kerr's *The Galloping Gourmet* late at night, and I watched them any time I managed to stay up late enough. I loved how those two characters stressed the use of fresh, healthy ingredients, but also used copious amounts of butter and wine in their recipes. Julia's on-air mistakes and Graham's tomfoolery taught me to relax in the kitchen. Mistakes happen.

My failures in the kitchen proved to be an excellent way to learn the art of cooking. If I botched a batch of cookies or made wallpaper paste instead of pasta, I remade the recipe until I got it right. I started a journal where I kept a list of cooking tips and annotated the recipes I made, being careful to include what went wrong as well as what worked. Just because vanilla smells divine, it doesn't mean more is better. I ruined a batch of homemade ice cream by doubling the amount of vanilla the recipe called for. I made note that you should grill a steak for five minutes on each side for rare, that an avocado will turn brown unless you sprinkle it with lemon juice, and that if you drop raw potato slices into an over-salted soup or stew, they'll absorb the salt as they cook. The bonus with that last tip was, I had some lovely rounds of potato to fry up for breakfast.

The more I cooked, the better I got at it, and the more I cooked, the more I *wanted* to cook. I also learned that making food comforted me in three ways.

The artistry of cooking is the first. I feel like a member of a dance troupe when I am in the kitchen: the recipe is the company director, the ingredients are my fellow dancers, and the rhythmic motions of dicing, measuring, and whisking are the dance steps. The director teaches the techniques but leaves room for creativity and experimentation. I learned how to express myself in whatever dish I made.

Secondly, I love to eat. A good meal makes me happy, and I eat for the sport of it. I enjoy how cooking and eating use all the senses. The sizzle of onions sautéing and the aroma filling the room draw people to the kitchen. We eat with our eyes as well. Putting green food dye in scrambled eggs doesn't change the taste, but would you want to eat them? A balance of colors on the plate or a dusting of minced parsley on a bowl of stew pleases the eye. Then there's the texture of the meal. Some don't mind the texture of snails or tapioca, but they're both a turnoff for me. Last, but most important, is the taste. I've been known to moan in pleasure with the first bite of something delicious.

And finally, I found comfort in the ghost of mom's presence by my side while I cooked. Cooking gave me a way to make up for lost time with her. However, my guilt sneered at me from the corner of the kitchen about how had I treated Mom when she was alive.

In one of the rare instances when I actually took an interest in my mom's life, I asked how her visit was with her childhood friend, Kay Erickson. I asked about Mrs. Erickson only because she sent me a birthday present every year. Unaccustomed to my attention, Mom launched into a description of the dishes her friend had cooked. In great detail, she told me about the barbecued salmon topped with avocado butter, roasted fingerling potatoes with fresh rosemary and unpeeled cloves of garlic, and the homemade strawberry ice cream they made for dessert. Weeks later, Mom mentioned that Mrs. Erickson was diagnosed with skin cancer. I asked when Mom found out about the cancer. She said she relayed the sad news to her while they were making the strawberry ice cream. I asked her, rather derisively, "Telling me about her avocado butter was more important than mentioning her skin cancer? Darn it, Mom. You describe every event in your life by what food was served." Now, with the way I talk, dream, and think about food, I had become my mother.

I made every beef stroganoff recipe I found. Some were better than others, but none matched my mom's version. Finding the right combination of ingredients seemed impossible. My vague memory of her stroganoff was different from anything I created. The recipe was like a word on the tip of my tongue that wouldn't come out. Undeterred, I plowed ahead.

In a flash of brilliance, I remembered I kept my mom's recipe box, an obvious place to find her beef stroganoff recipe. Her jumble of scraps of paper, recipes torn from the newspaper, and the backs of soup can labels were moldering in a box on a shelf in my kitchen. What a mess. She filed her oatmeal cookie recipe behind the Appetizers tab, and the fried chicken card was stuck to her biscuit recipe. I knew why. She always served her homemade buttermilk biscuits dripping with honey-butter along with her fried chicken. It took three sessions, but I managed to cull through the recipes and set aside the ones I wanted to make.

You guessed it—her beef stroganoff recipe wasn't in the box.

I learned that one trick to being a good cook is using the proper tools. Research on the best knives, pots and pans, and utensils taught me that quality comes with a large price tag. The stuff is expensive. I prowled kitchen stores like a lion on the hunt for good sales. Buying new clothes was once my guilty pleasure, but no more. Give me an efficient cheese grater, and I'm in seventh heaven. I became a connoisseur of cutting boards, lemon zesters, rolling pins, and meat thermometers. Wow! No wonder I was single.

The problem with cooking like a crazy person, if you want to call it a problem, is that you produce boatloads of food. With no one around to eat it but me, my freezer was crammed with surplus meals, cookies, and breads. Rather than filling more plastic containers, I brought my extras into the office and put them in the lunchroom without leaving a note. I often overheard colleagues talking about the wonderful pecan bars, roasted red pepper dip, or pull-apart sticky buns in the kitchen. They wanted to know who made them so they could get a copy of the recipe. My boss, Olivia, sent out an office-wide memo demanding that the person leaving food in the lunchroom show him- or herself immediately and that the person must start providing the recipes for the lunchroom cornucopia that appeared everyday. I raised my hand at the next staff meeting, confessed that I was the phantom provider of snacks, and passed out a sheaf of recipes. From then on, my coworkers would often stop by my cubicle to chat on their way back from the lunchroom. They would thank me, want to talk about food, and beg me to tell them what I was going to make next. My band of groupies encouraged the chef in me with their abundant praise.

An unexpected benefit of being the self-appointed company lunchroom baker and chef was that I got to know my colleagues on a different level. During their frequent stops by my office after they demolished my batch of macadamia nut snickerdoodles or Kalamata olive tapenade on crostini glazed with garlic, we talked about weekend plans, the upcoming football game, or the review for the latest movie release. At first, my cooking was the sole reason they stopped by my office. Over time, as they got to know me, they liked more than my food; they began to like *me*. My loneliness, in part, was solved. I had a batch of friends I could invite over for dinner. They always readily accepted my invitation.

I updated my dinner table by searching boutiques and antique stores and developing my signature style. The table décor needed to reflect beef stroganoff's rich, smooth texture. The trees were moving from lush green to a riot of all the colors of fall, so the changing season was my inspiration. I bought velvet placemats in a deep burgundy, olive-green napkins, and beaded napkin rings. In the window of my favorite antique store, a table was set with ochre-colored dishes, elegant stemware, and silverware with handles the color of espresso. I bought the entire display, and the owner threw in a pewter butter dish as thanks for my profligate purchase. I made a centerpiece with creamy pillar candles in the center of a wreath of Spanish moss and adorned it with acorns, magnolia leaves, and walnuts I had painted bronze. A beautiful meal would be the capstone to the ambiance.

My neighborhood farmers' market was held on Saturdays. The butchers, fish and cheese mongers, and produce sellers got to know my name from my frequent visits. I planned my dinner party menus in advance and gave the vendors my shopping list. During the subsequent week they would set aside a pristine salmon filet, a perfectly ripe round of Brie, an unblemished mango, or whatever other item was on my list. The wine merchant suggested a wine to accompany the meal. I was the general of an army of vendors, and my soldiers were eager to help, because they were regulars at my dinner table. To keep them on my team, I invited them often.

My favorite area of the farmers' market was the flower section. If I could afford the extravagance, flowers would spill out of vases in every room. Even at the farmers' market, a dozen irises were about the same price as a new television —well, maybe not quite, but they were still prohibitively expensive. Allowing myself the luxury of one bouquet for the dining room table, I made my flower choices like a judge at a beauty pageant. To make a colorful statement, each stem needed to possess an unblemished figure and be able to stand on its own in a group of other beauties.

In Search of Beef Stroganoff

The best flower vendor, appropriately named Petunia, offered flower arranging classes. Since I love flowers, I figured I should learn how to properly present them. The once-a-month classes were held in a neighborhood church hall in the afternoon after the farmers' market closed. For the price of admission, you brought home the arrangement you created. I was hooked after the first class and signed up for the year. Petunia was a talented teacher, and she could take a fistful of daisies and make a bouquet fit for a debutante.

One day during class, her stomach rumbled. She glanced around the room with an embarrassed half-smile. She explained that she didn't have time to eat lunch between the close of the market and the start of class. I offered to bring her lunch in exchange for a discount on the class tuition. Without hesitation she agreed, which surprised me. For all she knew, I planned to give her a peanut butter sandwich and a bruised banana in a greasy lunch bag. She saw my puzzled expression and said, "Oh, I heard about your knack in the kitchen from several of the other vendors. I've coveted an invitation to your apartment for dinner for months." From then on, Petunia was a regular guest at my table, and she always brought flowers.

I crossed off "Learn how to throw a dinner party" from my list of promises to myself.

For Thanksgiving, a number of my friends from work and the farmer's market had nowhere to go, or couldn't get away to be with family. I gathered them up and hosted an un-Thanksgiving dinner. Rather than the traditional meal of turkey, stuffing, cranberry, and yams, I made a Mexican fiesta. I didn't want my friends to taste my stuffing and feel nostalgic for their Aunt Betty's oyster and roasted chestnut version. I braised chunks of beef in hearty stock, lime juice, orange zest, tequila, chili powder and cumin for hours, and then shredded the tender meat for enchiladas. A pan of cheese enchiladas would satisfy the vegetarians. I rounded out the meal with an orange and jicama salad dressed with a zesty lime avocado dressing, corn fritters with a dollop of cilantro sour cream, and a batch of frozen margaritas. It wasn't a typical Thanksgiving meal, but no one seemed to miss the turkey.

My friends begged me to host an un-Christmas dinner. I agreed to cook as long as they suggested the menu. They had an animated debate about what they wanted me to make . . . Indian. Cajun. Italian. German. The conversation stopped when I said, "How about rib roast and Yorkshire pudding? Dibs on the end cut." Everyone nodded in agreement. A traditional Christmas dinner it would be.

As the year drew to a close, despite extensive experimentation with beef stroganoff recipes, the answer eluded and baffled me. Then I had an idea. I said aloud to my empty living room, "Maybe someone other than me needs to make it." I granted myself a hiatus and set out to visit every restaurant in San Francisco with beef stroganoff on the menu. My pursuit caused me to pad on ten extra pounds. Beef stroganoff is a caloric orgy. That's one reason the damned stuff tastes good. I didn't gain weight while I made food for others because, by the time the meal was on the table, the aromas had satisfied my appetite.

Sad to say, but no dive diner or bistro with white tablecloths ended my search. I left each meal full, yet unfulfilled.

Chapter 13: An International Quest

Appetite comes with eating; the more one has, the more one would have.

— French proverb

One of the very nicest things about life is the way we must regularly stop whatever it is we are doing and devote our attention to eating.

— Luciano Pavarotti

My first international destination was Austria. The almost fourteen-hour flight was agony. I sat between a rotund woman who should have purchased two seats and a man who forgot to put on deodorant. Sleep was impossible, so I daydreamed about Austria. *Sound of Music* visions of majestic alpine scenery, quaint villages, friendly eateries, and waltzes in the moonlight played in my head. That was when it dawned on me. Perhaps my problem in finding Mom's beef stroganoff recipe was that I had searched on the wrong continent. My parents had traveled to Austria before I entered this world. Maybe that was where my mom had found her recipe.

The trip took me to Salzburg for four days to do groundwork for a brewery that wanted to introduce their beer in the States. I met with the brewmeister to learn about the brewery's beer, brewing techniques, and current marketing strategies. My job was to feed the information to my company's marketing gurus so they could formulate the U.S. marketing, advertising, and public relations campaign.

The fun part was sampling beer with the jovial brewers. Could a brewmeister be anything but jovial?

While in Austria, I managed to find two restaurants with beef stroganoff on the menu. Both meals were excellent; however, I was disappointed to find that neither matched my mom's. Her version was home-cooked, so the secret must be that the recipe comes from a local, not a professional, chef. I found a tiny market on a narrow cobblestone street and implored the owner for her recipe. Despite her poor English and my nonexistent German, we somehow managed to understand each other. I clutched the recipe to my bosom as though I held the winning lottery ticket.

After four days of feeling like a wrung out dishrag when I arrived home, my internal clock adjusted back to local time. I hauled myself to the market to buy the ingredients for the Austrian shopkeeper's recipe. While standing in the meat department, to my horror I realized that half of the words on the paper were in German. Since I don't carry an English-German dictionary with me at all times—or ever, for that matter—I was stuck. I left the market and popped into a nearby bookstore to find one. Surreptitiously, I nestled in a corner and translated the recipe. Undetected by store personnel, I tucked the book back on the shelf and slunk out with a vague sense of guilt. It felt like stealing, but I merely stole the English translation of German for sirloin, sour cream, and onions. Nonetheless, I felt like a criminal. I saw the newspaper headlines in my head: *"Cook Convicted of Six Counts Grand Theft Noun Larceny."*

With my ingredients purchased, I strapped on an apron and set to work. The result was outstanding; the best I had made to date, but still not my mom's. The day after I made the Austrian version of beef stroganoff, I ran into one of the neighbors I had almost killed with my cooking at my first dinner party. I rarely saw her, and when I did, she kept her head down and pretended not to see me. My neighbors had turned down my invitations to dinner after that ill-fated night and avoided contact with me altogether. However, instead of dodging me that day, my neighbor asked what I had cooked the night before. The aroma crept its way under the door and into her apartment. She looked at me in disbelief when I told her what I had made. Pleased, and wanting to redeem my reputation as a chef, I delivered a plate of my stroganoff to her. The praise I expected at my disastrous dinner party was finally given to me for a plate of reheated leftovers.

My second business trip took me to France to research why a cycling clothing company's sales were poor in the States. The head designer showed me the company's line of jerseys, and I saw that he had failed to factor in the size of American cyclists. European riders are built like racehorses . . . sleek, trim, and sinewy. Except for a handful of elite riders, most cyclists in the States are built like Clydesdales, and fitting a wrist, let alone a bicep, through the sleeve of the largest European jersey was impossible. If American cyclists managed to zip up the jersey, most would look like a lumpy sausage. Photographs of typical American cyclists convinced the designer that the company needed to make larger sizes for the American market. I suggested launching an entire line targeting Clydesdale riders to give them the opportunity to wear European jerseys without the need for a starvation diet. He loved the idea.

That evening, I opened the windows in my hotel room and changed out of my work clothes to dress for a stroll and to find a place for dinner. The air was soft and warm and smelled French. My hotel shared an inner courtyard with the apartment building next door, and my neighbors' windows were open, too. I heard the distinct cadence of a knife on a cutting board coming from an apartment across the way. Chop. Chop. Chop. Chop. I left my hotel room but doubled back to grab a sweater in case the evening turned chilly. Returning to the room, I slammed into a wall of aroma. The chef next door had dropped chopped onions and garlic into a frying pan and was making dinner. How I longed to be invited over.

Since food is France's national sport, second only to soccer, I knew my search would come to an end in Paris. Beef stroganoff is Russian, not French, but Parisian chefs must know the trick. I combed the streets for a place to eat my first meal in the City of Light and spotted an enchanting café tucked in the Latin Quarter. They had what I wanted on the menu.

My first French meal was a disappointment. The food was worse than anything served in a school cafeteria. I studied the other diners in the café and realized they were American. I had picked a tourist joint that charged the unwitting patrons exorbitant prices for fake French cuisine. I had made a rookie traveler mistake. I needed to find a restaurant where Parisians dine, not where American tourists eat. I thought I was worldly, but I was appalled by how I blended in with my fellow patrons by looking like a sloppy American.

With the help of the hotel clerk the next evening I found the type of restaurant I wanted. The tiny brasserie was also in the Latin Quarter on an alleyway. Tourists would never find the place unless given specific directions. My minuscule Paris hotel room was almost bigger than the restaurant. Cozy and intimate, the mahogany paneling caressed the room. Stained-glass chandeliers swayed in the breeze from the open windows, and burgundy leather chairs begged for visitors. A toothpick of a woman showed me to a table near the front window.

My attire was clean, neat and presentable, but frumpy, compared to the French women in the restaurant. I wore a navy blazer, tennis shoes, jeans, and a T-shirt. The ensemble was appropriate for any American restaurant or theater; in reality, at home, I might be considered overdressed. In Paris, in that restaurant, I looked as though I had picked my outfit out of a ragbag. A French woman throws on a simple black dress, a string of pearls, and red lipstick, and looks as though she is Coco Chanel's best friend. I later learned their secret. French closets are impossibly small, and French couture comes with a shocking price tag. Rather than amassing piles of throwaway clothing like Americans, they buy a few well-made classic pieces. Their elegant style is effortless and inborn.

So I made a fourth pledge to myself while in Paris. I would work hard on developing a French woman's savoir-faire. Plus, I happen to look extraordinary in black—oops, strike that. The statement was too egotistical for my quest to achieve humility. At any rate, black camouflages extra pounds and hides all kinds of evils.

The café's stroganoff was spectacular, and I considered picking up my plate and licking it clean. But, alas, it was not my mom's recipe. I ate some of the best meals of my life in Paris, and dreams about the crusty bread make me long for a fresh baguette. Oh dear, I had become obsessed with food. Maybe I should see someone about that.

During my time in Paris, I noticed that the French live life at a different tempo than we over-caffeinated Americans do. I wondered if any Parisians held jobs, because at any time of the day sidewalk cafés are filled with men and women smoking, sipping wine, reading the paper, or having animated conversations using their hands. In the middle of a workday, department stores are packed. Smartly dressed women leisurely stroll arm-in-arm along the Seine. Unlike in any big city in the United States, where everyone walks as if they're running late for their heart transplant appointment, the pace in Paris is unhurried.

My next stop was London. I should have taken a chaperone with me, because I had too much fun. Really, I had too, too much fun. A small publishing company was gearing up for the release of a book they sensed was destined for bestseller lists in the States. I interviewed the author, drafted press releases, and scheduled the book signing junket. The work could have been handled by phone, and I wondered why Olivia insisted I do it in person. She mumbled that she owed the owner of the company a favor. I had a good idea what that favor was. The man blushed, and a faraway look veiled his eyes at the mention of her name. I suspected Olivia had broken his heart and she regretted it.

I loved the warm, inviting atmosphere of an English corner pub. Entering one was like a hug from a favorite uncle. (I don't have a favorite uncle, but I imagined if I did, he would hug me tight.) Not much of a beer drinker since college, I fell in love with English porter. The barkeeps weren't shy about pouring me more. The patrons were welcoming and happy to make room at the bar. The bartenders' warm smiles made me want to spill my life story. However, the numerous signs warning patrons to *"Beware of Dirty Bastard Pickpockets"* was disconcerting. Pickpockets weren't a problem for me while in London, but the signs made me cautious. I watched for the Artful Dodger around every corner.

In Search of Beef Stroganoff

Excited about their entrance into the American market, the publishing staffers were ready to celebrate. They invited me to do the pub scene with them after work. After a night of darts, drinking songs, and countless pints, my companions saw me to a double-decker bus to take me back to the hotel. The night was balmy for London in early spring, so I sat on the upper deck. Even if it were chilly, my beer-coat would have kept me warm. Too much stout and the swaying bus lulled me to sleep. We circled the city for an hour until we reached the final stop at the end of the driver's shift. He didn't know I was still on board and found me while he cleaned the bus. If his shift hadn't ended, I might still be on the upper deck. The cab ride back to the hotel emptied my wallet.

Americans make jokes about England's cuisine, but I found it delightful. It isn't merely gray meat, gruel, and suet. Charles Dickens gave his country's food bad press. The English believe in comfort food. After one okay meal of beef stroganoff, I decided to stick to bangers and mash, steak and kidney pie, and Cornish pasties. High tea is now mostly for tourists and the Queen, but I loved having afternoon tea in gardens and oak-paneled hotel lobbies. We Americans need to adopt the civilized tradition of teatime. Silver teapots, finger sandwiches, and scones with jam and clotted cream should replace our coffee in a paper cup and doughnut-on-the-run.

For my next assignment, I was sent to research and take photos of Amsterdam's bike problem. More precisely, I wasn't sent to the city for the problem with bicycles; they love their bikes. Amsterdam is home to more bikes than citizens . . . they do bikes as Rome does Vespas. The only difference is that, rather than changing flat tires or broken chains, people simply abandon their bikes. Bicycle skeletons are locked together five deep along the canal bridges, lampposts, and trees. They sully the city's romantic views.

City officials were at a loss about what to do with the wasteland of derelict bike carcasses, short of spending thousands of dollars on removal. They wanted to get to the root of the problem. The mayor's office put out a request for bids for a media campaign to address the issue. The president of my company was an avid cyclist, and he hoped my research would help nab the account.

I made the mistake of renting a car at the airport and relying on a map to guide me to my hotel in the historic town center. One-way streets with names that have more vowels than consonants suddenly became one-way streets going in the other direction. Bicycles swarmed around me like bees, and I almost collided with several daring riders who challenged my tentative driving. At last I spotted my hotel down a one-way alley, but I had to circle several streets before I was able to reach it. The hotel clerk sensed, by the wild look in my eye, that I needed a stiff drink and a good meal, so he handed me my room key and directions to a nearby restaurant. As long as it had a bar and I didn't need to climb behind the wheel, I didn't care where I ate. The car sat in the garage the rest of my time in Amsterdam.

Not fifty meters from the hotel was a restaurant that felt like walking into someone's kitchen for dinner. A Dutch woman with a shock of silver curls and skin like a twenty-year-old showed me to a table. She sat down across from me and recited the menu as if reading poetry. In excellent English, she said, "Remember what interests you as soon as you hear it, and forget about the rest. You won't remember it all." She was right. She stopped talking, and, as she predicted, I forgot what was on the menu, except for what I wanted to order . . . to start, the roasted paprika soup with crystalized ginger and pumpkin seed garnish, and then the fillet of beef with goat cheese and strawberry balsamic reduction sauce.

I asked her for a menu after I ordered, because I wanted to know what I had forgotten in an instant. She pointed toward the front door and said, "It is on that chalkboard. I change the menu almost daily. I can't afford to print it when something new is in season, when the butcher has venison, or my whim changes." I ate at the restaurant every night, and her menu did indeed change daily. With a shrug and a smile, she ignored my request to make the roasted paprika soup again. Sadly, I can't recommend the restaurant to anyone. The name has too many vowels, and the city's numerous one-way streets make giving directions impossible.

While in Amsterdam I didn't know if I should sightsee, shop, smoke pot, or visit an art museum when I wasn't working on the bicycle research project. The canal-laced streets offer diversions for all tastes, including prostitutes and live-sex-act shows, if one is so inclined. I wasn't, but I walked the streets of the Red Light District to prove to myself I was bold enough to venture in—only bold enough to venture in during the daylight, however. The girls in the windows were young, and their beauty surprised me. The women on display, like a candy store for men, were fit, cute, and wore wisps of clothing that showcased their ample physiques. I expected gaunt, drugged-out women with no self-esteem, not models torn from the pages of girlie magazines.

Amsterdam rejected our proposal, and instead built a gigantic sculpture out of abandoned bicycles to raise public awareness about the problem. The sculpture made a statement, but I thought the campaign was dumb. How would yet another jumble of bicycles encourage people to not abandon their bikes?

Chapter 14: Sins of the Past and My Attempt at Redemption

Hell is yourself, and the only redemption is when a person puts himself aside to feel deeply for another person.

— Tennessee Williams

In case you're wondering, I still wear my coat of humility with pride. I know I'm not the center of the universe and can't completely atone for the sins of my past, but I make an effort to be a good person.

I've talked about my inflated sense of self-worth in my youth. You must think I consider myself attractive as well. My mother called me beautiful. My pimply-faced high school boyfriend said I was pretty, but then his acne cleared up, and he became one of the popular kids. He didn't think I was so cute anymore and dumped me. With my promise to be more humble, I owe you a description of what I look like. In one word, I'm plain. My appearance isn't notable, and my features are ordinary. I'm not ugly, but I'm no great beauty either.

Thanks to my mother's $4,000 investment in orthodontia, my teeth are straight. I'll note here that my investment in my teeth was spending two years in junior high school without smiling. Thick glasses correct my horrible vision, but I wear contacts when I'm out of the apartment. My height, weight, and build are average, and my hair is nondescript. I never bought a prom dress, my name was missing from the nomination list for homecoming queen, and college boys didn't ask me on dates. I'm invisible when in a bar for happy hour, and I don't turn men's heads when I walk down the street. A construction worker did whistle at me one time—or, he whistled at the blonde behind me, but I'd like to think his admiration was directed toward me. I try to do the best with what I have. I dress nicely, style my hair, and put on makeup every day. Even with that, I am a regular looking person. How's that for humility?

My New Year's resolution was to fulfill the third promise I made to myself. I would become someone my mom would be proud of. She read to shut-ins, and I decided that volunteering at a nursing home was the perfect way to start. Besides, a space inside me craved the companionship of an older woman. I have always been more comfortable around people older than me than I was with my peers. Spending time with a senior citizen would be a way to learn life lessons from someone seasoned with the wisdom of time. Maybe I wanted a surrogate mother, but my ultimate goal was to be kind to another person.

There was a nursing home not far from my apartment. I expected to be welcomed there as a volunteer messiah for senior citizens. With a polite explanation, the administrator sent me away. She said I needed to produce a clean criminal background check before I could volunteer. I started to bluster, "What? Do I look capable of elder abuse?" But, swallowing the words, I trooped downtown for a background check.

The lobby of the Department of Justice was crowded with people who sported more tattoos than teeth. I clutched my handbag to my stomach. I was frumpy in Paris, but in the stark government fortress surrounded by the seamy oddballs, a fashion magazine editor would have no choice but to use me on their cover.

In Search of Beef Stroganoff

The nursing home called when my fingerprint clearance arrived, and I marched back. The receptionist peeked at me from around a floral arrangement on the front desk that was worthy of the Hall of Flowers. I waited for the administrator in the lobby, which was furnished with brocade sofas, oil paintings, and a marble floor so shiny I could have done my makeup in its reflection. The place was as elegant as an expensive hotel or exclusive country club. I couldn't imagine the cost. The nursing home surely stood in sharp contrast to the state facility where my college roommate's grandmother had lived.

The nursing home administrator said I could read to Astrid, a delightful woman in her eighties and one of their favorite residents. Astrid had few visitors, because her family lived in Minnesota and she would enjoy the company. The old-fashioned name conjured up the image of a sweet-faced grandmother, and I knew we would hit it off. The administrator did give me one warning. "Astrid isn't afraid to speak her mind. She's opinionated, can be crusty on the outside, and is quick to tell you what she thinks. However, she has the kindest heart of anyone I know."

I waltzed into Astrid's room and announced myself. Her room was as classy as the lobby. Aside from the hospital bed, you might have mistaken it for the master suite of a Nob Hill penthouse. Her flat screen television was the size of my apartment. Astrid was, indeed, a sweet-faced grandma-type who sat in a wheelchair with an afghan over her knees. However, she gave me one disgruntled glance and said, "I don't know who you are, and I sure as hell don't want what you're selling."

I gulped as the woman growled at me. With my voice shaking I said, "My name is Meredith. I'm not here to sell you anything; I came to read to you."

Chapter 14: Sins of the Past and My Attempt at Redemption

"You remind me of my smart-ass great-niece," she retorted. "Don't assume I want a floozy like you to read to me." She spun her wheelchair around and harrumphed. That hurt. I had expected to find a benevolent fairy godmother in the nursing home room, not an ogre.

Unsure of what to do, I pulled up a chair next to her and wrung my hands. I mentioned the warm weather we were having, commented on the elegant décor of the lobby, and rambled about the new exhibit at the Legion of Honor. While I made small talk, Astrid shot a dirty look my way every few minutes. The uncomfortable silence on her part made me give up my babble, so I sat with my hands tucked under my thighs. Astrid snorted when I left, and I told her I would be back the following week.

The same scene played out over several weeks. Busting through her crotchety shell was impossible. The friendly bullets I fired at her armor were ineffective. But I was determined to stand my ground. Books, playing cards, and a jigsaw puzzle didn't interest her. I tucked pictures from my travels in my bag, music to play, and stationery in case she cared to dictate a letter. The music was a bad idea. When I played my favorite cassette tape, she said, "Turn off that dreadful racket." I became a master at filling the void with talk about current events, the latest fashion trends, and what was on special at the market. Nothing worked.

"I've no idea why Astrid is snippy with you," the nurse said. "You must rub her the wrong way." The desire to win Astrid over followed me like the sound of footsteps in a dark alley.

Weeks into the ordeal of the uncomfortable silence while I sat next to her, I felt defeated and melancholy. Out of the blue, I told Astrid about Mom's passing and my remorse over being a selfish and miserable child. She listened while I talked for the better part of an hour without taking a breath. For the first time since our initial encounter, she looked me in the eye and said, “Your mother was a lucky woman to have you for a daughter, Meredith.” Astrid spun her wheelchair around and focused her glare out the window.

Eyes stinging with tears, I stumbled my way to the street. At the first opportunity, I collapsed on a stoop and bawled. How could she call me a good daughter after I confessed I behaved like a despicable person? What did she see in me that I couldn’t see in myself? Wait—she remembered my name? I blew my nose, and in a fog I made my way back to my apartment, where I consumed a bottle of wine. I admit I was self-medicating, and staring into the bottom of my glass was a coping mechanism for burying my pain and guilt. The wine was my heartache cure in a bottle.

We didn’t mention my confession during my next visit, and Astrid, as usual, was stony. The urge to say more about my regrets compelled me to speak. I needed to dust another sadness off my chest. “I could have prevented my college roommate’s suicide.”

While I talked, Astrid stared at her hands. At the end of my dissertation, I was drained and crying. Astrid said, “How kind of you, Meredith, to attend the poor girl’s funeral.” What? I confessed I deserved the World’s Worst Person award, and she thought I was *kind?* Was she crazy?

Over the subsequent weeks, Astrid listened to the rest of my sorrows about how I had lived my life in a self-absorbed vacuum. Sparing no details during the lousy boyfriend stories, my tears that time were caused by anger. I found myself furious about the situations all over again and more ticked at myself than with the ex-boyfriends. Astrid shrugged and said, “Good for you for wising up and dumping the sons of bitches." I recounted the story of my abysmal failure and ultimate firing from my first job because I stole time and office supplies from my employer. My out-of-control addiction to file folders, binders, sticky notes and rollerball pens had led me to a life of white-collar crime, and I needed to enter Organizers Anonymous for rehab. Pithy Astrid said, "Sounds as though you learned your lesson. My smart-ass great-niece isn't so sharp."

I volunteered to read to that old woman, but not one word was recited from a book. Our time together was cleansing my soul, unburdening my guilt, and healing my wounded heart. Astrid deserved an hourly rate for my therapy sessions.

She was as crusty as ever on my next visit. Impervious to her grouchy demeanor, I shared the story about my ill-fated dinner party and my epiphany after washing the dishes. "Astrid, I couldn't cook, I was a terrible hostess, and I need to find my mother's beef stroganoff recipe to feel close to her."

At the end of my story she was silent. I waited, expecting a succinct moral or encouraging words. I didn't get either one; she belted me with uproarious laughter. She caught her breath, wiped tears from her eyes and said, "That was a priceless story. You got your comeuppance, but saw the light because you made a lousy meal and a fool of yourself. Good girl, Meredith. Next time, bring *To Kill a Mockingbird* with you. The book is my favorite."

You didn't need a feather to knock me over. An eyelash would have done the job.

Chapter 15: A New Friendship

A friend is someone who understands your past, believes in your future, and accepts you just the way you are.

— Attributed to Abraham Lincoln

A friend is one of the nicest things you can have, and one of the best things you can be.

— Douglas Pagels

Somehow, in the process of unloading my life story to Astrid, I earned her trust. I floated a foot above the sidewalk on my way home, because I had made a step forward at last in becoming her friend. I combed my apartment and found Mom's copy of *To Kill a Mockingbird.* I figured Astrid would love what Mom had written to me on the inside cover of the book: *"This is my favorite, well, one of my favorite lines in this book: 'Until I feared I would lose it, I never loved to read. One does not love breathing.' Meredith, I hope you feel this way about reading. I do."* I counted the days until my next visit with Astrid.

The day finally arrived for my visit, and I checked my purse ten times to make sure Atticus, Scout, Jem, and Boo Radley were still tucked inside before I left for the nursing home. They were. Astrid's room was empty. Not worried, I assumed she was visiting a neighbor. After sitting alone in her room for five minutes, I began to pace.

Ten minutes later, I decided to check with a nurse. The head nurse knew me by then, and when I approached her desk, she paled. She said, "The doctor admitted Astrid to the infirmary during the night. A bout of the flu left her dehydrated and weak. She needs rest after her rough night."

I left the nursing home and found the stoop where I had stopped to cry before. My poor, dear, irascible new friend was not well.

Worry and angst were my constant companions until I learned Astrid had recovered. As my mother would say, I felt as though I had been dragged through a knothole backwards. I rushed to the nursing home room, and Astrid said, "Where the hell have you been?" She dismissed my stammered explanation with a gnarled hand. "Did you bring the book?"

With a light heart I opened *To Kill a Mockingbird* and read her Mom's inscription. Astrid said, "Your mom was a good soul. My favorite line is something like, 'You can choose your friends but you can't choose your family. They're your kin even if you don't acknowledge them and you look silly if you don't.' I'm glad you're finally acknowledging your dear mother."

We were engrossed in the book after page two, but by chapter four Astrid's chin was resting on her chest while she caught a peaceful catnap. Books do that to me as well. I'll never need a sleeping pill. Hand me a book, and I'm dozy in five minutes.

I collected my purse, left a note on her lap, and tiptoed to the door. As I reached for the knob, Astrid said, "How's the stroganoff search coming?" I apologized for waking her and told her my mission was at a standstill. She said, "I made a mean stroganoff in my day. Our neighbors always asked me to bring it to our little town's potluck suppers. My recipe is a legend, but I shared it with only one person."

I knelt by Astrid's side, clasped her hand, and said, "I hope one day you trust me enough to share your recipe with me." As I closed the door behind me, I swear I heard her snort.

I had learned from the nursing home administrator that Astrid was Swedish, grew up on a farm in Minnesota, and moved to San Francisco ages ago with her husband of 50 years. I regressed to my old snobbish habits for a moment and figured Astrid's recipe couldn't be what I had been searching for. I wanted the quintessential beef stroganoff, not one from a farmer's daughter. I didn't give her recipe another thought until I got home that night. If her recipe was that special, maybe I should hound her for it.

At first, I allotted an hour for my visits with Astrid. That hour evolved into two, sometimes three hours. If she dozed off, I left a note and crept out of her room. After *To Kill a Mockingbird,* we moved on to *Of Mice and Men*. We shared the same taste in literature. We read *A Tree Grows in Brooklyn*, and, to my surprise, when we finished the book, she asked me to bring a Stephen King novel. The woman loved lyrical prose, as well as page-turners with a little horror thrown in.

Occasionally we played cards, and I suspected she knew how to count cards like a card shark. We solved crossword puzzles together, but Astrid didn't understand the modern references in some of the crossword clues. She couldn't fathom why *user* was the four-letter answer to the clue *manual reader*. She had me beat on the clues about the Great Depression and World War II, so we made a good team. By now our friendship was as comfortable as a favorite sweater.

If I happened to visit when Astrid was in the community room watching her favorite game show, she would shush me without ceremony. Every senior citizen in the nursing home would be glued to the television for the half-hour show. If I did try to say something to her, I needed to shout, as the TV volume was deafening.

Astrid was also a rabid baseball fan. She wouldn't let me talk when a game was on television either, especially when her beloved Minnesota Twins were playing. She learned to love the game by watching her high school team. "Those strapping young farm boys knew their way around a baseball diamond," she said. "They won the state title my senior year. Plus, the centerfielder was a cutie." I bought her a Minnesota Twins baseball cap and pennant. I thumbtacked the pennant above her dresser, and Astrid wore the cap when she watched the Twins on television. She looked adorable.

I blurted out an awkward question one day because I was curious. "Why did you dislike me when we met?" She said, "I saw the chip on your shoulder from across the room. It wasn't a chip; the Rock of Gibraltar is more like it, and I couldn't be bothered. I've lived too long to put up with self-important do-gooders. I understand your past now; you've changed, and now I like you."

Astrid was a perceptive woman.

Chapter 16: Lessons

Challenges make life interesting, however, overcoming them is what makes life meaningful.

— Mark Twain

This day is all that is good and fair. It is too dear with its hopes and invitations to waste a moment on yesterday.

— Ralph Waldo Emerson

Astrid asked me if I owned a car, because she wanted to show me some places from her past. I confessed my car was a pile of junk on wheels and the battery was probably dead because I hadn't driven it in ages. I left her to ask the nurse if Astrid and I could go for a drive. The nurse said, "You need the doctor's permission. Astrid is sharp, but don't let that fool you; her body is betraying her. She is proud but not vain, and watching her body fail must be hard for her. But I know Astrid would love to go out with you. Did you know her birthday is next week?" The nurse called the doctor, who approved an outing on the condition that it wouldn't be too demanding. I sauntered back into Astrid's room and announced we were taking a road trip and I was taking her out to lunch for her birthday.

The next week, I pulled dust-covered Athena into the loading zone and hopped out to collect Astrid from her room. She was in fine form. She wore a paisley dress, and the nursing home beauty parlor somehow wrestled her hair into tight curls. She dabbed on a little garish pink lipstick while I pushed her wheelchair to the door. "Do you think I'm an invalid, Meredith? "My walker is in the closet." Geez, would she ever stop barking at me? I had assumed she was confined to the wheelchair, but she said, “Damn doctor doesn’t like me to walk much. Scared I’ll fall. He wants to do a hip replacement, but I won’t let ’em. I’m not a spring chicken, you know. I’d die on the operating table.” She flew down the hall pushing her walker, and I scurried to keep up. The nurse called after her, “No running in the halls, Astrid.” She might not be a spring chicken, but she was spry.

We started our outing at Tadich Grill for a lunch of their famous seafood cioppino. I gave Astrid a framed photograph that captured Golden Gate Park in all its glory at the height of spring. She said, “I know exactly where I want to hang this in my room so I can enjoy it every day. It is the perfect gift.” Over our meal, we decided that lunch at Tadich’s was a must for every birthday we celebrated together.

After lunch, I climbed behind the wheel and said, “Now where to?”

“You’ll see,” she replied. “I want to show you four places from my past. Go left at the light.” I put the car in gear and chattered like a kid on the first day of summer vacation. She remained silent except to give me directions.

Our first stop was where Astrid had gone to night school when she was first married. The building was now a dilapidated shell with a wrecking ball in its future. It was quiet in the parked car. Astrid drew a slow breath and said, “I, too, treated a classmate poorly. The young woman struggled to make the grade, and I found immense pleasure in besting her at every opportunity. The more I succeeded, the more the woman floundered. Rather than coming to her aid when she asked for help, I treated her with disdain. I was competitive to a fault, and she brought out a mean streak in me.”

The woman didn't show up for school one night, nor the next, nor the night after that. Astrid worried about her disappearance, regretted not helping her, and wondered whatever had become of her. Years later, a rags-to-riches story in the newspaper caught Astrid's eye. The article was about the woman who had struggled in Astrid's night classes. She had changed schools and was mentored by a talented teacher. She went on to get a master's degree in business at Stanford, founded an investment brokerage firm when she was in her forties, and was worth millions. She led the way for women in the early days of the male-dominated world of high finance.

"Don't blame yourself for your roommate's suicide, Meredith," Astrid said. "How were you to know the girl's spirit was broken? Not every bad relationship ends in tragedy. While you should have been more kindhearted, you learned your lesson and are working hard to become a better person. Or, at least, you have turned the page."

The next stop was in Golden Gate Park, with its tree-lined paths, cool lawns, and benches tucked in intimate nooks. The cherry trees celebrated the glorious spring day by wearing pink bonnets. After a long search for a parking space, I gave up, double-parked, and wrestled the walker from the trunk. Astrid ambled to the closest bench and waited while I parked in a garage a few blocks away. When I joined her, she said, "This park is where I almost had a love affair. As a new bride, I adored my husband, but when I met a dashing young man at night school, my love for Sven wavered. The man was debonair, bought me small gifts, and flattered me with pretty compliments. He knew how to turn a girl's head, and I became smitten. I invented excuses to cover for stolen moments in this park with the man. The way he made my heart flutter caused me to question my marriage. Maybe I married too young? The only boy I kissed was Sven. The almost-affair gave me doubts about every aspect of my life."

A fellow classmate suspected a romance was brewing between Astrid and the charmer. She pulled Astrid aside and said, "That man's amorous overtures are an attempt to con money from you, you fool. He's a heavy drinker, a gambler, mired in debt, and can't hold a job. Wise up, Astrid." Naïve and trusting to a fault, Astrid was an easy mark. She was also a hopeless romantic. The combination was ripe for stupid mistakes.

Raised in Minnesota as a good Lutheran girl, she frowned upon the drink and gambling. She was also smart and quick to see through his sweet talk after her friend tipped her off. Disillusioned and angry, she ended the relationship in no uncertain terms. Thankfully, she broke it off before she broke her sweet husband's heart; Sven would walk on the sun for her if she asked him to. She never risked losing his love again.

Astrid grabbed my chin and twisted my face so she could look me in the eye. "It's time you got off your fanny and found a man like Sven."

For our third stop, she asked me to pull up near a storefront. Astrid and her husband had owned the market on the ground floor of the building and rented one of the apartments above it. Now a Korean man ran the market, but Astrid owned the entire building. Smoked ducks strung up by their feet, bundles of herbs, and silvery dried fish hung in the market's windows. Strange-looking Asian vegetables were piled in bins on the sidewalk. Astrid said the apartment was where she experienced great joy, along with the darkest of days. Sven and Astrid raised a daughter there, only to have her taken away at far too young an age. The single tear on her cheek let me know she was too vulnerable to tell me what happened to the child.

Astrid said, "I, too, carried horrible guilt for the way I treated my mother when I followed Sven to San Francisco to open the shop he always wanted. Mother begged us to stay and argued that she would never see us again."

When her mother fell ill, Astrid boarded the next train to be at her bedside. She arrived home in time to ask her mother to forgive her for leaving town. Her mother said, "No, honey, don't say you are sorry. I'm a lucky woman to have you as a daughter." Those were the same words Astrid said to me after I bared my soul about my poor relationship with my mom.

We stared at her former home, and Astrid said, "Teenagers can be little shits. Mothers are used to their selfish behavior and know how to forgive. Hanging on to your remorse is unnecessary. Set aside your guilt about how you treated your mom, and embrace her memory. Needless regrets taint the past. Let it go, Meredith."

We moved on to the loading zone in front of the building where Astrid had worked as a bookkeeper. Like the night school, it, too, had changed, but this time the change was for the better. The offices had been converted into tony lofts with posh boutiques on the street level.

Astrid and Sven were desperate for money for their daughter's funeral. They wanted to bury her in their hometown, but shipping the body by train to Minnesota was expensive. They also needed money for their own train fare. As the bookkeeper, Astrid did the company's daily bank deposits and had unbridled access to the owner's account. In a rash and grief-stricken act, Astrid stole money from her boss so she could give her daughter the burial she deserved.

She paid back the money in full with interest, but years later her boss discovered her crime and summarily fired her.

"Strive to be the best employee, never repeat mistakes, and learn from those who know more than you," she advised. "You're lucky your boss didn't call the cops when you stole office supplies."

Our grand tour was over, and Astrid's parole from the nursing home came to an end. I pulled to the curb. "I hope you listened and learned," she said. "Leave the past where it belongs, and make a better future because of what you learned from your mistakes. I give you permission to let go of the guilt over your roommate's suicide and how you treated your mom. Let everything else go. Regrets will get you nothing but a goddamned ulcer.

"A wise man once said to me that, while you are building the resume of your professional career, you need to be building your obituary. Do things with your life that will make you look good in the article they write about you when you die. That way, you'll know you have truly helped someone. Your obituary will be the resume of your life. Make it productive and worthwhile. Dallying with me isn't enough."

Astrid had sacrificed herself and her afternoon nap to lead me on an exhausting yet poignant trip through the tangles and brambles of her past. The outing probably dredged up as many painful memories for her as happy ones. She wanted to teach me a lesson which was to quit beating myself up. A 2,000-pound burden lifted off my shoulders, while it felt as if the floor had dropped from beneath me. She found a way to let herself off the guilt-hook and paved the way for me to forgive myself too. Our two lives, two generations apart, shared many similarities. Her mistakes were akin to mine. The stories were different, but oh, so parallel.

I escorted her back to her room for a cup of tea and a nap. Back at home, I sat on the couch with my elbows on my knees and stared at the floor. It would take time to process Astrid's lessons. So what did I do? I dialed my mother's number. I knew the phone was disconnected, but I called it anyway. Over the robotic recording telling me to check directory assistance for the new number I said, "I'm sorry, Mom."

During the next visit with Astrid, I studied the photographs on her dresser. One was of an angelic toddler sitting on the market's stoop, holding a melting ice cream cone. Another photo was of her parents. I picked up a picture of a young man with a winsome smile. "That is a photo of my handsome husband from when he was on the high school baseball team," she said. "Cute, eh?"

I lingered the longest over the photo of Astrid when she was about my age. She looked like a beauty queen.

I visited her weekly; some weeks I went several times. Our relationship changed. We laughed more, cried some, and had a heated debate over using canned versus fresh tomatoes. Sometimes I accompanied Astrid to her physical therapy sessions, or, as she called it, her "pumping iron time." She kept up her strength, even while slowing down.

Every week I baked banana nut bread, blueberry muffins, or an assortment of cookies and nestled them in a basket lined with a crisp linen napkin to share with Astrid's fellow nursing home residents. Is there anything better than the smell of butter, sour cream, and vanilla? The nursing director admonished me, because so many of the people living there were on restricted diets and became upset if they couldn't indulge in what I brought. I had to find new recipes that avoided salt, fats, and sugar. It was a labor of love.

I quit bitching about my miserable life, because it was no longer miserable. My best friend was in her eighties, and by now I was making a comfortable living. I gave up my neurotic quest for my mother's beef stroganoff recipe and relaxed when I dined out. The pressure was off. Mom's recipe became a savory memory instead of a pointless competition with my guilt. The memories of my mom kept me company instead of haunting my dreams.

Chapter 17: Obituary Building

Many persons have a wrong idea of what constitutes true happiness. It is not attained through self-gratification but through fidelity to a worthy purpose.

— Helen Keller

I experienced some minor successes on my job. The French cycling account was the most notable. After a year on the job, Olivia promoted me to account manager. Although my new office was still not in a corner, it had a window, real walls, and a door. The total space was merely the size of Rockefeller's desk, but it was vast acreage compared to my former cubicles.

As an account manager, I wrote press releases, new business proposals, and ad copy. Writing was my favorite part of the job. I had pangs of guilt over being paid to do something I love. Olivia admired my writing skills and had my colleagues give me their work to edit. At first they were resentful and argued with me over the changes I made. I was gentle in my delivery, but my coworkers were defensive and at times hostile. Perhaps it was because they still saw me as the new kid.

Yet they slowly began to recognize the value of my edits and eventually were happy to seek out my counsel. Or maybe it was just that Olivia had told them to shut up. She more likely said, "Hush up," because it's more in keeping with her gentle style. I didn't mind the editing assignments, because I became a better writer with the practice.

One of my job requirements was to serve on a non-profit board of directors. Astrid had told me to build my obituary with good deeds, and now my company was obliging me to do it. The type of non-profit was up to me, as long as the mission fell within my company's philanthropic guidelines. I wanted to be involved with an organization that worked to improve the lives of senior citizens. I didn't care if the agency's work dealt with housing, providing meals, transportation, or healthcare, but it needed to be senior-centered.

Helping senior citizens was important to my mom. Because I wanted to make her proud of me, it was a noble endeavor in my quest to build my obituary and be a better person. Astrid's life as a senior was one of relative ease, minus the hip pain, but thinking about less fortunate old folks made my heart blue. I wanted to promote their health and happiness. I wanted to do it in honor of Mom and Astrid. I needed to do it for me.

Getting on a board of directors isn't as easy as it sounds. Most non-profits are particular about who sits on their board, and more than a few rejected me. I approached an agency that offered a variety of services to senior citizens, including rides to doctor appointments. The director and chairman of the board interviewed me. They were passionate about the agency's mission to the point of obsessive. The director had a commanding presence that made me want to sit near her to soak up her knowledge. The board chair was a prominent lobbyist and as smooth as a politician on the campaign trail, but not in a creepy way; he possessed John F. Kennedy charisma. The interview was like a chat with two friends, and I was invited to join the board.

The director gave me a binder filled with information about the agency and the issues their work addressed. Not wanting to make a fool of myself at my first board meeting, I did my homework. The agency's profile and outline of services confused me; I couldn't figure out how they assisted seniors. I understood the meaning of each word on the page, but the way they were strung into sentences made no sense. I blamed my inexperience.

I decided to keep my mouth shut during my first board meeting and learn by listening. If I opened my mouth, the director would surely recognize my ignorance and kick me off the board. The receptionist ushered the board members into the opulent boardroom as though we were royalty. Leather executive chairs gathered around a table the size of a football field. The artwork was museum-quality, and walking on the plush carpet in heels was a perilous exercise. The audiovisual equipment rivaled that found in any Fortune 500 company's boardroom. Tuxedoed waiters served the catered breakfast. *Wow!* I thought. *The agency must store buckets of discretionary money in the janitor closet. Where did the funds come from?*

The board chair opened the meeting, welcomed everyone, and introduced me. He asked me to say a few words about myself. Not expecting to be called on, I blabbered a few words about my background. I wondered what I had said and hoped I sounded intelligent. He then asked the committee chairs to give their respective reports. The board members were downright rude and interrupted the reports with condescending questions and negative comments. I sat on my hands during the presentations as my head swiveled back and forth between the speakers as if I were watching a tennis match.

The chair of the finance committee gave a vague, disjointed report. The fund development and public relations chairs reported jointly, because the committees were working together on a dinner dance and live auction fundraiser. Half of the room found fault with what the committee had accomplished since the last report. The member development chair droned on about updating the bylaws. I was befuddled . . . not one mention of senior citizen issues. Wasn't that why we assembled in that sacred chamber?

The board chair turned the meeting over to the director for her report. She spewed out what I assumed were the names of the agency's programs in an acronym alphabet soup and cited what seemed to me to be unrelated statistics. The board members let her speak without interruption. Their wide-eyed reverence made you think she was hand-delivering the Ten Commandments to Moses. They hung on each word like disciples. An eloquent speaker, she kept her audience rapt and bowed to their applause at the end of her report, but the gobbledygook she spewed made my eyes cross. Again, I reasoned my inexperience was to blame and I would understand with more time.

The finance chair approached me after the meeting to invite me to her committee. Knowing full well the finance committee would be a bad fit for me, I said, "I majored in business, but numbers baffle me, and I don't know the difference between a balance sheet and an income statement."

She patted my arm and said, "That's okay, Meredith. You don't need to know anything." I dreaded being on the committee, but since it was for the greater good, I didn't whine about my assignment.

As I predicted, I couldn't read, much less analyze, the reports distributed at the finance meetings. But I did know enough to recognize that the expenses were greater than the income. I asked about the negative cash flow, and the director gave me mumbo-jumbo about it happening every month but that the finances even out by the end of the year. "The problem is with the timing of entering the grants' contracts and performing services before getting reimbursed," she said.

See what I mean? Martian-speak. I found it odd that she asked us to return the handouts at the end of the meeting because they were "confidential and must not leave the building." What did she think I wanted to do, hand out her precious financials on the street corner? But I complied.

Try as I might, I couldn't understand where the money came from and how the agency spent it besides lavishing the board members with food and a palatial boardroom. I invited the director to lunch, hoping a one-on-one session would help clear things up for me.

She was pleasant and witty over lunch, as I knew she would be. Without my noticing until it was too late, she changed the subject whenever I turned the conversation toward the agency. It was like asking her what time it was and having her tell me how the watch was made. She regaled me with a story of how she had found a darling pair of shoes on sale, and she invited me on a shopping trip. The next tale was about the time she had dropped her purse in a canal in Venice. A dashing Italian man had swooped her bag from the water before it could sink, invited her for a drink, and attempted to woo her to his bed.

She twirled a strand of hair around her finger over and over and over while she talked. At first I found the gesture precious, but when I realized she twisted her hair only when pouring on the charm, the habit began to annoy me. She reminded me of my favorite line from *My Fair Lady* . . . "Oozing charm from every pore, he oiled his way around the floor."

Chapter 17: Obituary Building

The director went on a six-week medical leave and was vague about the reason. I assumed it was a female issue and sent her flowers and a card. At the board meeting after she returned from leave, a new member was sitting at the head of the table. I sat next to my committee chair and leaned over to ask her who it was. She said, "She's not a new member. That bag of bones is the director."

I couldn't believe this was the same person. The skin on the director's face was so taut she looked like a mummy wearing pink lipstick. The finance chair said, "She dumped her husband of thirty years, lost twenty pounds, and had a facelift and a boob job. I suspect she had a tummy-tuck too. No one with three kids has a stomach that flat."

I had wasted my hard-earned money by sending her flowers to wish her speedy recovery from self-mutilation. From her tone, I sensed the finance chair was shaken out of her charm-induced coma and no longer cared much for "that bag of bones." Maybe I had found an ally.

Rather than handing back the financials at the end of the meetings, I would tuck them in my briefcase when no one was looking. Astrid had been a successful business owner and bookkeeper; maybe she could help me read the reports. Astrid and I pored over them, and she pointed out entries that raised concern. I decided to consult my boss Olivia as well. "Don't ask me about financials," Olivia said. "I don't know how to balance my checkbook."

I went to the next meeting armed with the list of questions Astrid had helped me compile. The finance chair let the director answer. With a winning smile she talked in circles. I tried to follow along but was lost midway through her sentences. I asked for clarification and received jargon and more intelligent sounding nonsense. My fellow committee members nodded their heads in solemn understanding of what the director was saying. She had mastered the art of confusing the masses into conformity.

The director interrupted my third question and announced that the meeting was over. “Meredith, you know we promise our board members that we begin and end our meetings on time.” With a smile and a sleight of hand she dismissed my pesky questions. It felt as if a thin shroud of dishonesty had blanketed the meeting.

Chapter 18: Finding a Man

Falling in love consists merely in uncorking the imagination and bottling the common sense.

— Helen Rowland

I don't think any day is worth living without thinking about what you are going to eat next at all times.

— Nora Ephron

I had shut men out after my two devastating boyfriend experiences, so I shunned advances from, or even friendly banter with, men unless our interactions were work-related. Even in those conversations I came off as unapproachable. They all must have thought I liked men about as much as I liked taking out the garbage. If they did, they were correct.

I heeded Astrid's advice and decided to get off my fanny and find a new man. But I didn't go to bars or sign up for a dating service. I wasn't adept at flirting, so how was I supposed to let a man know I was interested? Handing him my phone number seemed too forward.

So I decided that meeting the right man merely entailed opening myself to the possibility that somewhere on our planet a guy has my name written on his heart. With gentle hope, I began to look at men differently. If I found myself attracted, I wondered, "Is he the one?" I decided to let finding a new man play out on its own, and when a good man knocked on my heart, I hoped I would be at home.

At first I brought a book or newspaper along when I went out alone to restaurants. I wanted to appear to be an out-of-town businesswoman forced to eat by herself, rather than a nerd with no friends. After a while, I didn't care what others thought, and I enjoyed my surroundings over a leisurely meal. I liked to eat alone, because I love people-watching. I learned how to figure out who found new love, who imparted bad news, what tables talked business, and who let a spat ruin their night out. Spying is a fascinating hobby.

I discovered a new restaurant on Union Street near my apartment with the dreamy name of Reverie. The fireplace crackled, and candlelight bathed the tables that were cloaked in white. *Life Happens Around the Table* was spelled out over the mantel in an eclectic collection of letters from old storefronts. A note on the bottom of the menu read, *Our food is seasonal, organic, sustainable, and locally grown.* I hadn't seen the term 'sustainable' on a menu before. One bite of the bread from the breadbasket made me swoon. I restrained myself with herculean willpower and didn't consume every piece of bread and then ask for more. Like the bread in Paris, it was crusty on the outside and like a cloud on the inside. If the bread was that good, I knew the meal would be spectacular, and I didn't want to fill up on bread. I was sorely tempted to dump the remains of it into my purse.

Reading their autumn menu was like skimming a list of my favorite meals. It offered Guinness stew topped with poppy seed dumplings, a pulled pork sandwich smothered in barbeque sauce with apple coleslaw piled on top, coq au vin with asiago polenta, and slow-cooked ribs with garlic fries. Beef stroganoff wasn't on the menu, but deciding what to order was easy when I heard about the special of the day. I couldn't resist the chicken potpie with a side of creamed spinach and an heirloom tomato salad. That was it. I love comfort food, and I wasn't disappointed. The piping-hot ramekin held succulent chicken in a sauce redolent with sage, thyme, and rosemary and was topped with a buttery crust. The pastry shattered like flakes of mica when my fork broke the surface.

I sipped an after-dinner cappuccino and watched the chef make his way around the room. His animated conversations with the diners let me know that many were his friends or repeat customers. I smiled and watched him in profile. My, he was handsome, in a roguish way. Because he was busy talking, I could stare at him unnoticed. He must have felt my eyes boring into his head, because he turned in my direction and caught me gawking at him. I averted my eyes and pretended to admire the artwork. I groaned inwardly; I needed to start being subtle when I studied people.

He wended his way closer to my table. I'm sure he heard my pounding heart and noticed my palms dampening the tablecloth. I fidgeted like a high school wallflower hoping to be asked to dance. *What will he say to me? What will I say to him? Oh God. I hope I won't get tongue-tied. That has happened to me before, you know.*

He made his way to my table, but I kept my eyes glued to my plate. He said, "Welcome to Reverie. I hope you enjoyed your meal. Please do come back." I nodded that I would, and when I lifted my eyes to speak to him, he had vanished. *That didn't go well, did it?* Embarrassed by my shyness, not to mention my fleeting infatuation with him, I paid my bill and left a hefty tip. Of the hundreds of meals I had eaten while dining out, that one was the best.

I found myself daydreaming about Reverie and replaying the meal over and over in my head. Okay, to be honest, what I replayed was my one-sided conversation with the chef. The image of his profile haunted me, and his seductive aura was etched on my brain. I wondered how long I should wait before visiting the restaurant again. But that thinking was silly. It wasn't like when a guy tries to figure how long to wait before calling a girl for another date. Still, I didn't want to seem too eager. I chided myself. *Too eager for what? Another excellent meal?*

I decided a week was ample time to wait. I starved myself all day in order to leave room for dinner *and* the entire basket of bread. I was ravenous and should have eaten during the day, because the first sip of wine shot straight to my head. In three bites, I inhaled a piece of bread to absorb the alcohol. I ordered the house-made lobster ravioli in a silky lemon cream sauce. The pillows of seafood ambrosia gave off a rather erotic aroma. Although the portion was generous, I still wanted a second helping. But I didn't ask for one, because I had saved room for the warm apple torte topped with vanilla gelato I had spotted on the dessert menu.

Like my first time at Reverie, the chef emerged from the kitchen and greeted the diners, like a replay of the scene from my previous visit. I veiled my eyes to prevent the chef from catching me ogling him again.

I chugged the rest of my wine for fortitude, and when he paused at my table, I was ready for him. I gazed up at him as he said, "Welcome back. I hope you enjoyed your dinner. I made the ravioli this morning."

"Thank you," I said. He smiled and moved on to the next table. *Thank you? Thank you? Was that the only brilliant sentence I could come up with? Thank you? How lame.* He didn't make the ravioli for me alone, of course. I kicked myself under the table. *Thank you?* Those two words echoed in my head far into the night. It was hardly clever repartee. I was pathetic.

Chapter 18: Finding a Man

Falling asleep was difficult that night. Maybe I ate too much rich food. Sleep was folding me in her arms when my eyes flew open and I sat bolt-upright in bed. He had said, "Welcome back." *Oh. My. God. He remembered me.*

The day after my second meal at Reverie, I wandered the rows of vendors at the farmers' market, as I did every Saturday morning. Chicken-hearted as I was, I crouched behind a pile of potatoes when I spotted Reverie's chef buying crabs from the fishmonger. *What am I afraid of?* Shoppers stared at me while I duck-walked along the side of a display table to peek at him from around its corner to watch his beautiful back as he made his selection. He turned and saw me. I pretended to tie my shoes, which was crazy, because I clearly wore slip-on loafers. He smiled at me, waved, and moved on. *I know how to impress a guy, don't I?*

Business travel kept me in Germany for two weeks, and I am happy to report that, because of my therapy sessions with Astrid, I didn't feel compelled to eat beef stroganoff while traveling. The trip was hectic and left little time to think about Reverie or its talented chef. I called the restaurant for a reservation as soon as I got home, and the first one available was for Tuesday. "I'll take it," I said. "How about eight o'clock?" The lone open reservation was for the third seating at ten o'clock. The hostess explained that a rave review in *The San Francisco Chronicle* swamped the restaurant with new customers. "Good problem to have," I said and hung up the phone. *Rats. I have to wait a week for dinner.*

Fortunately, the week flew by while I played catch-up on a thousand phone messages. On the night of my reservation, I changed my outfit six times and fretted over which shoes to wear—cute flats or high heels. Have I mentioned my unhealthy shoe fetish yet? I can't pass a shoe store without going in, and I never met a sale rack I didn't like.

I opted for painful high heels and the simple black dress I had bought on my last trip to Paris. The look I was after was Audrey Hepburn. Those French women had nothing on me. For good measure, I stopped at a drug store on the way to the restaurant to buy a red lipstick. I hoped it wouldn't stick to my teeth. Not a good look when trying to impress a chef.

Eager, I arrived at Reverie early. As the hostess warned, every table was occupied. The room was filled with the gentle clatter of fork on plate and the hum of conversation. I loitered near the front door while I waited for my table and watched young couples passing by on the street. The sight made me acutely aware that I was dining at Reverie alone. I turned when I heard a champagne bottle pop open. Ah, a celebration was taking place. I watched a man in his seventies slide a ring box across the table to a regal woman with silver hair. I almost clapped, but decided it would be too much. Reverie was an ideal setting for a sweet marriage proposal. My heart ached a little.

The veal I ordered was sumptuous, as were the endive leaves stuffed with a pomegranate and avocado salad, the roasted vegetables on the side, and basil rice pilaf with roasted hazelnuts. With a hunk of French bread, I mopped up the last of the lemon-and-caper-infused sauce that had blanketed veal. I had eaten myself into a stupor. No wonder I was gaining weight. Since no one was waiting for my table, I sat back and savored the last inch of my wine.

Alone with my thoughts about Astrid, I vowed to go to the nursing home the next day on my lunch hour for a dose of her gruff witticisms and florid stories. That was dangerous, as my one-hour lunch break often turned into a three-hour visit with her. Wrapped up in our conversation, we would lose track of the time. I had sent her postcards from Europe because I wanted her to know she had traveled with me in my heart.

I reflected on how my life had changed after meeting Astrid, and how happy I was that my cocky pain-in-the-ass attitude had vanished. I slipped on occasion, but I tried to catch myself when I did. Comfortable in my skin for the first time in my life, Astrid kept me grounded and humble. My role model imparted her wisdom in five words or less. She was chatty at times, but when she had a lesson to teach, she did so tersely. Her words and tone might have offended me, but I learned to have a thick skin around her. She didn't want to insult me; she just wanted to make her point.

Rousted from my musings by a wall of white coat standing before me, I jerked to attention and scanned the room. The only other people in the restaurant were the newly engaged couple drinking more champagne.

"May I join you?" the chef asked.

Rather than answering, I pulled out the other chair at the table.

"Thanks," he said with a smile. "I'm beat. The increase in business from our review in the paper is running us ragged. I haven't sat in a week." He set a bottle of wine on the table and pulled a corkscrew from his pocket. "Can I buy you a drink?" he asked as he poured.

Mute, I nodded. Where was my voice? I resisted the urge to polish the wine off in one gulp. I knew it was expensive. How did I know? My budget didn't allow for wine that good.

We were quiet for a minute, and then he combed his fingers through his mop of hair and said, "You've become a regular. I'm glad you like my place. My name's Adam."

Stammering, I said, "I'm Meredith, and this is the best restaurant in town. You are an alchemist in the kitchen." I didn't exaggerate. *Wow, wait a minute.* I strung words together and uttered an intelligent sentence in his presence. I even managed to squeeze in a big word correctly. I'll confess to you that the word 'alchemist' was in a crossword puzzle, and I had to consult a dictionary. An alchemist is a person with the power to transform an ordinary item into something special. Feel free to use the word.

We talked about food and Reverie for an hour while the hostess and kitchen crew waited in the shadows. I noticed the late hour when I heard a discreet "Ahem." Adam's staff wanted to head home, and I didn't blame them. They probably hadn't sat down in a week either. Glancing at my watch, I realized in horror I was due at the office in seven hours. I grabbed my purse, thanked him for the wine, and said I would be back.

My heart skipped in triple-time on my walk home. Or maybe it floated on air outside of my body. He was wonderful. I was vocally constipated around him the first couple of times, but he turned me into a chatterbox that night. Our conversation was light and effortless, and I couldn't wait to tell Astrid about him .

Chapter 19: Reunion

Friendship is a strong and habitual inclination in two persons to promote the good and happiness of one another.

— Eustace Budgell

At the nursing home, Astrid and I hugged as though separated for three years rather than three weeks. She filled me in on the happenings with her fellow residents.

Her deaf-as-a-doorpost neighbor had celebrated a birthday; chocolate cake had been served. The man who moved as if his battery were running low had had a tense visit with his estranged daughter. Another neighbor had become a great-grandfather for the sixth time. Yet another had lent her a book on tape, describing it as "delicious," and Astrid had listened to the book while I was in Europe. She slapped my knee and laughed. "The old biddy loaned me a titillating and scandalous romance novel. Once the shock wore off, I got a kick out of it." I made a mental note to buy a lusty novel to read to her. Everyone deserves a little romance, including a woman in her eighties. I looked forward to reading one myself.

With unconcealed enthusiasm, I described Reverie, my delicious meal, and Adam. As was my wont with Astrid, I relayed the nice parts, as well as how I felt foolish when he rendered me speechless. "He's a masterful chef," I said, "a fascinating conversationalist, and, quite frankly, devilishly sexy." Although smitten with Adam, I didn't know what he thought of me. "Maybe he figures I'm either a loser who's forced to dine alone or a self-proclaimed food snob. I *do* dine alone, and I guess I *am* a food snob. He probably read through me."

"If that's the case," Astrid responded, "you found yourself a perceptive man, Meredith. I want to meet him."

Once again I kicked myself. Why hadn't we gone on more outings? She was cooped up in the nursing home and lived vicariously through me while I gadded about the world. *How thoughtless of me.* I brought out a notepad, and we brainstormed places to visit. At the top of the page was a meal at Reverie. The rest of the list looked like a school field trip calendar. I dashed off a note to her doctor asking permission to make weekly jaunts, left the note at the nurses' station, and checked my watch. My one-hour visit with Astrid had, indeed, turned into three hours. I prayed I wouldn't be fired.

Chapter 20: Food and Cheer and Song

If more of us valued food and cheer and song above hoarded gold, it would be a merrier world.

— J.R.R. Tolkien

The following week, I hadn't yet received the doctor's permission to take Astrid out, so I made a reservation for myself at Reverie, and that time I requested the last seating. I set aside the menu, because I had it memorized, and ordered the beef stew with dumplings laced with poppy seeds. My dinner plate was worthy of the cover of a foodie magazine. The meat was like velvet, and the baby carrots tasted as if they had been yanked from the ground that morning. I inhaled my dinner and then waited for the dining room to clear. Why were these people lingering over brandy and chocolate mousse? Wasn't there someplace they needed go, like to bed?

At last, a frazzled Adam emerged from the kitchen. He scanned the room, and when he saw me, lines of fatigue vanished as he threw me a lopsided grin. Without asking, he pulled out a chair at my table and crumpled on to the seat. "Boy, am I glad that's over," he said. "I need to hire more help. You want a job, Meredith?"

I snickered and said, "A short time ago you wouldn't have wanted me for a busboy, let alone help you in the kitchen. The Health Department would have closed you down." Without thinking, I continued, "I nearly poisoned my neighbors once but have since taught myself to cook. I went on an absurd obsessive-compulsive search for my mom's beef stroganoff recipe, but I realized that finding the recipe wouldn't replace my mom."

Adam pressed two fingers to the inside of my wrist to pause the story and said, "I'll be right back."

He returned with a bottle of wine and two glasses. I waited until he popped the cork before I continued. I laid out my sordid tale and included how I had unburdened my guilty conscience to Astrid one story at a time. I described her healing power of giving me permission to forgive myself. He fetched another bottle of wine, dismissed the staff, and locked the front door.

He returned, and I continued my monologue. As with Astrid, I narrated my life story through my bad behavior and the hard lessons learned along the way, but that time the tale did not include self-pity. I even divulged my weight gain from eating out so often. During my recitation he nodded solemnly, sighed during the sad parts, or shook his head when amazed. He let out a low chuckle when I described Astrid's sharp tongue and how she had no problem putting me in my place.

At the end of my story, Adam said, "I would hire you this second, I'll help you find your Mom's recipe, and I want to meet Astrid. Will you bring her to Reverie?"

"I'm already planning on it," I replied. "She wants to meet you, too. I'll let you know when we're coming."

He helped me to my unsteady feet and saw me to the door. I had consumed more wine than I should have, yet my head was oddly clear. He offered to see me home, but I waved off his offer with a shrug and an "I'm okay." I wanted the time alone on the short walk home to think. The fall evening was chilly, and Adam wrapped his chef's coat around my shoulders when he saw me shiver. The gesture confirmed to me he was a gentleman, as no former boyfriend would have dreamed of doing that. The jerks would have chastised me for not bringing a coat.

I wasn't too inebriated to notice that the white T-shirt he wore under his coat molded his body. The sight of his biceps, not the wine, made me tipsy.

Chapter 21: Astrid Meets Adam

The meeting of two personalities is like the contact of two chemical substances: if there is any reaction, both are transformed.

— Carl Jung

The doctor finally gave me permission to take Astrid on excursions; he didn't approve of evening outings, but he didn't disallow them. Without receiving further clarification in case the doctor said no, I called Reverie to make a reservation for two. Knowing Astrid ate dinner on the early side, I made the reservation for five o'clock and asked the hostess to give Adam a message regarding the date and time.

My dented car and I picked up Astrid. She wore a crisp linen dress and a smudge of blush. I detected a spritz of perfume when I hugged her. She smelled as fresh as a field of lavender—my favorite. She set out to impress that night, but not to impress me. Her sights were set much higher.

We parked in the garage near Reverie and made our way across the street. Astrid grabbed me when a taxi honked and swerved around us. She left finger-shaped bruises on my arm. Peeking through the window, I saw that the restaurant was empty. "Oh, no, I must have the day wrong," I said. "Reverie is closed." I rattled the locked door and jumped back when it flew open and Adam, dressed in a tuxedo, welcomed us. I was flabbergasted. Astrid regained her senses first and said, "Nice joint you have here." I introduced her to Mr. Wonderful, also known as Adam Mason.

Chapter 21: Astrid Meets Adam

Adam had canceled the evening's other reservations, so the restaurant was ours. He had spent the afternoon cooking, and right before we arrived he had stripped off his chef clothes and donned his tux. At our table next to the crackling fire he popped open the bottle of champagne chilling in a bucket, poured three glasses, and dropped a plump raspberry and a sprig of mint into each one. Astrid set her glass aside and said, "Thank you, but I never drink before five o'clock." (It was 4:57.)

"Anything close to five o'clock is wine o'clock as far as I'm concerned," Adam said, "but I'll wait."

We sat in silence and watched the seconds tick by. The clock struck the hour, and Astrid downed half of her champagne in one swallow. Adam bravely kissed her on the top of her head and disappeared into the kitchen. (If I had tried to kiss her when we first met, she would have snapped at me.)

Astrid leaned over to me and whispered in a voice audible a mile away, "He's a keeper." I nodded my agreement vigorously. We heard "Oh, shoot!" from the kitchen, and then Beethoven's *Moonlight Sonata* softly filled the room. I pushed the breadbasket to Astrid and mumbled with my mouth full, "You have to taste this . . ." An amazing aroma heralded the arrival of a plate of fried calamari sprinkled with Parmesan and minced tarragon. I glanced at the appetizer and then watched Adam retreat to the kitchen.

I love calamari, but, it often disappoints me. If not prepared properly, it turns into deep fried sections of garden hose. I've never attempted to make calamari, because it intimidates me, and all those slimy tentacles make me squeamish.

Adam's calamari, however, was nirvana. I popped a calamari ring into my mouth and wondered how something could be so crisp and tender at the same time. The lemon infused batter was tinged with a hint of cayenne pepper, and the calamari was nothing like a garden hose. A butter lettuce salad with toasted almonds, ripe pear, Gorgonzola, and a drizzle of delicate champagne vinaigrette were next. I was getting full, but ready for more.

Astrid and I talked about her family, my upcoming trip for work, and the rather insipid book we were reading and planning to dump. We also planned our trip to the de Young Museum. She was most interested in the French Impressionist works of art, and I wanted to be sure to find pieces of their somewhat limited Hudson River School collection.

The kitchen doors banged open, and our main course arrived. Astrid was thunderstruck by the meal Adam served us. I was speechless, too, but not for the first time around that man. He made beef stroganoff for us.

He served the stroganoff over buttered noodles, with a side of roasted asparagus bathed in a garlic and rosemary sauce. He returned from the kitchen with another plate, shrugged off his tuxedo jacket, and joined us. Again he said, "Oh, shoot." He darted out of his chair and back to the kitchen and returned in a flash with a ruby-red Cabernet Sauvignon. I sighed as tears stung my eyes.

"My regular customers were angry when I canceled their reservations without explanation," Adam said. "I hope they'll return."

"Your regulars will want to adopt you if you serve them that calamari," I replied. We dug into the beef stroganoff. Though not my mom's version, the meal would inspire poets. In truth, Adam had served poetry on a plate.

Chapter 21: Astrid Meets Adam

It had taken weeks for Astrid to warm up to me, but it took only twelve seconds for Adam to worm his way into her heart. They talked as though I had vanished from the room. I learned more about Astrid over dinner that night than I had done in the hours I had spent with her over the past months in her nursing home. She was a charmer. I swear I saw her bat her eyes at him, the big flirt. He was gallant, engaged, and absolutely endearing. I officially fell in love with him while they talked.

He pushed away from the table and picked up plates that were all but licked clean. The aroma of coffee and the pleasant fragrance of toast wafted from the kitchen. Mr. Tuxedo pushed a cart out of the kitchen with demitasse cups of espresso, three crème brulées, and cordial glasses of Grand Marnier. The sweet burning smell we detected was the vanilla sugar top he browned with an acetylene torch.

With her mouth full of dessert, Astrid asked Adam to pass the artificial sweetener for her coffee. She winked at him and said, "That is how I keep my girlish figure," and took another bite of about 2,000 calories. The button on my skirt was about to pop, but I devoured every morsel of my dessert, and Astrid scraped her dish clean with gusto.

I glanced at Astrid while Adam and I discussed the merits of fresh versus dried tarragon. Her chin was on her chest, and a snore purred in her nose. *Time to go.* I nudged her awake while Adam retrieved the walker from the back of the restaurant. "Let me pull the car across the street," I said as I dropped my credit card on the table and grabbed my keys.

Adam and Astrid were in an intense conversation and looked rather guilty when I returned. *What the heck? What was that about?*

My credit card was where I had left it. No insisting on my part convinced Adam to let me pay for the meal. With a crooked smile he said, “My treat. This was more fun than I’ve had in years.”

Astrid announced that she needed to use the restroom. “As I always say, never pass up the opportunity to use the loo. You don’t know when the next chance will present itself.” When she returned to the dining room, she had freshened her lipstick and rouge a bit too heavily.

Adam escorted us to the car and, with a bow, kissed Astrid’s hand. Even in the dim light, I saw that she was blushing. Except for knights, actors, and karate students, no one bows these days. Knights might not even do it anymore. Adam proved that chivalry wasn’t dead.

The nurses were likely to have my hide when we returned to the nursing home, for I had kept Astrid out for an hour longer than what had been granted. During the drive there we giggled like naughty schoolgirls breaking curfew.

The automatic doors to the nursing home opened with a deafening whoosh—so much for slipping in unnoticed. However, applause welcomed us in when we crossed the threshold. Some of the staff had gathered to welcome Astrid home. They knew about our dinner date and were glad we were late, because it meant she had fun. They didn’t scold me. Astrid was a celebrity, and I was a hero.

On the ride up in the elevator to her room, I said, “I think you have a new boyfriend.”

“No,” she countered. “I know *you* have a new boyfriend, Meredith. And he makes a fantastic beef stroganoff.”

Chapter 22: A Bold Move

I ran up the door, opened the stairs,
Said my pajamas and put on my prayers,
Turned off my bed, tumbled into my light,
And all because he kissed me good-night!

— Author unknown

For it was not into my ear you whispered, but into my heart. It was not my lips you kissed, but my soul.

— Judy Garland

I fell into bed with my head swirling. *Adam closed Reverie for the night for me. Maybe he closed Reverie for Astrid, not me. But if he did it for Astrid, he ultimately did it for me. Right? Did I gush too much about his cooking?*

My rattled head was fraught with self-doubt. In a bold move, I decided to ask him over for dinner. *Am I crazy? Inviting a professional chef to dinner? I need to study up for that one.* I spent a sleepless hour wondering what to serve. I gave up, deciding I needed Astrid's counsel.

By noon the next day I had gathered the courage to call Adam. My hand quivered while dialing the phone. *Silly me, I should have known he'd be busy with the lunch crowd.* So I had to leave a message.

Three unbearable hours crawled by without a return call. A mantra in my head said, *Why did I tell him I gained weight? What a fool, fool, fool I am.* Describing extra pounds was hardly the way to attract a man.

In Search of Beef Stroganoff

The phone rang at last. It was Adam. Stumbling over each other, we said, "I'm glad you called." We stepped on each other's words for several seconds, but he stopped me and said, "You first." My invitation for dinner was memorized, but I forgot every word of my well-crafted speech when I heard his voice. I managed to spit out, "Would you like to come for dinner?"

He answered, "No." I was ready to slam down the phone until he said, "No, Meredith, I wouldn't like to come over for dinner. I'd *love* to come for dinner."

We agreed on the following Monday, his night off. I panicked, as it gave me little time to prepare. I raced to the nursing home, and Astrid helped me to plan the menu, decide what I would wear, and pick out the music to set the mood. The music was easy . . . Beethoven, as he had played for us the night before. The question of what to wear required more time. Astrid voted for a simple skirt and blouse. "You should show off those legs," she said. I vetoed her and opted for jeans and a V-neck cashmere sweater.

The most fun was talking about what to serve. The conversation made my stomach growl. I suggested a rib-eye steak bathed in a Cabernet reduction. What man doesn't love a steak? And Cabernet? Maybe I could roast a whole chicken with halved lemons, garlic, and rosemary nestled in the cavity. Astrid didn't like the idea of garlic perfuming my breath. I thought about poaching a whole salmon and serving it with creamy herbed vinaigrette, but worried the apartment would smell like a fish market. I love my recipe for curried pork tenderloin with grilled brandied peaches. However, curry gives me the hiccups. I couldn't have that.

We ended up opting for Astrid's first suggestion. Don't laugh—we decided on spaghetti and meatballs. "Best to stick with the basics rather than being hoity-toity," she said. "Men love spaghetti, even fancy-schmancy chefs."

We changed the music from Beethoven to Pavarotti. Our evening would open with chilled Prosecco, a sparkling Italian wine, accompanied by a variety of cheeses and olives from my favorite deli in North Beach. Halved cherry tomatoes topped with tender mozzarella, a basil leaf, and a drizzle of olive oil and aged vinegar would be sexy to eat in one bite. It looks like an Italian flag on a plate.

The first course would be cantaloupe wrapped in paper-thin prosciutto with a squeeze of lime juice. A hearty salad would accompany the spaghetti and meatballs. Vanilla gelato topped with strawberries marinated in balsamic vinegar would be our dessert. Crazy as it sounds, the recipe I found called for a grinding of black pepper over the top. At first I was hesitant to do that, but the pepper gave the berries an unexpected zing. I debated buying an espresso machine, but decided instead on a robust dark-roast coffee and thick sweet cream from the farmers' market. Coffee was a must, because I wanted the guy to stay awake.

With our dinner date still a few days away, I set the table. I played with the ambient lighting and crowded the dining room with candles. Every woman knows candlelight is flattering. I stood back to admire the room, which looked as though I was planning a séance, not a seduction. I blew out half a dozen candles and turned up the chandelier a notch. The effect spelled romance.

Not wanting to overprepare, I did one trial run on the dinner. The meatballs were ground veal, pork, and beef, and I baked them rather than fry them. The result made them tender, not rubbery. The sauce was an aromatic blend of tomatoes, onion, and earthy mushrooms. I brought Astrid a plateful to see if she approved. As only she could, she gave me a brusque nod and "It's good." I wore her words as a badge of honor.

No Italian meal—or any meal, for that matter—is complete without a crusty hunk of good bread. By this time the hostess at Reverie knew me, so I phoned her and asked if I could surreptitiously buy a loaf of bread from them, and I explained why. She giggled and agreed to meet me on the corner with a baguette. The morning of my careful attempt at romance, we met, and I handed her money for the bread. The exchange looked like a drug deal. If a narc busted us, he would find I scored bread, not crack.

I spent the day in the kitchen and left ample time to clean up and dress for dinner before Adam was due to arrive. I allowed myself too much time and had nothing to do but pace and carve a rut in the floor. The doorbell rang, and I jumped two feet. After checking myself in the mirror for the hundredth time, as elegantly as possible, I swung open the door and accidentally whacked my knee. While rubbing the dull throb, I managed to gesture for him to come in, and I said, "You smell wonderful." With that, he wrapped me in his arms.

We carried our Prosecco to the living room and swapped stories about food, our families, and decided we both wanted to adopt Astrid. With Pavarotti playing in the background, the discussion turned to music, art, and the theater. My nervousness vanished as our conversation flowed without pause and wrapped my soul in velvet. Like a lovesick cartoon character, hearts and birds fluttered around my head. I hoped Adam didn't notice.

We sat down for dinner, and I passed Adam the breadbasket. He complimented my baking skills with his first bite and said the bread was as good as his. "It should be," I said. "It *is* yours. I bought it off your hostess in what looked like a drug deal." The comedy of my subterfuge, or the wine, made me giggle, but I put a cork in my twitter before he thought I was a ditz. I changed the subject. "Cooking for you made me a nervous wreck. Thank goodness Astrid helped me plan the evening."

"I suspected her hand was in this," he replied. "I was anxious, too." Noticing my worried frown, he added, "Not about your cooking, Meredith. I was worried I tried too hard to impress you with the dinner I made for you and Astrid." We lingered deliciously over every course.

Adam shared with me that he hoped to open another restaurant. The hours were grueling as a chef and restaurant owner, but making his customers sigh with content over a perfect meal energized him. Reverie was his baby, and he nurtured the inviting atmosphere that appealed to his sophisticated clientele. He designed the restaurant to be elegant, refined, and serene. But he wanted his second restaurant to be different from Reverie. The dream wasn't clear, but he knew the new restaurant needed to be playful and bustling.

I described to him how I grew from being a whiz at opening a tin of tuna for dinner to someone who derives tremendous pleasure from cooking. Food means more to me than fuel for the body; feeding my friends nourishes my soul. I love to pamper people with food. A delicious meal holds magical powers and can turn a bad day into a good one. It intrigues me how cooking brings me in touch with my mom and how she guides me in the kitchen. I laughed and said, "The idea to bake the meatballs instead of frying them was sent to me from heaven."

Against my protests, he insisted on helping with the dishes. He looked adorable with a dishtowel tucked in the waist of his pants for a makeshift apron. I was enchanted.

To be accurate, I was more enchanted than ever. When the kitchen was tidy, he took my hand while we sat on the couch and nibbled on biscotti dipped in my homemade limoncello. The recipe said to let the lemony liqueur age for eight weeks, but it had only aged six days. "That's okay, Meredith," he said. "Let's sample it again after it ages longer." He wanted to hang around long enough for my limoncello to age. Thank the Lord.

The anticipation of our date and all of the preparation for it finally caught up with me. Adam noticed me stifling a yawn and said he ought to head home. We glanced at the clock. It was after two a.m. Although seven hours had passed as though they were mere minutes, I was loath to say goodbye. At the door, he folded me into his arms for the second time that night, but this time he gave me a lemon-scented kiss.

I closed the door, fell back against it, counted to ten, and raised my arms above my head in triumph. I let out a thunderous, "Woo-hoo, I'm in love!"

Within seconds Adam was back at my door. "Are you okay? I heard you shouting." I assured him it was just me sounding happy.

I blew out the candles and went to the bathroom to wash my face. My reflection in the mirror startled me. Even without makeup after washing my face, I was rather pretty. Love had a Pygmalion effect on me. My eyes were a brighter blue, my forehead smoother, my smile brighter. Maybe the cause wasn't purely love.

After my mom died, I had set out to transform every part of my being into a better person. Changing the ugly parts inside my body and mind was altering my outside too. Before I met Astrid, I was meek and lacked confidence and covered up those flaws by being brash. She helped me to understand my value and place in the world. Instead of plain, I looked happy. By looking happy, I was more attractive. Go figure. It called for a shopping spree to celebrate. I had my eye on a panini press. Highlights for my hair were in order too. Yup, I was in love. Call me Captain Obvious.

Part II: Astrid's Story

Chapter 23: A Full Life in Brief

An autobiography is an obituary in serial form with the last installment missing.

— Quentin Crisp

Over the weeks and months I spent with Astrid, I learned more about her life. It was as though she read a chapter from her autobiography to me every week. We set aside our novels, games, and crossword puzzles and settled into her tale. The characters in her story became my adopted family. She painted pictures in my mind of the farm, her schoolhouse, the movie theater, and the boy she had fallen in love with. I fell in love with him too. Her story was a warm embrace.

She was the eldest of five children and saw herself as their leader. Her siblings would have called her just plain bossy. Her family had a farm on the outskirts of a small town in Minnesota named Garden Valley. Honored members of the community, her family held the small-town equivalent of celebrity status, as they owned the largest farm in the area. Astrid's parents were simple, God-fearing, and humble. They were strict yet loving, and didn't tolerate a sassy mouth. I didn't mention it, but I thought she should have paid more attention to their "no sassy mouth" lessons. She and her siblings were taught that the surest way to heaven was a compassionate heart and a pure soul.

Astrid's tight-knit community would run to help a neighbor in need. She grumbled when she followed up that statement with . . . "Unlike nowadays, when people don't know their neighbor's name." Every occasion, from the birth of a baby to a death in the family, gave rise to a potluck supper. Tables were improvised from old doors and sawhorses, strong coffee was brewed, pies were baked, and picnic baskets overflowed. Astrid gained notoriety for her beef stroganoff at those potluck suppers. Neighbors raced to the table to grab a serving of her dish. If you tarried, you'd be out of luck and find the dish scraped clean. She kept her stroganoff recipe a secret. It brought her local fame, and she didn't want to be bumped out of the spotlight by anyone.

In high school she found, as she put it, "the boy of my dreams." Sven Johansson lived on a farm as well, and the classic Nordic angles of his body contrasted with his face's gentle features and his soft manners. However, in grammar school, Sven had teased Astrid with unmerciful persistence. Astrid hated him, and whenever the teacher wasn't looking she stuck out her tongue at him or hid his textbook. They were adversaries with an unspoken rivalry over doing multiplication tables, winning the spelling bee blue ribbon, and scoring the highest marks on tests.

As they grew older, Astrid and Sven's relationship evolved. Instead of sitting by her to tug on her braids, Sven sat near her to brush his hand against hers "by accident." He possessed an uncanny ability to find her when she went to the movies or the library. At the end of the school day, he raced to offer to carry her books home. She snubbed him at first, but his dogged determination ate away at her resolve until she agreed. The walk home lasted a little longer each day as they slowed their pace to a crawl to be together for as long as possible.

Sven played center field on the high school baseball team, as Astrid had mentioned when she told me about her love of the game. Astrid was the team's most loyal fan, which is saying something. The town treated the team like heroes. The bleachers were half-filled at the team's practices and at capacity for the games. Every game made the front page of the local newspaper, and the townsfolk were depressed for days after a rare loss.

To raise money for a new Bible study classroom, the church organized a picnic basket auction. Each of the town's eligible girls filled a picnic basket, and the lucky bachelor who won the bidding on a particular basket could enjoy the privilege of eating its contents with the creator. The girls toiled and fretted over making the most bountiful basket. Hours were spent planning the menu and ironing napkins. They waited to pick strawberries until they were crimson and vied for the plumpest chicken from the butcher. Tearful girls summoned their mothers to the kitchen if a cake fell flat or the cookies burned. Brothers were banished from the bathroom to make way for the girls' last-minute primping before the auction. Making the finest basket was a serious cutthroat competition.

The bidding for Astrid's picnic basket was fierce. "I was quite a looker in my day," she said with a wink. "Old age is not my best feature." Sven outbid his competitors, and her basket fetched the highest price of the day. With reverence he carried the basket to a shady spot on the church lawn and spread out the blanket, where they sat at opposite edges. Sven stared at his lap, and Astrid picked at the hem of her skirt. His money bought him a picnic supper and an hour of uncomfortable silence. The easy banter they shared on their way home from school had disappeared into bashful nerves. "We were awkward that day, because the picnic was our first real date," Astrid said. "And if you're wondering, yes, beef stroganoff was tucked in the basket. I wrapped the dish in layers of newspaper to keep it warm."

In Search of Beef Stroganoff

At a high school dance during their senior year, Sven asked Astrid to join him on the floor. Uncoordinated dancing smoothed when they found each other's rhythm and moved in sync to the music. With her in his arms, he summoned his courage and said, "I love you." She said, "I know." He gave her ponytail a quick tug, and from that moment on they were inseparable.

Sven was a farm boy, but he wanted a different life. He wanted to sell quality meat, fruits and vegetables, but not grow them or raise livestock. He worked weekends at the town's only grocery market, and his bank account swelled with the savings for his dream of buying his own market in a big city. He kept his vision a secret, even from Astrid. He knew his parents would disapprove and was certain his friends would laugh at him, so he secretly scoured the newspaper for notices of markets for sale.

Not long after high school graduation, he found an advertisement for a corner market in a bustling working-class neighborhood in faraway San Francisco. The owner of the market had died, and his children didn't want to carry on the family business. The market with an apartment above it was exactly what Sven wanted. He had saved enough money for the down payment, two train tickets, and a gold ring.

Sven invited Astrid on a date for dinner at the historic Hotel Duluth. He planned to ask her to marry him over dinner, but he knocked over his water glass when he reached for her hand to propose. While the waiter changed out the tablecloth, Sven decided to postpone the proposal until after dinner, giving Astrid time to forget his blunder. They listened to a jazz combo in the hotel's famous Black Bear Lounge after dinner. Legend had it that in the Roaring Twenties a bear smashed through the hotel's 15-foot-tall plate-glass window and ransacked the lobby. A policeman shot and killed the bear, the hotel had it stuffed, and it became the centerpiece of the lounge, thus giving it its name.

Between sets, Sven nervously told Astrid he was buying the market in San Francisco. She asked, "But what about us?" Sven didn't answer her, but instead placed around her neck a gold locket engraved with initials. "It is lovely, Sven, but the initials are wrong," she said. "The engraver put a 'J' for my last name."

"I know," he said. "That's because I want your last name to be Johansson. Will you marry me? We can pick out your wedding ring together."

Astrid answered him by simply throwing her arms around his neck.

Telling their families they were moving to San Francisco was hard. Their parents pleaded with them not to leave, but they wouldn't consider staying. With resignation their parents accepted their move away. To ease their sad hearts, Astrid's parents threw them the most elaborate wedding the town had ever seen.

Astrid's departure from the farm was hardest on her youngest sister, Mildred. She wouldn't come out of the house when it was time for the newlyweds to catch the train. Not wanting to leave without saying goodbye, Astrid went in search of her sister and found her sobbing into her pillow. Mildred wouldn't turn her head. Astrid smoothed her sister's hair and promised she would write to her every week, which only made the crying louder.

On an impulse, Astrid fished in her pocketbook and found the recipe card for her beef stroganoff. She told Mildred that she was giving her the recipe for safekeeping and that, whenever she missed her, she could whip up a batch. The weeping subsided as Mildred twisted around and hugged Astrid so tight she thought her heart would break. Astrid kept her vow and wrote to Mildred every week.

Astrid paused her story. "Giving the recipe to my sister wasn't really a sacrifice," she said. "Mildred didn't know I had the recipe memorized. Promise to keep that secret safe when you meet her."

Nodding, I swallowed a tear, because the only likely place I would meet Mildred was at Astrid's funeral. I hoped that day was as far away as never.

The newlyweds talked about their new life in San Francisco during the train ride. Sven was eager to clean and stock the market, and Astrid wanted to play house. She admitted to Sven she was a little afraid of the city. She visited Duluth a handful of times, but it was so different than where they were headed. Sven assured her that, side-by-side, they would make their way together.

Sven and Astrid settled into the two-bedroom apartment above the market. They used their parents' wedding gift of money to buy furniture and a sewing machine. They scoured thrift stores to make the money stretch as far as possible. Astrid's nesting instinct was strong; she made lace curtains for the windows, a slipcover for the secondhand divan, and quilts for the beds. She made the apartment a cozy, comfortable nest while Sven ran the tiny market.

Astrid's fears about living in the city vanished within weeks. "Maybe I'm not such a farm girl after all," she thought. San Francisco's rhythm beat in time with her pulse. She loved the diversity, the cramped and dusty shops, the traffic noise, and the option to visit a world-class museum on a rainy afternoon. Astrid and Sven couldn't afford the theater often, but Astrid saved a dollar a week in a coffee can, and they saw the hottest show at least once a year. They also took in the latest movies at the local cinema. The cable car cost a dime, another dime for the movie tickets, and a nickel for a pack of chewing gum. A mere twenty-five cents gave Astrid and Sven a grand night out. On occasion, they stopped at the neighborhood pub for a nightcap and to listen to music.

To supplement their modest income from the market, Astrid decided to attend night school to learn bookkeeping so she could find a job and do the market's books at night. She sailed through the coursework and graduated with honors. The multiplication table competitions with her former nemesis-turned-husband paid off. The night school helped her find a job near their home. The company's owner was as kind as Ebenezer Scrooge, but they needed the extra income, so she suffered his temper willingly.

Astrid was frugal. She used meat bones from the market that customers didn't deem fit to purchase for their dogs to make savory broths, and she added any unsold past-prime produce to create delicious soups. She made their clothes, darned their socks, and had their shoes repaired by the cobbler rather than buying new ones. The tissue paper dress and shirt patterns she used to make their clothes stood in for toilet paper when money was scarce. It was the happiest time of their lives.

Much to the young couple's delight, Astrid became pregnant after many months of trying. Complications during the last month of her pregnancy confined her to bed rest, which was like a prison term for her. She gave birth to a sweet baby girl, and they named her Mildred. Because of that, Astrid's sister almost forgave her for leaving. Almost.

Although their neighbors loved the market's former owner, they took in the new family as one of their own. Astrid found that delivering casseroles to neighbors and potluck suppers wasn't confined to her farm community. When their baby was born, the new parents were flooded with a soup kitchen's worth of food, and Astrid had to beg the neighbors to stop. Nonplussed, they continued to deliver hot dishes and kettles of stew.

Astrid was guilty of doing the same thing. She made beef stroganoff and delivered it to neighbors whenever an event called for celebration or solace. Her reputation for beef stroganoff followed her to San Francisco. The neighborhood women were proud of their cooking, and Astrid earned their respect in their world of potluck suppers. As when she lived in Minnesota, she wouldn't acquiesce and share her secret recipe.

A Swedish towhead, Mildred had upturned lips, translucent skin, and ice-blue eyes. She delighted her parents and the elderly Chinese babysitter they hired when Astrid went back to work. Mildred grew up on a diet of Swedish meatballs and dim sum. Astrid and Sven didn't eat anything more exotic than spaghetti while growing up, but Mildred was as familiar with the city's diverse ethnic cuisine as she was with Swedish pancakes.

As the daughter of bright parents, Mildred shined in school. She had heard about her parents' spelling bee competitions in grammar school, and Mildred insisted on staging their own competitions in the tiny kitchen. She excelled at spelling, but math was difficult for her. Multiplication tables and long-division problems were etched into the top of the kitchen table from Mildred's heavy-handed problem solving. Homework was a time of bonding, learning, and frustration.

Astrid and Sven's happy life above the market came to a sudden and tragic end when Mildred was in the fourth grade. On her way home from school one day, a taxicab swerved onto the sidewalk to avoid hitting a stray dog. The cab pinned Mildred to the granite pillar of the bank on the corner, and she died at the scene. Astrid and Sven became mute and moved as if they were in a trance. Sven closed the store for a month. No one knew how to console the grieving parents; the entire neighborhood was grieving.

Astrid never rode in a taxi again. The memory they evoked was unbearable. I told her she had left bruises on my arm when the cab honked at us when we crossed the street on our way to Reverie. "I thought I might have, Meredith," she said. "Sorry about that."

Years passed before life returned to normal for the bereaved parents. How their marriage survived the pain is a miracle. Perhaps it lasted because, like ghosts, Astrid and Sven haunted the motions of life. As they traveled through a long, depressing tunnel, they gradually reassembled the shards of their lives. They found they were still in love, and laughter crept back into their home.

Sven retired after 50 years of running the market and hired a young man with a pierced eyebrow to run the operations. By that time, Astrid and Sven owned two additional and equally successful stores. Their grab bag of employees became like family. The rough-and-tumble group would gather at their dinner table on Sundays and helped to fill the void created by Mildred's death. Astrid was their confidant, advisor, and surrogate mother. Many of the employees were working at the market only until they made it big on the stage or went on tour with the Rolling Stones.

At age 68, Sven was diagnosed with pancreatic cancer, which cruelly took him from Astrid mere months after the diagnosis. On the day Sven died, Astrid's sobbing echoed down the hall and reverberated in the street. Within minutes, three neighbors were by her side. The apartment building's paper-thin walls made for an information pipeline more efficient than the nation's telephone system. To preserve a sense of privacy, neighbors ignored marital spats, corporal punishment of wayward children, and the normal bickering that occurs in families. Astrid's crying sounded different from anything like that, and the neighbors could not turn a deaf ear to the mournful sound.

Sven was laid to rest in Minnesota alongside their daughter, and once again, Astrid was numb. Her sister Mildred closed their parents' farmhouse and took the train back to San Francisco with Astrid. Mildred took command of the household and attended to the revolving door of well-wishers bearing casserole dishes while Astrid stayed in bed for days.

On a Saturday morning, Astrid bathed, put on a fresh dress, tied on an apron, and declared she was ready to run the three markets. With her mouth agape, sister Mildred couldn't fathom what happened overnight, so she asked. Astrid said, "My daughter and husband are dead, but I am not. Time to stop acting as if I died too. If their legacy is to live on, I need to be in charge. By me doing so, from his corner of Heaven, Sven will be pleased."

Astrid sent Mildred home and gave the market's employees a 10% raise. They were loyal and hardworking, and deserved to make more money than the paltry wage Sven had paid them. Astrid quit her bookkeeping job and positioned herself alongside the eyebrow pierced manager to run the markets together. She stopped her story short and said, "I hate body piercing with a passion."

Within a few months she had a handle on the business, made a business plan, and mapped out her future. Her business sense was better than Sven's, but her old-fashioned sensibilities had made her hold her tongue when she had disagreed with his decisions. Sven, while a smart man, was weak when it came to suppliers and costs, and he paid what they asked. Because the vendors knew that, they gouged him. Astrid stepped in, and that nonsense stopped. She asked the vendors what other markets were paying for the merchandise. Suspecting they had lied to her, she asked her competitors, who were also her friends, and learned the truth. Armed with the information, she bullied her suppliers until they reduced the prices. The black profit line on the bottom of her income statement became blacker. In six months' time, she amassed enough money to open another store. Within another six months, she opened two more. Astrid was on her way to becoming a wealthy woman and had the means to buy the entire building that housed their first market.

Because a capable manager was in place and she had the money to do so, Astrid visited her hometown of Garden Valley often. She reconnected with friends, made new ones, and was a favorite guest. Astrid traveled with two large suitcases, one for her clothes and the other filled with gifts. She was Aunt Santa Claus, even in June. She also visited her siblings, who were scattered across the country and came to know her nieces, nephews, and a handful of great-nieces and great-nephews. One of her teenaged great-nieces liked to challenge Astrid to verbal duels and tussles about politics. Astrid enjoyed the battles, because the smart mouthed girl backed down every time and ended up agreeing with her.

Twenty years after Sven's death, Astrid's health began to fail. In her early eighties, the stairs were difficult to manage, climbing out of the bathtub was a challenge, she fell asleep without warning, and her hip pain was nearly crippling. Mildred badgered her for months, and Astrid finally agreed to move out of her apartment. They toured a number of facilities until they settled on an elegantly appointed nursing home with a pleasant staff. It wasn't home, but Astrid knew she could carry out the last days of her life there. Mildred helped her sort through the fifty years of memories gathered in the apartment. Junk was purged, items parceled out to family members, and the rest was sold. Once she was settled into the nursing home, Astrid sent Mildred home.

Unable to bear parting with the original market, Astrid leased it, along with her apartment, to an Asian couple. She sold the other markets and gave her employees generous severance packages. Her one regret over selling the markets was putting her employees out of a job, so she made sure they had a safety net until their next jobs came along.

Astrid's old neighbors made the trek to the nursing home, but entertaining her friends left her exhausted. As time wore on, the visits went from frequent to seldom to never. The older neighbors died off, or health issues prevented them from making the trip, and the young ones were busy raising the next generation. Astrid didn't mind, as it left her with time to contemplate her life.

That was when I waltzed in and thought I would bring joy to her days. How was I to know that *she* would be the one bringing *me* joy?

Part III: Our Story

Chapter 24: Romancing the Media

Today's restaurant is theater on a grand scale.

— Marian Burros

Since I worked during the day and Adam worked six nights a week, finding time to see each other was difficult. The solution was to work together, so I bused tables at Reverie on busy nights. The long days were excruciating; I worked ten hours at my day job and three more on my feet at the restaurant. I would fall into bed and practically be asleep before I turned out the light. But the exhaustion was worth it, because Adam and I could at least be in the same building.

At work, Olivia pulled me aside and said, "I'm concerned about your health, Meredith. You're pale, thin, and have dark circles under your eyes. The careless errors, missed appointments, and unanswered phone calls aren't like you. Are you okay?"

"Oh, yes I'm okay," I replied. "In fact, I'm better than okay. I'm in love."

Not wanting to lose my job, I cut back at the restaurant, but I had a brainstorm. Reverie was successful, but more media coverage and special events could change its course. Adam knew how to plan an event and make amazing meals, but a public relations firm was needed to create more hype about Reverie, and I knew the person to do the job: me. My hidden agenda was we could be together and I wouldn't get my sorry ass canned from my real job.

Adam agreed he needed marketing help, because his aspiration to open another restaurant required money—

gobs of it. To make more money, he needed to fill every table every night. My boss, Olivia, was happy to have a new client for the agency, even if not in her division, so she loaned me to the department handling their San Francisco clients to work on Adam's account. I spent a week working on the marketing and media outreach plan and conducted research to find the right reporters and contacts to approach. My temporary boss blessed it before I told Adam about it. He raised an eyebrow over the number of hours my plan would keep him away from Reverie, but he agreed to do it.

I launched a media blitz, but it fell flat. Not a single media outlet showed interest in Adam or Reverie, or seemed to care about food in general. Badgering news editors did nothing but annoy them, and reporters ignored my numerous phone calls. I turned to Olivia for help. She suggested I bribe them with a free meal. Excellent idea. Adam and I planned a special luncheon for members of the press, food editors, television station directors, and public radio hosts. The invitation made it clear that there wasn't a catch and they weren't going to have to listen to a sales pitch. All they had to do was to show up with their appetite.

The lure of a free meal worked. It also helped that Olivia made a few phone calls to her media contacts. They may not have answered my phone calls, but they always picked up when she called. Reverie was almost full on the day of the media party. When Adam served his lobster ravioli, the room fell into an awe-filled silence. I waited in the corner to see what would happen when the lunch ended. I hoped that at least one person from the media would go up to Adam afterwards. More than one did. Nearly all of them did. Adam was handed business cards and was urged to be in touch. Adam didn't contact them, but I did. It was easy to talk to them about him, because I was in love and he was my favorite subject.

It took quite a while to capture the media's full attention, and I was about ready to give it up. I was finally able to convince the public television station to include Reverie on their show that featured local restaurants. But my first true success was getting Adam a guest appearance on the morning news and a local talk show for a cooking demonstration. The camera loved him. So did the female television anchor and talk show host. I needed to beat the eyelash-batting women off with a stick. The television station's sister radio station liked what they saw, and the ratings were excellent, so they had him as a guest on their afternoon talk show. After that they gave him a trial half-hour Saturday morning spot to discuss food, wine, and cooking. Listeners called in with questions, and some of the callers, including a few men, brazenly flirted with him on air. The nerve. The show was so popular that the radio station gave him a permanent spot in their line-up.

My efforts with the media, which was in great part fueled by Adam's charisma, started to gain momentum. I persuaded *The Chronicle's* food critic who wrote the rave review of Reverie to co-write a series of articles with Adam on hot trends in the food industry. The managing editor liked the series, and he offered Adam a weekly column. He called it *Life Happens Around the Table.* The column enjoyed a sizeable following, and I'm sure his photo next to his piece won over his female fan base. He wrote about the fruits and vegetables that were in season, cooking techniques, and hints on entertaining, and he included one of his prized recipes every week. Once a month he subtitled his column, "The Chef Recommends . . ." where he would feature five gadgets he considered must-haves in every kitchen. Adam told his readers where to buy them and, if need be, how to use them. One week, the five items were his favorite mandolin slicer, a microplane zester, nesting mixing bowls from the Museum of Modern Art, a pasta maker, and a food scraper to transfer chopped items from the cutting board to the pan. The owner of a local kitchen store begged Adam to tell him what items were going to be featured in the column beforehand so he could be sure to have enough in stock. People took Adam's recommendations seriously.

Adam asked me to edit his column before he submitted it to the paper, but one week when I was out of town I didn't have a chance to review it. I almost spewed coffee across my kitchen counter when the piece hit the paper. He asked his gentle readers to send in their favorite beef stroganoff recipe. He would make the recipes, and an expert judge, his girlfriend, would declare a winner. The winning recipe would be published in his column, and the winner would be treated to dinner for four at Reverie on the night he made the recipe as the special.

Dozens of recipes were submitted; Adam hadn't expected such a large response. A few of the entrants enclosed provocative photos, which I promptly shredded. He culled through the entries, tossed the ones that sounded awful, eliminated duplicates, and narrowed the recipes down to a manageable number. Mapping out a plan on how to make the recipes, he estimated that he would need one month to work through the entries. As the expert judge, I braced myself for four weeks of massive calorie intake. I abhor running, but I laced up my sneakers to prevent the pounds from holding a convention on my thighs. What a miserable occupation—I would have rather cleaned the toilet than put in the miles.

Chapter 24: Romancing the Media

The contest was a romp in culinary taste testing, and I loved judging the recipes. The beef stroganoff recipes came in many different varieties. Some called for sirloin, others were made with hamburger, and one person had the nerve to submit a recipe for lamb stroganoff. Lamb? It doesn't work. By week two, I couldn't stomach anymore beef stroganoff. In the search for Mom's recipe, I sampled dishes for months, but breaks between the tastings gave me time to breathe. With the recipe contest I endured sour cream, various cuts of meat, and egg noodles night after night.

Lucky for me, halfway through week three, one lucky entrant nailed it. The sauce was to die for, the seasonings were exceptional, and I declared it the winner. Adam protested, because he insisted I needed to judge the rest of the recipes first. Too bad. My search for beef stroganoff was officially over and out. I was sick to death of it. Sorry, Mom.

I also hired a designer to help establish Reverie's online presence. To add to the website's classy, sleek sex appeal, I sprinkled photos of Adam on every page. A professional photographer did photo shoots of him shopping in gourmet markets, standing alongside a farmer in a field of tomatoes, caramelizing onions in the restaurant kitchen, and posing bare-chested by a pool making a grocery list. The shirtless photo was shameless of me, I know, but I also had him dress in his chef's coat, tuxedo, suit and tie, and blue jeans with white T-shirt. He exuded animal magnetism, and his website made him a local household name—with the ladies, that is.

As part of the media outreach to bring more attention to Reverie, Adam hosted wine and food pairing events as fundraisers for a variety of local charities. The ticket price was outrageous, but invitations to the parties were sought after like the mother lode during the Gold Rush. I flooded news desks with press releases and media alerts. Newspapers and local magazines usually sent reporters and photographers, as the attendees were celebrities, politicians, and other city notables. Plus, as I had learned, reporters love a free meal. Articles on the parties and photo spreads were printed on the newspaper's society page and in the "About Town" sections of magazines.

At the food-pairing events, wineries vied for the honor of being the night's featured wine. Adam would give a talk about what he was serving, and the vintner discussed the wine. My favorite event was the occasion when he paired champagnes with oysters on the half-shell, caviar, and lobster macaroni and cheese. No, I take that back. The best one was the martini night, when he made killer Kobe steak kabobs, roasted root vegetables, and portobello mushrooms stuffed with crab. One bite of the steak would have converted any staunch vegan to a bloodthirsty carnivore. Since I was officially working that night, I nursed one martini. Even the one made my knees wobbly. As my mother would say, "It's like giving mittens to a one-armed man. One is enough, and two is too many." If I had consumed one more, you would have found me under the table.

The Oktoberfest was the rowdiest event. Adam made potato soup, bratwurst, red cabbage, and Spätzle, with a tender apple strudel for dessert. As German beer flowed, the oom-pah band led the inebriated crowd in drinking songs. A harpist played during a port tasting night, with an elaborate spread of different salty cheeses, dried fruits, and roasted nuts to complement the sweetness of the port. We hired a professional cigar roller for those guests who wanted to enjoy a fresh cigar outside after their glass of port. On the tequila and salsa night, which included a Mariachi band,

Adam served ceviche, tamales, and grilled citrus-marinated chicken. We knew how to throw a party.

In addition to being a food and wine connoisseur, Adam was also an olive oil snob. I rolled my eyes when he suggested an olive oil tasting night, but I unrolled them when he said, "Homer called it 'liquid gold,' so quit smirking." He heaped baskets with thin slices of his baguettes, he filled bowls with olive oil from California, Spain, Italy, Greece, Australia and South Africa, and he paired each variety of oil with a wine from the same region. A light supper followed, with dishes featuring olive oil as a key ingredient. The meal needed to be light, because everyone was stuffed with bread like a Thanksgiving turkey.

With all of our media and special event efforts, if you wanted a reservation at Reverie, you had to plan weeks ahead of time.

Chapter 25: Inseparable

Love is a flower. You've got to let it grow.

— John Lennon

Gravity cannot be held responsible for people falling in love.

— Albert Einstein

You know you're in love when you can't fall asleep, because reality is finally better than your dreams.

— Dr. Seuss

Adam and I saw each other or talked on the phone every day. My day was incomplete until I heard about his. I made mental notes about what I wanted to remember to tell him and jumped when the phone rang, hoping it was Adam. I thought about him to distraction. Good grief . . . I even doodled his name during meetings. Afraid the magic spell we were under would be broken, I hadn't yet told him I loved him. I wouldn't risk it. Our chemistry was precious to me, and I wanted an "and they lived happily ever after" ending to the fairytale I was living. *God, I'm a dreamer.*

During bouts of insecurity I wondered why he hadn't said he loved me either. Only recently opening myself to the possibility of love, my heart was still vulnerable. Hell, I wrote the owner's manual for a fragile heart. He hadn't taken me to meet his parents yet either. Maybe it was because I was keeping him too busy with the public relations junkets. But isn't meeting the parents a logical step in the progression of a relationship that has been going on for over six months?

The hostess at Reverie was darling. Maybe she was his true love. I saw the way she ogled him. I shook off the possibility that Adam and the hostess were an item when, stupid me, I remembered her boyfriend. She told me she knew he was about to propose to her, because she had overheard him on the phone with his brother.

I fretted about the wealthy women who came to Reverie and openly flirted with Adam. The grace and charm they acquired through money and good breeding had to be tempting to him. The glint in the socialites' eyes said they would be willing to strip for him at the least provocation. Did a rich trendsetter tempt him? I contemplated tailing those infatuated women to see if they tried to weasel their way into his bed. I'm not above stalking, you know.

But, lucky for me, when I was feeling the most insecure about our relationship, Adam had the gift of saying or doing the right thing. A hand to the small of my back as he passed. A wink from across the room. "You look beautiful," whispered in my ear. A stolen kiss nuzzled on my neck in Reverie's kitchen. With that, my worries would vanish.

Given our conflicting work schedules, we made the most of our time together. After the restaurant closed, I made a late night meal for him, or he cooked for me, but we mostly cooked together. We dubbed his Monday day off dinners "Silly Supper." We would pile cheese, fruit, crackers, and bits of leftovers on the coffee table and watch television while we ate whatever we were in the mood for. We often wandered the aisles of our favorite bookstore and took our selections to the park. I wanted Adam to read to me, but he thought that was corny. We loved the theater and went as often as our schedules allowed. Like Bogart and Bacall, we went to jazz clubs and listened to music while enjoying a martini. Some days we stayed in and watched sports on TV. Correction: He watched the game, and I feigned interest. I was willing to fake enthusiasm when his college football team scored, because it made it possible for me to lounge on the couch beside him.

My severe shortage of friends was no longer a problem. Adam's friends adopted me into their circle. Most worked in the food or wine industry. They loved me because I loved to talk about food and cooking. His college friends enjoyed swapping college party stories with me. Adam would drop everything for a friend in need. We spent many weekends helping his—now *our*—friends move into new apartments. Given his friends' ages, he was the caterer for numerous weddings and baby showers. I bought wedding and baby gifts in bulk. I went from having three friends to having dozens.

It was hard for me when my job started sending me overseas again. Before I met Adam, I looked forward to each trip. I pored over guidebooks in case I had time to sightsee, researched restaurants, and learned about the country's history, food, and culture. I learned a few phrases of the local language so I could at least ask for directions to the metro station if I got lost. After meeting Adam, an assignment in Europe was met with dread. I resented Europeans, because they forced me to be away from him. Unreasonable, I know, but I disliked them.

The best parts of my trips were the homecomings. The anticipated reunions made me giddy. Much to my fellow passengers' discomfort, I hogged the airplane bathroom before we landed. I couldn't let Adam pick me up at the airport with my clothes, hair, and makeup looking as if I had waged war with my airplane seat, even though that was precisely the case.

One aspect of traveling I did enjoy was finding a local delicacy and a bottle of regional wine to bring home to Adam. Home from the airport, I would ask him to close his eyes, feed him a bite of what I brought, and ask him to guess what it was. With maddening frequency, he knew. Damn chefs. He said, “I love it when you travel.” Seeing my crestfallen look, he hurried to add, “It turns me on when you feed me when you return, Meredith.” He redeemed himself before I threw the hunk of cheese I had hand-carried from Parma at him.

Chapter 26: A For-profit Non-profit

Fraud and falsehood only dread examination.
Truth invites it.

— Samuel Johnson

I continued to serve on the non-profit's board of directors, but had to miss a few meetings when I traveled. Missing the meetings didn't bother me, however, because my lack of board experience made me tense and my fellow members were unfriendly. My questions about what the agency was doing to help seniors and my nitpicky comments about the finances seemed to annoy everyone.

The director was short with me as well. I think she suspected I kept the financial handouts at the end of the meetings. She watched me as though I were a felon casing a jewelry store. What she didn't know was that I was sly and would have made a good secret agent. With stealth, I continued to slip the financials in my briefcase when the meetings were over.

The director called me to her office after a board meeting and asked the board chair to join us. Her expression was disturbing when she closed her office door. Since her facelift, I didn't like any look on her face, but the one that day was scary—it felt like a summons to the principal's office. "Please sit down, Meredith," she said.

With eyes bugged, as if she had sat on a thumbtack, she stared me down. "I need to ask you to resign from the board," she tersely announced. "You have missed many of our meetings, and we require that our board members be fully engaged. Because of your travel schedule, you haven't fulfilled your commitment to us." The chair shook my hand and said, "Please contact us when you are able to meet our expectations."

I had managed to get myself fired from a volunteer job. Ridiculous. I consulted my calendar and counted the handful of meetings I had missed. I pulled out the minutes from the board meetings, and after an hour of study I proved to myself that other members had missed more meetings than I had. It appeared that the director didn't appreciate my questions about the agency's finances and wanted me gone. I wouldn't sleep until I found out why.

I arranged the financial reports I had filched from the meetings in chronological order. With the textbook from a college accounting class as my reference, I tried to teach myself how to read the financial statements. I made notes, tracked trends, examined the credit line balance, and averaged the monthly donations. The income was more than the amount spent on programs, but the agency was in the red and the line of credit was maxed out. The numbers added up, but the story didn't. Apparently money was being siphoned off the agency.

I asked Adam to review the reports, and he agreed that something about the finances wasn't right. "I think the director is threatened by you, and that's why you were fired from the board," he said.

As a finance committee member, I was privy to the director's salary. Her income was modest, as was warranted at a non-profit. But she owned a luxury car, designer clothing, traveled the world extensively, and diamonds dripped from her ears like an Oscar nominee. How did she pay for it all? Before she hated me, she had dropped $300 for a pair of jeans while we were on a shopping trip together.

I hadn't spent $300 on my entire wardrobe in the past year. Her ex-husband was an electrician; even with their combined income before the divorce, how did she afford to outfit herself in such style?

I called the finance chair, hoping for corroboration, collaboration, or confirmation of my suspicions. I don't know—maybe it was another "C" word I was after. No, I wanted validation. The finance chair cut me off when she realized where the conversation was headed, citing ignorance about what I was talking about. It puzzled me, because I thought she shared my misgivings over the agency's finances. We hung up, and it dawned on me that she was afraid she was culpable (ah, the other "C" word). Charged with the oversight of the agency's finances, she could be liable for failing in her duties. Maybe her hands were dirty. She wasn't an ally; she was one of the enemies. I wanted to bring *her* down, too. I set the financial reports aside and turned on my computer.

I found a website that publishes reviews and financial data on non-profit organizations. I downloaded and printed information about the agency, such as annual reports and audits. Rather than helping, they made the picture fuzzier. Most of their money came from federal grants and donations. With about three clicks of my computer's mouse I found a telephone number to report suspected fraud to the Office of Inspector General. A sick suspicion gnawed in my gut, and I knew I needed to make the call.

A courteous person answered the phone, and I rattled off my suspicions. I described the plush boardroom, the elaborate meals and board retreats, the evasive answers to my questions about the agency's spending, and the financial ambiguities. For spite, I mentioned the director's extravagant lifestyle and her $20,000 worth of plastic surgery. She thanked me for my call and said they would review my complaint and contact me if they needed further information.

Then, the Feds went silent. I waited two months and called again. I was told an investigation was opened but the details were confidential. The woman on the phone gave me the impression that the investigation would take months, if not years. I did what I could about the matter. My conscience was clear, but the nagging feeling that the government was being duped remained, along with my worry that seniors weren't being helped.

Because my job required it of me, I needed to find another non-profit that would accept me as a board member. Olivia introduced me to the executive director of an agency that connected seniors with transportation, doctors, and other services. I was invited to serve on the board, and I was relieved when I understood what the board members said at the meetings. The director didn't speak gibberish, I could wrap my brain around the agency's funding and expenses, and I could stop by its programs whenever I wanted to. My favorite program was one that asked nail salons to donate gift certificates for manicures and pedicures. It's difficult for someone with arthritis to reach their toes, let alone cut their toenails, so it felt reassuring to be associated with an agency making a difference.

A nightmare about the other non-profit haunted me for days and created a knot in my stomach. In the dream, the director's petrified face floated over Astrid's nursing home room. About the time I was able to shake off the image, Special Agent Martinez from Washington D.C. called. He was coming to town to investigate my report and asked if I was willing to meet with him before he began the process at the agency. Boy, was I willing. I gathered my files and met with him in a federal building that looked more like a prison than an office. He grilled me for three hours in a windowless conference room. His suit jacket fell open, and I jumped when I saw the gun in a holster at his hip. *Fraud investigators are armed?*

He had planned on staying in town for a week to complete the investigation. His son's third birthday party was Saturday, and he needed to leave by Friday. He was still in town on Sunday when he called me again with more questions. I asked about his son's party. He said, "Couldn't leave. The investigation is more involved than I thought it would be. My son is disappointed, and my wife is probably interviewing hit men." My suspicions were confirmed; all was not kosher at the agency.

The media were alerted about the investigation, and the director was on the evening news. She shrugged off the fraud allegation by flippantly blaming a few minor accounting errors and said they would repay the government. How would the agency's donor base like their contributions being used to pay back the Feds, rather than promoting the agency's agenda?

The board chair called me late one night and blamed me for leaking the investigation to the media. It sounded as though he had been enjoying one too many martinis. Damn. Why didn't I think of calling the local news stations? I worked in the business after all. And then, radio silence from all parties. I didn't hear from Special Agent Martinez, the director, and nothing more appeared in the newspaper or on the evening news.

Chapter 27: The Mother

A mother's love for her child is like nothing else in the world. It knows no law, no pity, it dares all things and crushes down remorselessly all that stands in its path.

— Agatha Christie

Besides a passion for food, Adam and I shared something else in common. He was an only child as well. His dad was a retired high school principal, and his mother had taught history for forty years. His parents had met while working at the same school. Adam said his dad was a lovable pussycat, and, rather than dreading a summons to the principal's office, the students sought him out. He was an aberration in academia administration. He was adored as their principal and wrote excellent letters of recommendation for college. Adam believed his dad's letters helped many of the students get accepted into Ivy League schools.

The school mourned for days when his dad announced his retirement. The booster club and PTA threw him a retirement party in the school gym. Teenagers as well as and former students in their fifties attended his send-off party. Two years later, when Adam's mom announced she would retire, the school didn't give her a retirement party, but her students threw a blowout beer bash at the house of the captain of the football team. Neighbors had to call the police to break up the party.

After seven or eight months of seeing each other, Adam finally invited me to dinner at his parents' house in Palo

Alto, an hour south of San Francisco. He warned me that his mom wouldn't like me.

"Ha!" I retorted. "What's not to like?"

"Just so you know, my high school girlfriend called her 'Attila the Hun,' " he said. But I wasn't worried. I had grown into a likeable person, more or less.

The night of the dinner, I brought his parents homemade English toffee and flowers to endear myself to them. His dad greeted us at the door and crushed me in a hug. He held me at arm's length, studied me, and declared to Adam, "Gorgeous." Adam's mom came out of the kitchen and walked past me without making eye contact in order to hug her son. As only a mother can do, she gave his cheek a tender pat. She finally greeted me with a sneer and a resentful nod. *Uh-oh.* We were off to a bad start. I wasn't uptight about meeting Adam's parents until I saw the disapproving curl of her upper lip. Her frigid reception made me a dust devil of nerves.

Adam followed his mom to the kitchen while his dad led me by the hand to the living room for cocktails. The room's centerpiece was a classic 1950s cocktail cart with a martini shaker, an aluminum ice bucket, and highball glasses embossed in gold with pheasants.

"May I fix you an Old Fashioned, Meredith?" he asked while I sank into the sofa. The spongy cushions swallowed me, and I feared I would need help climbing out. An Old Fashioned was a new drink to me, but I said I would love one. "Coming right up," he said. "Because I like you, I'll treat you to two maraschino cherries." At that moment I knew why his student's loved him; he was cuddly in a rumpled-uncle kind of way.

He prattled away, not noticing I was too nervous to speak. I was angry with Adam for abandoning me. He later admitted to me that he had kept his mother away from me until I had a cocktail under my belt. The Old Fashioned was tasty, and I didn't notice my glass was empty until his dad took it from my hand to refresh my drink. The bourbon warmed my core and filed down the edges of my anxiety.

Adam raised an eyebrow when he saw the Old Fashioned in my hand while he and his mother joined us. His dad made two more drinks, and Adam said, "Be careful, Meredith . . . that drink is lethal. Trying to kill my girlfriend, Dad?"

Adam's mom glared at me and snorted. The cocktails worked a miracle on my nerves, and I hoped her drink would thaw the block of ice around her. While the three of us visited, she bristled on the arm of her chair and scowled. White knuckles clenched her drink, and it looked as though the glass might shatter. My attempt at charisma and humor worked on Adam and his dad, but his mom remained as cold as the Antarctic. Her body language seemed to say that she thought I was too glib for my own good. Indeed, Attila exuded hatred from every pore. So I said yes to another drink.

Adam's talent in the kitchen came from his mother. She created a lovely meal. Don't ask me what she served; I have no idea. I don't remember the drive home either. I don't recall anything after Adam's dad handed me the third drink. The Old Fashioned cocktails made me legless. However, vomiting four times in the middle of the night was a vivid memory, and an epic hangover in the morning clanged against my brain. I can hold my liquor, but Old Fashioneds are out of my league. I swore off drinking, but I'm afraid that only lasted a week.

Deathly afraid I had made a fool of myself, I ignored Adam's multiple phone calls in the morning, because I assumed he was calling to break up with me. Also, my head exploded when I tried to lift it off the pillow to answer the phone. I managed to call in sick to work and didn't have to fake it. I must have sounded as if I were about to croak.

At noon, I finally fell out of bed, made a cup of tea, and ate a stale cracker. Adam banged on my door and yelled my name. I looked as though a bus had dragged me across town, so I scanned the kitchen for somewhere to run. With no escape route to be found, I answered the door. Adam stormed in and said, "Why didn't you answer my calls, Meredith? Are you sick?" I decided to buck up, and I confessed I was hung over and apologized for my behavior at his parents' house.

He laughed, which made the pounding in my head worse. I stuck my head in the freezer to numb the pain. "You were fine last night," he said. "Actually, you were a trooper. You weren't embarrassing; you were effervescent. My dad loves you."

"Oh yeah?" I said with a raised eyebrow, which made my head hurt more. "What about Attila? She like me?"

"I went to their house this morning and chewed out my mom for her bad behavior. I demanded she apologize and that she better be nice to you in the future. I said if she didn't, there would be hell to pay. She's the role model for overprotective and doting moms around the world and is convinced no woman is worthy of my attention. She likes to scare women off. Maybe the three Old Fashioneds helped, but you didn't let her intimidate you." Adam patted my shoulder.

"You have no idea," I said. "She made my toenails curl."

He invited me to dinner at his parents' house the following weekend, and I was determined to stand up to his mom and garner her respect. Again, his dad greeted me with a hug that squeezed the air out of my lungs. Rather than ignore me, Adam's mom offered me a handshake that crushed my fingers into chalk-dust. The reception was cool, but she didn't bare her fangs or slash at me with her claws. She grudgingly offered an apology for her rude behavior, but added with a voice this side of a snarl, "You have to prove to me you make my son happy."

I picked up the gauntlet with a resolute look in my eyes. And I didn't drink that night. I wasn't going to make that mistake again. I needed to keep my wits about me. What did Adam's sweet dad see in the witch? Thank the stars she wasn't my history teacher in high school. I had a hard enough time passing classes with teachers who liked me.

Adam's mom warmed up to me after a month of me tiptoeing around her. Perhaps 'warm' is too strong an adjective to describe how she behaved toward me. She thawed around the edges, and she smiled at me from time to time. Attila the Hun was downgraded to Attila the Tolerable.

I invited Adam's parents and Astrid for Easter dinner and banned Adam from helping with the preparations. Changing out my velvet placemats and wintery table décor with a fusion of spring color, I covered the table with a mint-green tablecloth and tied six chives as a napkin ring around polka-dot napkins. I wanted to evoke the idea of an Easter egg hunt in the grass. My grandmother's floral dishes were again pressed into service. For the centerpiece, I placed thin slices of lemons, limes, and cucumbers in a glass vase filled with water and arranged an armload of tulips in unimaginable shades of pink. Filling every vase I owned with flowers, the apartment was like Macy's windows at Easter. With my décor refreshed by spring's bounty, I said to myself, *Bring it on, lady.*

Adam's mom nodded her approval at my apartment, but made no comment on the paycheck's worth of flowers. Astrid gushed over every blossom, my table, and the meal of glazed ham with cranberry chutney, twice-baked potatoes, and bundles of pencil-thin asparagus wrapped in bacon. The conversation was animated around the dinner table. Adam's mother forgot she disliked me for a moment and even laughed at one of my jokes. Another chunk of ice fell off of her.

After dinner, Adam announced it was game time. I cleared the dishes and served coffee and key lime pie while Adam and his dad set up the trivia game. "You, mom, and Astrid are a team," Adam said. "Watch out. Dad and I will cream you."

What he hadn't counted on was my mastery of minutia. Armed with my years of reading, crossword puzzles, international travel, and movie-watching, I handled the geography, entertainment, and literature questions with ease. Adam's mom and Astrid were whizzes in the history category and knew most of the science questions. Except for Astrid's knowledge of baseball, we failed in the sports category, so Adam and his dad trumped us on those. The competition was intense. Adam accused me of cheating when I nailed the answer to "What was Fred Astaire's sister's name?" The question crops up in crossword puzzles now and again, so I knew the answer. (In case you don't know, her name was Adele.)

We won the game, and Adam's mom clutched Astrid and me in a hug while Adam and his dad moped. Hold on—Adam's mom *hugged* me. It took a second to sink in. *She hugged me? Really?* I made a breakthrough at last. She had asked me to prove I made Adam happy, but, as it turned out, I won her approval by crushing him in defeat and making him sulk. When she hugged me a second time, I looked at Adam over her shoulder, and he gave me the thumbs-up. His dad and Astrid did the same. The iceberg, also known as Adam's mother, thawed a bit more.

To keep up the momentum, I invited her to lunch with Astrid and me. They gabbed like old pals over lunch, as though I weren't there. Polishing off my grilled swordfish, I tuned them out, but snapped to attention when I heard my name. Adam's mom had said to Astrid, "Meredith makes Adam happy. You know, I've never seen him this way. He struts around as though he won big at the craps table, and his silly grin makes him look like he drank too many of the casino's free cocktails." She smiled at me and said, "Okay, Meredith. You win. You proved to me you make my son happy." She abdicated her throne to me and conceded she was no longer queen of the realm in Adam's heart.

Chapter 28: A Novel Idea

There are three rules for writing the novel.
Unfortunately no one knows what they are.

— W. Somerset Maugham

There is nothing to writing. All you do is sit down at a typewriter and bleed.

— Ernest Hemingway

In utter loneliness, a writer tries to explain the inexplicable.

— John Steinbeck

I love the printed word. It fascinates me how, when strung together well, words paint pictures and evoke a range of emotions: love, hate, joy, and sorrow. Good writing makes the reader experience the character's feelings and carries them along in the surf of the story. You feel a jilted lover's rage or grieve alongside a mother who lost her child.

Bad writing, however, wastes a reader's time and leaves one to wonder why the writer squandered the paper and ink. Writing is like playing with building blocks to make a beautifully structured story. Fitting words together is an art, and, when done well, the engineering behind the construction is transparent.

I had always fantasized about writing a novel and seeing it on a bookstore shelf. The only person I shared that dream with was my high school English teacher. I worried he would laugh at me, but he didn't. He said, "Read every day, write every day, and it will happen. You have talent and a distinctive voice. Find something to say."

The problem was, I couldn't think of anything to write about for a short story, let alone for a novel. Until Astrid shared her life story with me, my chances of a book signing tour were slim. A story based on Astrid's life was rattling around in my head. I wanted to write it as a tribute to our friendship and as thanks for the warmth and light she had brought into my life. The work would pay homage to my mom, too. I had an idea to have my mom as a fictional character in Astrid's story. She could be the sweet to counterbalance Astrid's acerbic, yet kind, nature. They could be two unlikely best friends. I wasn't sure where the storyline would go, but I knew writing about my mom and Astrid would be cathartic.

Adam closed Reverie for a week so he could visit his ailing uncle in New York. Without weekend plans, I stocked up on food and wine and chained myself to my desk to see if I could make some literary magic. The challenge was to find the right combination and rhythm of words. At first I nurtured my writer within, then I wheedled her, then I used brute force to make her give me words to type. It started out slowly. No, not slowly—painfully. I wrote a couple of paragraphs and was pleased with the result. Pleased, that is, until I reread what I wrote and found it was rubbish. Hoping inspiration and creative guidance would find its way to my fingertips, I kept typing.

Saturday was wasted on hollow writing, only to delete the words on Sunday. By mid-afternoon on Sunday, I was near tears and considered throwing the foolish notion of writing a novel in the trash, along with my stupid paragraphs. I had a bad case of writer's remorse. I unshackled myself from my chair and poured myself a whiskey, even though it was barely three o'clock. I figured, if a stiff drink was good enough for Hemingway, it was good enough for me. I also hoped the whiskey would help ease the knots that had developed in my shoulders, because I had sat hunchbacked and dejected over my computer for hours.

My blank computer screen stared back at me while I sipped the bracing whiskey. I heard a voice and glanced around to find out where the sound came from, but the room was empty. The woman's voice came from inside my head. She gave me an opening line, and I typed the sentence before the words escaped me. I heard another sentence, and another, and another. At times the words floated onto the page like delicate petals. Other times they bounced into sentences like a Midwest hailstorm and formed paragraphs. The paragraphs turned into a page. One page became three.

Astrid gave me the concept for the story, but the voice whispered what words to write, as if I were a steno taking dictation. If I hadn't been wearing grubby sweats and my unwashed hair hadn't been pulled back in a messy ponytail, I would have looked like a Madison Avenue secretary wearing a pencil skirt and a crisp white blouse.

The voice kept talking when I took a bathroom break, and I had to race back to the computer to type her words. The voice took coffee breaks without letting me know, and I worried she might not come back. When she did, I greeted her warmly and kept typing, thankful that she hadn't quit her job without giving me notice.

I worked late into the night and called in sick in the morning. If I had stumbled into work, I would have been worthless—not because of the sleepless night, but because I would be waiting for the voice to start up again. Better to fake the flu than be fired for listening to voices inside my head.

I knew Astrid's story well, but the voice wasn't asking me to write her biography. She wove elements of Astrid's life into a tale of love, mistakes, and redemption from the perspective of a Midwestern farm girl living in San Francisco. My mom was worked into the story as Astrid's supervisor who then became her best friend. The voice was secretive about where she was taking me. Afraid she might refund my ticket and kick me off the train, I didn't ask. Like an obedient passenger, I boarded and transcribed the description of the view and the conversations around me.

If I wasn't a sane person, I might have worried that I was becoming schizophrenic, hearing voices and all—well, not voices, but one voice. After hours at the computer, I needed a break. I stretched out onto the couch and was asleep in seconds.

Several hours and a long shower later, I was certain the pages would end up in the trash bin, along with the other drivel I had spewed onto the pages. Maybe my secret voice was as bad a writer as I was. When I read my words, the writing was raw in areas, but I'll admit it was damn good. My new invisible writing partner and I were onto something.

With a little cajoling my poltergeist voice dictated more sentences and paragraphs. I didn't need to be chained to the desk; not even a charge of TNT could move me from my spot. Sometimes I quieted the voice and let my own be heard. The voice's timbre was the same as mine on the computer screen. Maybe the voice I was hearing was mine all along.

I wrote until I finally did light a stick of dynamite under myself and went to bed. My paying job wouldn't like me moonlighting as an unpaid writer and would want me fresh for work.

While I was concentrating on the task at hand at work the next day, the voice butted in and talked to me. Not wanting to disturb my coworkers, she whispered random ideas, entire sentences, or sometimes just one word. I kept a notepad close by, because the words were fleeting. If not caught on paper immediately, they disappeared like an intense dream upon waking. Images vivid in sleep become intangible and indescribable over coffee and the newspaper in the morning. I watched the clock until quitting time and raced home to transcribe the new ideas the voice whispered in my ear.

When not at work, I spent hours on the computer. Sometimes I edited existing copy, and sometimes I wrote new material. At the end of the week, when Adam came back from New York, I handed him thirty pages to read. He didn't know I liked to write, nor did he know about my fantasy of seeing my words in print. I kept quiet about the voice, because he might have had me committed. His eyes were teary as he set down the last page. "You've captured Astrid's spirit and spark."

Emboldened, I confessed I had heard a mysterious voice in my head and waited for Adam to call the men in white jackets, but he didn't. Instead, he said, "The same type of divine guidance comes to me in the kitchen at times. I read that creative types such as artists, writers, sculptors, and dancers describe the phenomenon as a force outside their body that uses them as a vehicle to bring art to life. The ancients believed the gods guided artists' hands. The creative process is mysteriously elusive or about as subtle as a sledgehammer. It is like capturing lightning in a bottle." I wasn't crazy; an otherworld deity inspired me. "I hope my goddess has talent."

Chapter 29: Tat

A great chef is an artist that I truly respect.
— Robert Stack

In order to be irreplaceable one must be different.
— Coco Chanel

The media outreach efforts promoting Reverie continued to be successful, and the wait for a reservation had become months long. It was like a piranha feeding frenzy. The junket I put together for Adam kept him away from the restaurant too much, and he needed help. He didn't trust anyone else in his kitchen and was reluctant to hire another chef. But doing everything himself was impossible. He also knew it would be smart to have someone trained and ready to step in if and when he opened a second restaurant.

After weeks of interviews and tasting sessions, he found a chef he was comfortable handing his apron over to. He hired him after sampling his short ribs, brussel sprouts with bacon and cayenne pecans, and beet salad with goat cheese. The chef, named Tat, was an old school punk rocker who had held onto his younger years as a wannabe rock star for far too long. He wore ripped jeans and was covered in tattoos and piercings, so I was skeptical about Adam's decision to hire Tat at first. I don't understand the popularity of tattoos. I never saw a tattoo on a body part and thought, *Well, that's a vast improvement over just plain skin.* In keeping with the upscale restaurant and its patrons, I preferred that the new chef be clean-cut like Adam.

However, as I got to know Tat, I found that his soft-spoken and bashful manner belied his edgy appearance. He was a kind soul, loved tearjerker chick-flicks, and often emptied his wallet when he saw a homeless woman on the street. He was a superlative chef and could create sublime dishes with his eyes closed. Five ingredients were turned into a masterpiece by his hand. He was a sweet man, but, with his gross piercings and graphic tattoos, I refused to put Tat's photo on the restaurant's website.

Astrid looked puzzled as I described to her the new chef's unconventional appearance, generosity, and exemplary skills in a professional kitchen. She asked his name. "I don't know his real name," I said, "but he goes by Tat, short for 'tattoo,' I presume. He's covered with them, so the name is appropriate."

"He sounds familiar," she said. Yet how could someone who looked and dressed like Tat sound familiar to Astrid? It's not likely they ran in the same circles.

I invited Astrid to Reverie for dinner to meet Tat and to tell her she was the inspiration for my yet unpublished novel. Adam was helping a friend move, so Tat was working solo. Over dinner I launched into a description of how I had stared into the abyss of my computer in an attempt to write a novelized account of her life. She didn't consider hearing a voice in my empty apartment grounds for criminal insanity. Astrid grumbled about being an unworthy heroine of my novel, but asked me to read the story to her on my next visit. I agreed on the condition that she would give me more material about her life. The flood of words from my phantom writing partner had slowed to a dribble.

Astrid rattled off stories nonstop while we relished the appetizer of bacon-wrapped scallops and made yummy noises over the Hungarian goulash. I jotted notes while she rambled. Toward the end of our meal, I spotted a white chef's coat. With a start, I sat up, but slouched back down again when I remembered Adam wasn't working that night.

Tat worked his way around the room, greeting the diners. Astrid gasped when he came up to our table. Afraid she was ill, I grabbed her hand. She stared at the chef with her mouth hanging open. "Frank? Is that you?"

Tat pulled out a chair and landed with a thud. "Holy shit. Is that you, Astrid?"

It turned out that Tat had been the eyebrow-pierced manager of Astrid's market. The last time they had seen each other was at the party Astrid had thrown on the day she sold the markets. It had been next to a miracle that Astrid and Tat had run into each other in a city filled with thousands of people and almost that many restaurants.

I had already devoured my plate of goulash, so I eyed Astrid's plate while she caught up with Frank, Tat's real name. Without looking at me, she pushed it over in my direction. I learned that Frank had used the severance pay Astrid had given him upon his termination as her manager to backpack his way through Europe. He also spent some time in Kenya, which was where he started stretching his ear lobes for his nasty gauge earrings. At that time no one in the States had seen gauge earrings except in issues of *National Geographic*. His ears drew more than a few gaping stares, even in quirky San Francisco. He added quite a few exotic tattoos to his collection while in Kenya as well. Tat was not afraid to break social conventions.

Tat wanted to break into the European music scene, but, while he was a minor success in Paris, true fame eluded him. To supplement the money he earned from his occasional music gigs, Tat found a job in the kitchen of a tiny café and fell in love. His passion wasn't for a woman, but for a sauté pan, chanterelle mushrooms, and every other food item in a French chef's arsenal.

The café's owner adopted Tat as a son and invited him to live with the family above the café. Recognizing Tat's potential as a fine chef, the owner loaned him the money for culinary school. Tat attended a nine-month program at *Le Cordon Bleu* and earned *Le Grand Diplome,* certifying that he was a master of cuisine and patisserie.

Tat set out to find a job as a full-time chef. With glowing letters of recommendation from his teachers in hand, a boutique cruise ship line for the affluent was quick to hire him. The ship was more like a large yacht for wealthy people who had no interest in owning their own boat. His ship sailed from France to Spain, and then on to Italy, Tunisia, and Sicily. He started out as a line chef and worked his way up to executive chef. Word of his prowess in the kitchen made its way to the States. Many passengers sailed on his cruise ship based on what they had heard about his food.

After fifteen years of being out of the States, his wanderlust diminished, and he yearned for home. An American passenger offered Tat a job as his private and corporate chef and moved him to San Francisco. But Tat's punk rock wardrobe and anti-establishment leanings soon clashed with the corporate environment. Because his boss insisted he fit into their mold, Tat quit without notice. That was when he answered Adam's ad in the newspaper.

Chapter 30: A Catered Affair

But I always say one's company, two's a crowd, and three's a party.

— Andy Warhol

With Tat established in the kitchen at Reverie, Adam could pursue his other passion: catering. He soon became *the* chef to hire for ritzy dinner parties, intimate gatherings, and art gallery openings. He commanded high prices, and each event brought him closer to the money he needed to open another restaurant. San Francisco socialites would have happily knocked out each other's teeth over who booked an event with him. The ladies sidled up to him in the kitchen at neighbors' parties, stuck out their fake boobs, and tried to get on his calendar.

That wasn't the only thing of Adam's they wanted to get on. One woman sent him a pair of her lace panties with her check for her party. The underwear was clean, but, *ugh*. He never took another catering job from her. One night he caused a scene between two women who had events planned for the same night, and they both wanted him. *Sorry, ladies, he's mine.*

A prominent retired San Francisco businessman and his wife hired Adam to cater their formal fiftieth anniversary party at the Legion of Honor. Christophe, the husband, had made millions importing inexpensive French wine to the States and selling it with a huge markup. His wife, Celeste, spent her days attempting to spend every dollar he made. They collected art and antiques and bought estates in Tuscany, Normandy, and the Alps as if they were cheap garage sale finds. They also donated thousands of dollars to the Legion of Honor as easily as if it were a Salvation Army bell-ringer at Christmas. Adam spent hours with Christophe and Celeste, the florist, the graphic designer, the rental company, and the venue while they planned every aspect of the golden anniversary party.

Adam invited me to go with him to one of the planning meetings. I went into the meeting skeptical and fearful of Christophe and Celeste's wealth. But I was wrong. They were warm, genuine, and couldn't be more gracious. Hearing that I worked in public relations, Celeste wanted to hire me to help promote her endowment for art restoration and preservation in developing countries. Christophe offered the use of any of their homes if Adam and I wanted to have a getaway.

The Legion of Honor has grand halls and intimate spaces that recall the glory days of wealthy San Francisco patrons of the arts. You can fit 250 of your closest friends for a sit-down dinner in the three adjoining Rodin galleries. Adam was a walking time bomb of nerves as he planned the party, because it was the largest, most important event of the year, and of his career. He rented a sleek professional kitchen that came with a catering chef and a staff of forty cooks and servers. It looked like a science lab, or the modern kitchen of a Hollywood movie star. Building the kitchen must have depleted the nation's supply of stainless steel.

Celeste insisted I come to the party and bring a guest. Astrid and I wouldn't know anyone there, but we didn't care. We wanted to mingle with money, art, and San Francisco's A-list. I told her I needed to shop for a dress. "Come check my closet, dear," she said. "I know I have something for you to wear." *Oh, great. I'll be attending the year's biggest event wearing a musty dress borrowed from an old lady.*

Boy, was I wrong. The back of Astrid's closet was like the costume vault on a Grace Kelly movie set. The floor-length dresses were of timeless style, sewn with millions of tiny hand stitches. Seeing my surprise over the couture treasures in her closet, Astrid said, "Back in the day, my figure looked like yours. Once we could afford the tickets, Sven and I loved fancy dress parties. I even attended a few galas after he died, and I sure turned many an old man's head." I modeled Astrid's gowns like a little girl playing dress-up. Except for needing to be taken in a little at the waist, the gowns looked and felt as if they were made for me.

Deciding which gown to wear was nearly impossible, but I opted for the black dress with a beaded bodice and silk moiré ballerina-length skirt. The almost-off-the shoulder neckline made my neck appear long and graceful, and when I pulled my hair into a French twist, Audrey Hepburn nodded her approval from Heaven. I considered taking up smoking and waving a cigarette holder as she had done in *Breakfast at Tiffany's*.

Astrid decided to wear her electric-blue lace dress with dyed-to-match low mules. The dress hung from her shoulders in a graceful column and made her look like the grandmother of a Grecian goddess. I commented on the color, and she said, "Most little old ladies wear beige lace and blend into the background. I like to make a splash. Don't want to be mistaken for a corpse." Everyone would notice her when she wore that dress.

I convinced Astrid that we should hire a car or limo to take us to the party. She balked at first, because she considered them too closely related to taxis. She relented when I explained that I would have to park my car and make the long walk up hill to the front of the Legion of Honor in high heels. "Well," she responded, "if we're going to hire a driver, he better be driving a limo, and he better be good-looking."

No expense was spared for this party. A string quartet played, champagne flowed, and guests stopped talking to grab more of Adam's appetizers as the waiters passed by. The flower arrangements rivaled that of a state dinner. The Rodin galleries reverberated with excitement and celebration. Christophe looked dashing in his tux and gold cummerbund and bowtie, but I didn't care for Celeste's gold lamé sheath dress. She looked like a life-size Oscar statuette wearing a wig.

After the cocktail hour, Christophe asked the guests to be seated for dinner. Candles and crystal goblets sparkled on the tables. The diners enjoyed Adam's meal under the watchful eyes of the figures in Rodin's statues. Between the salad and main entrée, the hosts made the rounds of each room greeting their guests. As major benefactors of the Legion of Honor, they encouraged us to support the museum. It was more a mandate than a suggestion.

Adam made an appearance after the entrées were served. Celeste crooked her arm around his elbow and led him on a tour of the tables as though he were her own son. He excused himself before he got to our table, as it was time for Christophe and Celeste to cut the multi-tier anniversary cake. Because wedding cakes were not his specialty, Adam had commissioned it from You Sweet Thing bakery in Atherton. The cake's white frosting was covered in hundreds of gold birds made of marzipan, which made it look ready to take flight on the wings of the doves. The cake topper was a crystal birdcage with two lovebirds in it. I had Adam ask the bakery to hide Christophe and Celeste's initials on the cake, as my mom used to do. She would have loved that over-the-top confectionery creation.

Chapter 31: My Big Idea

Everyone is in love with his own ideas.

— Carl Jung

An idea that is not dangerous is unworthy of being called an idea at all.

— Oscar Wilde

I kept Tat out of the spotlight while promoting Reverie, but one night, when I was thinking about him, I hit on an idea for Adam's second restaurant. While Reverie catered to San Francisco's well-to-do, Adam could use Tat as the bait to attract a different market segment: the up-and-coming young professional crowd. Tat was pushing middle age, but his funky style would appeal to those wanting an alternative to an intimate restaurant. I mulled over the concept and toyed with it in my head. Adam said he wanted another restaurant with a playful atmosphere. What if it was hip like a European underground nightclub? Tat's know-how from his time in such places would help pull it off. The restaurant could serve dinner and then later morph into a late-night venue with music. Hmmm . . . intriguing. Or idiotic. I wasn't sure which.

I wrote up my ideas and researched the demographic profile of my target age group. I looked online at our potential competition and searched for pictures of English and Irish pubs. With a workday looming, I forced myself to bed, where I fidgeted for an hour. Too many ideas played hopscotch in my brain. With a groan, I gave up hope for sleep, got on the computer again, and became convinced I was brilliant. I might not be a restaurateur, but I knew how to find a market niche and fill it. I wanted to share my idea with Adam but didn't dare call him in the wee hours of the morning. Plus, the idea needed to percolate more before I mentioned it to him. In daylight, the notion might seem ludicrous. With all my thoughts jotted down, I was blessed with merciful sleep when I turned off the light.

The next morning, while blow-drying my hair—which happens to be my best thinking time—I came up with more nuances for the new restaurant's concept. I put down the dryer to type up the new ideas. I then re-wet my hair and started over, because it had dried in weird angles. I needed to redo my makeup, too, because the water had run down my forehead. It was a small price to pay for beauty, but it made me late for work.

Before sharing my idea with Adam, I ran the concept by Olivia so she could either validate my belief that it was good or give me her frank opinion that it was rot. Her expression remained impassive while I pitched my idea, and it made stomach bile burn in my throat. I feared she would hate the restaurant's concept. When I ended my presentation, her silence caused me to squirm in my chair. Olivia nodded and without a word, rose to her feet and started to applaud. I jumped up, let out a holler, and asked for the afternoon off.

I headed to the nursing home to tell Astrid my idea. She was a tough critic, so if my proposal passed muster with her, the new restaurant was sure to succeed. I outlined the concept and told her Olivia endorsed it, and all that stood in the way was Adam's approval. Oh, and the small matter of the financial means. Bouncing on the balls of my feet, I waited for her reaction.

She grunted and said, "I happen to be a rich woman. If he wants to do it, I'll be his silent partner."

In Search of Beef Stroganoff

Adam had the day off, so I dug my phone from my purse and made a lunch date with him. We met at a deli near his apartment and bought sandwiches and pasta salad for a picnic lunch in the park. We found a secluded bench and basked in the soothing winter sunshine over an egg salad sandwich. I had to choke down my lunch, because I was anxious to tell him about my idea.

"To what do I owe this pleasure, Meredith?" he asked me. "You've never asked me on a picnic."

"Tat kept me awake in bed for hours last night," I said. Adam jumped to his feet. "No, no, no, it's not like *that!"* I continued. "He gave me an inspiration for your second restaurant, and it was the *idea* that kept me awake last night." Adam sat back down with a thump. I told him my idea for the pub-style restaurant and added elements that dawned on me while I talked. Unable to sit, I paced and made wild gestures with my hands to help him see the clear picture in my head.

Adam was quiet during my rant. When I stopped talking, I was panting. *Geez, I need to exercise more.* I stood in front of him with arms akimbo and waited for his response.

"It could work," he finally said. "I wish *I'd* thought of it. Now I need the money and superhuman strength to pull it off."

"Eat your Wheaties." I threw my arms around his neck. We were off to the races.

Yet there were many more obstacles to wade through, climb over, and duck around to make the restaurant a reality. The next one was Tat's approval, because he was a critical element in my grand scheme. Adam and I made the presentation to him together. I wanted Tat to know Adam didn't think it was a harebrained scheme. As soon as we finished speaking, Tat said, "That's brill. Count me in."

Chapter 31: My Big Idea

We spent several hours planning our strategy. I asked Adam and Tat what they might put on the menu. They popped out answers like contestants on a game show, on the theme of pub food with a twist. Fish and chips in microbrew beer-batter would come with a selection of dipping sauces and traditional malt vinegar. A chicken wing plate with Asian, Cajun, Indian, and sticky barbeque would go alongside the usual spicy buffalo wings with bleu cheese dressing. They would lace comforting mac and cheese with bits of jalapeno peppers and minced cilantro. Steak and kidney pies made with stout served in individual ramekins could be a weekly special. With a nod to tradition, a grilled cheese sandwich and creamy tomato soup would come with a chocolate malt.

The conversation made my mouth water. I offered my services as official taster and volunteered Astrid as well. I did have one request. The menu could not, under any circumstances, include beef stroganoff. I was sick of it, and it wouldn't pass my lips for a long time, if ever again.

A bar with a full complement of craft beers on tap, mixed drinks, and an extensive wine list was easy to pull off, because of Adam's solid relationship with the local breweries, distilleries, and wineries. He threw in the idea of brewing his own beer as the signature libation. Adam and Tat decided to take a beer making class and work on the right combination of hops, malt, and yeast. The way they talked, it sounded as though they had taken the class already. I guess when you love combining fine ingredients, the line between food and beverage is easily crossed. I designed the décor in my head and tuned out their beer talk.

My arena was the marketing, advertising, and media relations. By now I could do it with my eyes closed, and my extensive notes on the plan would guide me. Olivia offered to help come up with a name for the place. She said her frequent travel made her well versed in the European bar scene, and she thought the name should be authentic. I scratched my head. A classy lady like her doing pub-crawls didn't fit her style in my mind. She amazed me.

Tat had possibly the hardest job, which was finding the venue. A centrally located space conducive to a dining/music scene with a dash of funk might be hard to get. The space should be underground, or at least partially so, to create the proper mood. It must appeal to young professionals wanting an alternative to high-priced restaurants, pizza joints, or dank corner bars. Tat said he was up to the task.

Quality music would draw customers in for more than just dinner. Tat was still connected to the music scene in the States and Europe and rattled off suggestions. During dinner, the music shouldn't overshadow conversation or the meal itself. It could be traditional English and Irish folk, mellow jazz, classic blues, and country fusion—not intrusive, but a memorable sound. The pub would transform after dinner into a rocking venue for different types of performers, where the music would be the centerpiece instead of the background. We wanted a strong representation of musicians from overseas, especially from England and Ireland, in keeping with our pub theme.

The décor was tricky and caused an argument. I saw vintage tin beer signs, sawdust on the floor, and a salvaged bar and front door from an English pub. Vintage record albums, instruments, and old European subway maps could line the walls. A dartboard was a must. Because Adam was a classy guy, he envisioned brass fixtures, rich velvets, and intimate seating. He wanted a Prohibition-era speakeasy or dinner club ambiance. Tat, with his punk rock background, saw a garage band atmosphere with corrugated sheet metal walls, chrome fixtures, avant garde art, and hard edges.

We decided to table the décor discussion, because we were at an impasse. The venue itself would give us direction. I understand now why some parents can't settle on a baby's name until the little one pops out of the oven. Maybe that would be the case with the décor and the venue's name.

Adam and I argued about Astrid's offer to be his partner. "I am above accepting handouts," he said, "and I'll find a way to finance the place on my own."

"You're an obstinate fool," I countered, "and it could be years before your dream comes to bear."

We bickered for an hour. I offered the proceeds from the sale of my mom's house. He refused my money, too. "Money has a vicious habit of changing good relationships into nightmares." I surrendered, because winning the battle was unlikely for me. Exhausted and energized at the same time, we parted company.

At the nursing home, I updated Astrid on the progress we had made with the restaurant plans. In my best offhand and nonchalant manner, I said, "Adam won't take your money."

She scowled. "Let me talk to him." She phoned him. "Don't be an ass," she told him. "Take my money." I laughed out loud when I heard Adam's meek voice on the other end of the line say, "Okay, partner."

How did she ever change his mind with seven words, when nothing short of seven thousand words from me didn't budge him? She was one formidable woman. Remind me to never enter into a debate with her. I'd lose.

Adam drafted a business plan for the restaurant and would tweak it once a location was selected. He realized that, even with Astrid as his silent partner, they would need additional money for remodeling the new venue. I suggested contacting Christophe and Celeste for a loan. Rather than enlisting them as partners or stockholders, Adam and Astrid could pay off the loan with a percentage of the restaurant's monthly profits. Celeste agreed before she finished reading the plan. Christophe said no, but said he would reconsider once a location was found and his lawyer and investment advisor had read the plan.

Because Reverie was flourishing from our media blitz, we scaled back our efforts in that arena. We needed to work on our various assignments for the new restaurant. We wanted to do it right, because a great deal was at stake. Restaurant failures are as frequent as restaurant openings. Patrons are fickle, music critics are cruel, and judgmental food critics like to write acerbic reviews.

Chapter 32: The Perfect Place

You want to be where you can see
Our troubles are all the same.
You want to be where everybody knows your name.

— Gary Portnoy and Judy Hart Angelo
Lyrics from *Cheers* TV series theme song

Like a battering ram, Tat burst into Adam's apartment while we were eating dinner. Breathless, he said, "Grab your coats. I found the perfect place."

We downed our wine, because it would have been foolish to waste the expensive Pinot Noir. We left our half-eaten dinner on the table and ran out the door in his wake. During the cab ride, Tat explained that his buddy's band was practicing in a vacant pub the owner rented out by the hour. Tat's friend had told him the pub had been on the market for a long time, the asking price was cheap, and the acoustics were fantastic.

Tat directed the cabdriver to the neighborhood called South of Market—or SoMa, as locals call it. It was a once-thriving warehouse and light-manufacturing district. It was also home to seedy motels and a working-class population who lived in modest Italianate and Victorian row houses. It had a significant population of transient seamen, homeless people, a gay community, and a high crime rate. Businesses had moved out of San Francisco in search of cheaper rent, and by the 1950s the area was one notch above a slum. In the mid-1960s, free-spirited hippies, in the days of sex, drugs, and rock and roll, found a place to drop out of society. A counterculture music scene gave the area an edgy vibe in the 1980s.

But, similar to what happened to SoHo in New York in the 1970s, the neighborhood was now in transition. Developers were converting the vacant warehouses into loft apartments and artist studios. Artists craved the crisp natural light that streamed into the lofts' floor-to-ceiling windows. Because rents were relatively affordable, the refurbished apartment buildings and Victorian houses were filling up with young professionals. With a long way to go, the neighborhood was developing a sense of pride. *Perfect.*

Many of the buildings' facades were of classical Italian Renaissance design. Symmetrical columns flanked the doors, and ornate cornices made hooded eyebrows over the windows. Fire escapes zigzagged their way down the fronts of the warehouses and rundown apartment buildings. Some facades were painstakingly restored, yet others had boarded-up windows. Cigarette butts and trash littered the sidewalks except in front of the art galleries and new boutiques. The adult video shop next to a store carrying high-end handbags and shoes was odd.

In the fading daylight, we stood before the pub Tat found. The façade was in shades of grey, but we could tell it was once rather grand. Window boxes, long devoid of flowers, were above the leaded glass windows. Coats of arms in stained glass graced the top panel of the bank of windows. The front door's black paint was peeling, and the tarnished brass hardware made the door look as if it were scowling. *MAC'S PLACE* in faint gold lettering was above the windows, and *Live Music Daily* was above the door. The signs reminded me of the typeset of headlines in old newspapers. We stared in disbelief.

Chapter 32: The Perfect Place

Because Tat's friend's band was practicing, the front door was unlocked. We stepped into squalor. The pub was worn, tired, and sad from neglect. Although dust covered every surface and the corners of the room were crowded with cobwebs, the pressed tin ceiling was in remarkable condition, given its age. Tacky girlie posters and broken neon beer signs covered the walls, and the bar reeked of stale beer and cigarettes. At first glance, the space lacked promise.

"Check this out," Tat said as he flipped a light switch. Adam and I drew in a breath. A sturdy mahogany bar with a cluttered white marble top ran along the length of the room. The Guinness beer pull was the only one left. A mirror behind the bar was flanked by cabinetry with glass doors; a few panes were broken, and the doors hung on their hinges like drunken sailors. Above the mirror was a pendulum clock with its hands frozen at 4:03. I wondered what had been happening at 4:03 the day the clock stopped. The pub was dilapidated, but through the layers of dust you could conjure up a vision of its glory days. It needed work. It needed more than work; it needed love. Tat was right. He found the perfect place.

We followed Tat down a narrow staircase to a dingy basement, ducking our heads to prevent knocking ourselves silly on the oak transom. A storeroom opened up at the bottom of the stairs. Decaying cardboard boxes, chairs with broken legs, flimsy tables, and other detritus were shoved in one corner, making room for the band to practice in the opposite corner. The walls were brick, and the floor was uneven cobblestone. Six bare light bulbs hanging from frayed wires cast odd shadows around the room.

Tat's friend had told the owner we were coming to look at the pub, and, sure enough, the owner was right there to give us a hard sell. He had tried to unload the property for more than a year and was eager for a buyer. Knowing some of the pub's history, he told us the neighborhood had been home to a melting pot of immigrants, flophouses, and dockworkers. The working class living in the area patronized the pub and held jobs in the district's manufacturing industry.

Mac, the stout Irish proprietor, was a legend. He was quick with a joke, knew everyone's favorite beer, and served bowls of nourishing soup to anyone down on their luck. He strived to keep the bar open when his patrons and the jobs moved elsewhere, and in doing so he died a penniless man. A shady outfit, perhaps with Chinese Mob ties, purchased the bar and catered to a sketchy group of regulars looking for a cheap drink, prostitute, or drug deal. The pub closed when even the criminal element was afraid to enter the neighborhood after dark.

The current owner had learned from a City Hall insider that revitalization money was earmarked to pour into the neighborhood. He bought Mac's Place, hoping to flip it and making a quick profit. The area was turning around, but his finances had run out. He needed to sell the building fast and was willing to negotiate the price.

Beneath the grime, the bar had what we were looking for: history, character, and charm. Adam agreed to meet the owner at his office the following day to work out the details. It was late, but with Tat in tow we took a cab to Astrid's to let her know we found the perfect place. It was past her bedtime, but she was still up and watching a movie with fellow residents in the community room. We told her the name of the old pub. "Oh, yes, I know Mac's Place," she said. "Sven and I would listen to music at the pub after taking in a movie. You're right; Mac's is perfect."

Chapter 32: The Perfect Place

She asked me to fetch her purse from her room. She rummaged in her massive handbag and handed Adam a blank check. “Make it happen.” With an abrupt spin of her wheelchair she turned back to her movie.

Chapter 33: Renovation Begins

Architecture in general is frozen music.
— Friedrich von Schelling

Adam and Astrid met with a lawyer to draw up a partnership contract, and they didn't want me at the meeting. Which was okay by me. I hate the legal side of business deals, preferring to be creative, innovative, and cutting edge. Legalese makes my eyes cross. I should care about such matters, but I don't. Yet perhaps I should have paid more attention to the partnership agreement, because months later their meeting with the lawyer had a profound impact on my life.

Christophe agreed to be the financial backer for the renovation after he and Adam hammered out the terms of the loan. Celeste wanted to have a say in the design, but Adam was somehow able to get a clause in the deal that stated the investors could not have any creative input. I don't know how he slipped that in, but it was a brilliant move.

The real estate transaction progressed without a hitch. The building permits and liquor license were another matter. The road was paved with confusing, frustrating, maddening red tape. At times we were ready to abort the idea. The city and county acted as though they wanted to deter businesses from opening. You would think the tax revenue was needed, but no. Obstacles were erected at every corner of the bureaucratic maze.

Once we navigated our way through permitting hell, renovation could begin. On a tight budget we did some of the work ourselves on weekends, lunch hours, and Adam's day off. The first job was to haul out the trash, the broken chairs and the worn, outdated Formica tables. While Adam did the heavy lifting, I vacuumed every inch of the place and chased spiders from the corners. The former owner said Mac's Place had stopped serving alcohol during Prohibition and instead served simple meals of soup, stew, and sandwiches. Adam found empty moonshine bottles in the basement, and we suspected that, far from the eyes of the police, Mac continued to ply his patrons with booze downstairs.

We saved cleaning the carved bar for last. We wanted to enjoy polishing the old wood and buffing the marble. Refinishing the bar would remove its layers of varnish but would also strip it of its personality, so we let it be. The mirror behind the bar was missing a good bit of its silvering, but the crazing on the glass added to the room's charm. We replaced the cabinet's broken glass panes, and the clock went in for repair. The clockmaker said it was at least one hundred years old.

With the space clean and uncluttered, the real work could begin. We hired an architect who specialized in historic restoration. He toured Mac's Place and said, "You have yourself a treasure." We didn't need to move or erect walls, but electricity and plumbing had to be brought up to code. The architect helped us locate materials and fixtures that were either vintage or in keeping with the period. With his help I won the argument with Adam and Tat about the décor. It started out as an Irish pub, and so it would remain. I tried not to gloat, but I did anyway.

Adam and Tat teamed up with an interior designer to plan the kitchen's renovation. Adam insisted upon a professional-grade kitchen but without the usual cold, industrial feel. He kept the wood floors, and the only stainless steel he would allow in the space was on the appliances. The design called for Carrara marble countertops with a subway tile backsplash. All shelving was to be open for easy access and to keep the countertops uncluttered. Pots and pans would hang from a wrought iron rack above the island. There would be stations for prep, sautéing, grilling, and garnishing. An area that served as a place to prepare desserts by day would become a salad station by night. The kitchen was small and required an economy of movement; no wasted steps. As my mother and Benjamin Franklin would say, "A place for everything, everything in its place."

The revolving door of contractors had worn a path on the floor. Adam and I decided to strip the paint from the front door and window boxes ourselves, so we could stay out of the way of the renovation but keep an eye on its progress. Plus, the workers constantly riddled us with questions and needed us close at hand.

Gallons of paint stripper later, my muscles were sore, but my arms were sculpted from the hours of scraping. Thick coats of black paint had camouflaged a small brass plate on the door. With the precision of a surgeon I removed the paint. The plaque read, *Mac's Place, Est. 1915*. Adam and I nodded to each other knowingly. I shed my protective gloves, fished my cell phone from the pocket of my overalls and called Olivia. "No need to come up with a name for the pub," I said. "We're keeping it 'Mac's Place.' " We left the painting of the front door and window boxes to the professionals. I filled the freshened window boxes with red geraniums and screwed the plaque back on the door. I touched it for luck every time I entered the pub.

Chapter 33: Renovation Begins

We hired a well-known graphic designer, Paige Phillips of Paige Design, to recreate the name above the windows. I chuckled over the play on words with the name of her business. Her *MAC'S PLACE* and *Live Music Daily* in shadowbox gold lettering was an exact duplicate of the original sign. Adam and I crossed the street to admire Paige's work and called Tat to join us. We stopped a stranger and asked him to snap our photo to document the moment and our silly grins.

By now you must be wondering what happened to my day job and to Adam and Tat's night jobs. Frankly, our jobs suffered. Sleep, the laundry, apartment cleaning, and any semblance of a life also suffered. We ate, slept, and lived according to the demands of the renovation project. I would pack grubby clothes in a duffle bag, change at the end of the day in the ladies room, and head straight to Mac's Place to do another eight-hour workday. We were dead on our feet, yet euphoric. Work on my novel suffered too; about 150 pages languished in the corner of my desk. The voice inside me called out to me daily and said, *Where the hell are you?* I told her to pipe down. No time for writing. I had a pub to renovate.

Adam and Tat discovered the impossibility of being in two places at once. Tat suggested hiring a chef for Reverie, and he knew the man for the job. He had worked with Tat on the cruise ship and had confided that he longed to live in America. He was born and raised in France, but, because his parents are American, he had dual citizenship. Adam was desperate, and, because he trusted Tat's judgment, he asked Tat's friend to be on the next plane to the States.

I kept up my visits with Astrid and frequently brought her to Mac's Place to see our progress. True to her word, she remained a silent partner. I expected her to rattle off strong opinions about the renovation project, but she only admired the work and complimented the craftsmen. She was in awe of the energy we invested in the rehab, but she pleaded with us to take a break, warning that frayed nerves lead to short tempers.

Word spread about Adam and a silent partner opening a restaurant/nightclub in a restored building. Word got out because I had put it out there. Adam hired my firm to handle the publicity for Mac's Place, and Olivia gave the account to me to work on. I used every trick in my public relations bag to pique interest in the place. Adam included before and after pictures of the renovation in his newsletter, and his readers followed the progress like soap opera junkies.

One day on the bus on my way home from work, I eavesdropped on two young women in navy blue suits. They were talking about the upcoming grand opening of Mac's Place and the rumor about the bar once being a speakeasy. They planned to attend together if they were lucky enough to receive coveted invitations to the grand opening. I grinned the whole way home.

Chapter 34: The Devil is in the Details

Beware of the person who can't be bothered by details.
— William Feather

Countless details must be considered when making a restaurant concept into reality. At every turn we faced another decision. The logo was the easiest. Paige suggested using the block capital letters "M" and "P" from her recreated *MAC'S PLACE* sign, for their simple yet bold statement. Other decisions, from utensils to toilet tissue holders, required hours of research and shopping.

One night Adam called me and said, "Meredith, we need to talk." My heart sank to my feet, and my hands shook. I had heard that line before, and I hated it. We had been dating for months, but in my mind his cold tone said, *Breakup looming*. The phone line was silent for half a beat too long before he said, "We need to talk about what the waiters should wear."

I sank into my chair. His tone wasn't cold; it was merely businesslike. The answer to his question stumped me, however. Formal wasn't right, but nor were a leather jacket and torn jeans. I called upon Olivia for help. "That's easy," she said. "White shirt, skinny tie, black suit jacket with narrow lapels, drainpipe trousers, and Cuban-heeled boots. You know . . . like what the Beatles wore on their 1964 *Ed Sullivan Show* debut. Did I tell you I was in the audience that night?"

That was exactly what the waiters' uniforms should be. Although the target market we wanted to reach wasn't born when the Beatles had burst onto the music scene, everyone from all generations knew the band defined excellence in music. Besides, the basement music venue's distinctive atmosphere was not unlike the Cavern Club in Liverpool, where the Beatles had begun their musical odyssey. She added, "The bartenders need to wear white Oxford shirts with the sleeves rolled up above the elbow, flat-front grey wool slacks, with a crisp white dishtowel tucked in the waistband." I ended the call with Olivia by setting a date for lunch to hear more about the story of how she had happened to be in the audience the night the Beatles stormed America.

Adam and Tat took a beer making class but soon realized that producing enough beer to supply Mac's Place would be a full-time job and require a commercial brewery. So Adam convinced a local microbrewery owner to license one of his varieties for Mac's Place to call its own. The brew Adam selected was smooth with hops and had an undertone of citrus. The ale was colored like a burnished redhead. Tat planned on serving it with a slice of Mandarin orange he was planning to order from orchards in the Sierra foothills for his chutney recipe.

Adam and Tat, without consulting me one bit, named the beer "MP" for Mac's Place. It sounded like "Military Police" beer to me, but I kept my mouth shut, since they were elated with their clever name. Adam ordered pilsner glasses embellished with the "MP" logo in gold. The glasses were expensive, but, again, I kept quiet, because Adam was proud of his selection.

Adam and I suspected that Tat hoped to be music director as well as head chef. But the notion made us uneasy, as his musical taste was the opposite of what we had in mind. That was confirmed to me one night when he turned on the stereo. It blasted head-banging music that flattened me to the wall. I shouted over it, *à la* Astrid, "Turn off that dreadful racket!" It made my teeth hurt.

A talent agent who seemed to understand what we wanted in terms of music sent us demo tapes. Adam and I took a blessed night off from the renovation, knowing we found the man to book the music after hearing a couple of the demos. To gather strength before calling Tat to tell him he wouldn't be in charge of booking the musicians, Adam made two gin martinis. Knowing my quirks, he made mine with an olive, an onion, and a lemon twist. *Sweet man. I like garnish-overkill in my martini.*

Adam dialed Tat's number and broke the news to him. We expected him to be disappointed, so his reaction surprised us. He was actually relieved that we hadn't asked him to be the music director. "Too much pressure," he said.

Adam selected plates, silverware, and chunky glassware that brought to mind an English train station lunchroom. Another decision: tablecloths, or no tablecloths? Pubs don't use tablecloths, but Adam adamantly contended that white linen softened a room. I argued that tablecloths said "fancy restaurant," and thought we should convey a "make yourself at home" ambiance.

One evening after work, I wandered into an antique store to kill time, because Adam was at work and I needed a break from the construction. A sturdy masculine oak pedestal table caught my attention. I was struck with a marvelous idea, or at least I thought so. Mac's Place should have mismatched tables and chairs, like what you might find in the kitchen of an Irish farmhouse. Antique tables and an eclectic mix of chairs need no help in saying, "Make yourself at home." I bought the table, reasoning that, if Adam thought my idea was dumb, I still wanted to own it.

In Search of Beef Stroganoff

I stopped by Reverie to tell Adam my notion of mismatched chairs and tables. If he doubted my idea, he was afraid to say so, because the excitement in my eyes and the tone of my voice said, “I’m right about this.” I haunted antique stores and bought tables and chairs that spoke to me. I still can’t pass an antique store without checking the furniture selection. I suspect antique storeowners in San Francisco call me the Oak Table Lady. If so, I’m proud of the nickname.

On my lunch hour one day, I stumbled upon an antique store that specialized in instruments and music memorabilia, and I snatched up several pieces for the walls of Mac’s Place. On my way out the door, an upright piano bare of ornamentation caught my eye. Her simple square legs tapered at the bottom, and she looked like a workhorse. The shop owner said the piano was from the early 1900s and was plain, but a fine instrument. A piano tuner had cleaned her up and was surprised that the old gal was free from termite damage. The shop owner had purchased her from a defunct smoke-filled jazz club, the type you now see only in black-and-white movies. Beyond that, he didn’t know any more about its history.

Mac’s Place needs that piano, I decided. Without a second thought I whipped out my credit card, scheduled the delivery, and said a silent prayer that the piano would fit down the stairs. Since Adam had his way with the glasses and beer name, I figured it was *my* turn to do something without consulting *him*.

The basement’s cobblestone floor posed a tripping hazard and a nasty lawsuit. A lawsuit didn’t concern me as much as the possibility of it causing Astrid to fall. Our architect devised a clear raised floor so you could see the cobbles but not injure yourself walking across the room. In a departure from the Irish pub décor upstairs, we outfitted the basement like an intimate 1960s nightclub. Naugahyde easy chairs, small sofas and ottomans in jade-green, mustard-yellow and cobalt-blue mingled in circles. Hurricane lanterns with candles made shadows flicker on the walls. We nestled a vintage bar in one corner so thirsty music lovers didn't need to run upstairs for a drink. The front of the bar was reminiscent of a Cadillac Eldorado with its black tuck and roll upholstery and shiny chrome trim. I hung reproduction Beatles concert promotion posters around the room and on the stairway. In a word, it was retro. In another word, it was boss.

The renovation took a physical, emotional, and financial toll on us. As Astrid predicted, the early mornings and late nights, nonexistent weekends off, and endless decisions frayed our nerves. Our energy was siphoned off, drip-by-drip. Adam, Tat, and I argued about small matters. We argued over large issues, too. We argued for the sake of arguing. For Pete's sake, the pettiest argument was about where to hang the chalkboard for the list of the daily specials. The stress was weighing on us. In the right light, I saw that Adam's hair was peppered with gray. My face was haggard in every light. We had started the project with a full tank, but redlining the engine for months drained us of fuel. We needed a break, but someone kept moving the finish line when our backs were turned. It was like riding a roller coaster going a hundred miles per hour at a standstill.

Adam and Tat were like sandpaper on silk to my nerves. Everything they did or said bugged me and made me cross. Rather than dealing with my irritation directly, I buried it, blindly adhering to the misconception that if you don't acknowledge conflict it doesn't exist. I complained to Astrid that Adam and Tat irritated me but I didn't want to confront them about the situation. She said, "Ignoring conflict is an effective way to create more. Talk to the boys. You'll *all* feel better." I wondered what she meant by "you'll *all* feel better," but I heeded her advice and aired my grievances.

I didn't know it, but Adam and Tat harbored dozens of issues with me as well. They were annoyed at my snarkiness but kept quiet about it, fearing an ugly round of fireworks among us. We did more than air our grievances—we ran them through a NASA wind tunnel. The ensuing argument was so venomous the construction workers ran for shelter under my sturdy oak tables. Tat never raised his voice, so my jaw dropped when he pounded his fist on a table while yelling at me. "Quit being a control freak, Meredith. You need to chill!" I hate that expression.

Astrid was right. Bottling our gripes gave them the moist conditions to multiply like bacteria. In the end, the blitzkrieg was healthy. In the course of World War III, I found out that Adam and Tat had individually grumbled about me to Astrid. *That's* why she had said, "You'll *all* feel better."

Down to the last details, we hired experts to set up the lighting and sound system for the stage of the Cavern, as I called it, although we didn't call the basement that officially; the Cavern in Liverpool wouldn't like it if we purloined the name. The dark shadows that huddled in the corners presented a challenge to the lighting guys. Working in their favor was the rosy hue cast on the stage by the pitted brick walls. The sound engineers' work was easy, because the acoustics were remarkable. If you whispered into the corner of the room, it sounded as though you were shouting. The venue would be great for listening to music, but the crew asked us to invite friends over for a sound test. The mere presence of bodies, tables and chairs would muffle and buffer the sound and bounce it off the walls in a different way than when the room was empty. We needed to throw a pre-party party. Fantastic idea.

No permit was in place, but we changed out of our work clothes, threw on makeup (me, not Adam), and made a dozen phone calls. "I'll perform unplugged," Tat said. "I bought a new twelve-string guitar." Adam and I were askance. Would we be safe with Tat as the inaugural headliner? Yet Adam whispered to me, "He deserves this." I reckoned that, if Tat played an acoustic guitar, it couldn't be that bad. At least I hoped not.

With no time to prepare food, I ordered sushi takeout and bought six bottles of sake and two cases of Japanese beer. Our friends, Olivia, and a few of the pub's neighbors arrived at the appointed time. The Cavern echoed with laughter and was more like a family reunion than a sound system beta test. Astrid circulated the room like Greta Garbo at a Hollywood party. Adam and I supervised the proceedings while our guests filled their plates and poured drinks.

Later that evening he leapt on the stage like a movie star about to accept an Oscar rather than a frazzled restaurateur about to unveil his baby to our friends. My sweet Adam said, "This evening was made possible because of the vision, ambition, selfless behavior, incredible bitching, and endless nagging of one special person." He called me to the stage. As much as I wanted to, I refrained from giving him a whack upside the head as I mounted the stage and acknowledged the plaudits, because our closest friends were cheering. True, I was bitchy and a nag of late, but did he need to blab it to everyone?

"The next person I want to acknowledge," Adam continued, "is Astrid Johansson. She's the bang behind the buck on this project. Her financial backing, generosity, business savvy, and faith in me made Mac's Place a reality. She holds strong opinions and is quick to call you an ass, if deserved. I know, because she called me an ass on more than one occasion. She signed on as a silent partner, and she kept her word. She let this place soar on its own. Oh, and Astrid claims she doesn't approve of the drink, but I beg to differ. She butted in line to be the first to pour a cup of sake tonight. What a hypocrite."

With that, Astrid stood and proclaimed, "The next round is on me."

"Now I would like to introduce Tat, the inspiration for this place. Apparently, my muse"—Adam glanced in my direction—"was awake for hours one night thinking of nothing but Tat, Tat, Tat, instead of me. Imagine the bruise to my ego that revelation caused. I must admit Tat is a handsome guy."

A cacophony of catcalls and hooting broke out. Astrid was the loudest.

"Settle down, people!" Adam shouted over the din. "There is plenty of Tat to go around. So, without further ado, I give you our headliner for the night, Frank Simpson, who goes by the stage name of 'Tat.' He's a chef extraordinaire, and he tells me he plays a decent guitar. You be the judge, but from what I know about him, he's probably correct."

Adam made his way down from the stage, stopping for hugs and high-fives with every step. I grabbed him, and we leaned against each other at the back of the room as Tat bounded onto the stage with rock-star flair. He perched on the stool, and the crew adjusted the backlighting and focused a spotlight on his guitar. His first song was an acoustic version of "All My Loving," a fitting song choice for our American incarnation of the Cavern; the Beatles had opened with it during their *Ed Sullivan Show* debut.

Because of his appearance, I had pigeonholed Tat as a punk rocker. The pierced eyebrow, the tattoo of a skull on his neck, the leather jacket that looked as if it had done a spin in a food processor, and the pink tinges on the tips of his spiked hair were my first clues. The final clue was his gauge earrings. The holes in his lobes were the size of Kentucky, and when I looked at his ears, my stomach did a weird flip-flop. I presumed the only music he produced was the sort that made you want to bang your head against the wall or do psychotropic drugs to help endure it. What I learned that night was, he was a consummate musician with a sultry voice and more depth as an artist than I had ever imagined.

For more than an hour he worked his way through two-dozen Beatles songs, mostly from the early days, giving each of them his own twist. He did his version of "Ticket to Ride" at a plaintive tempo, which made tears sting in my eyes. Every song he played held a double meaning for me, particularly "I'm So Tired" off *The White Album,* which perfectly expressed my emotions and weary body. The audience sang along to his rousing rendition of "With a Little Help from My Friends."

Tat ended the set with "All You Need Is Love," and the crowd erupted in applause. I was dang proud of him, and I knew he needed to be a regular performer at Mac's Place. I had to invent a way to clone him so he could be in the kitchen and on the stage at the same time. I hoped he wouldn't abandon us when he realized punk rock wasn't his genre, switched to classic rock from the sixties, and was discovered by a record label.

I pulled Tat aside when he stepped off the stage and said, "I did you a disservice when I met you, and was quick to judge your outward appearance. You, my friend, are an accomplished musician and tender spirit. I owe you an apology."

"That's okay, Meredith," he said. "Everybody does. No surprise with the way I look. You saw through my carefully designed facade."

Olivia joined us. She said to Tat, "If John Lennon were alive today, he would be pleased. I should know; I dated him for more than a year." Hearing the full story at our lunch date would be delicious, to be sure.

Chapter 35: The End of the Tunnel

I've got a theory that if you give 100 percent all of the time, somehow things will work out in the end.

— Larry Bird

At long last, the menu was finalized, the first month of musicians were identified, and the final inspection was scheduled. Petunia, my flower vendor friend, was set to make the centerpieces and an arrangement for the bar. The pub wouldn't normally have flowers, but the grand opening called for them. We decided on rustic arrangements of English lavender, stalks of wheat, and delphinium in Mason jar vases tied with a raffia bow.

Close enough to completion, we set a date for our soft opening, when we could work out any problems that came up. We invited a few friends and the construction crew. Three weeks later, after the snags were resolved, we would have a full-blown invitation-only event. The invitation list mostly comprised young professionals whose names I had culled from the ranks of non-profit boards of directors. Art museums, the opera, ballet, and other prestigious agencies in town were represented.

Ticket sales were agonizingly slow, which made us more irritable, if that were even possible. If you poked a pin into the tension around Mac's Place, it would have popped like a balloon. Sick with worry about the ticket sales, I chewed my fingernails down to the quick. The deadline was a week away, and we had received a mere seven responses. Disheartened, I curtailed my daily inspection of the mailbox to avoid the sick feeling it gave me.

The day before the deadline, I braced myself and went to the post office to check the mail. The post office box was crammed with RSVPs, and the event was sold out with a waiting list of twenty. I hate to admit it, but my generation puts everything off until the last minute.

Rather than calling Adam, I made reservations for a room at the St. Francis Hotel in Union Square and dinner reservations at their Oak Room. The next call was to book appointments at the hotel spa. My credit card balance would suffer, but I was ready to splurge. I called Tat to let him know the party was sold out and asked him to forgo his day off to cover for Adam at Reverie. He assured me he wouldn't let on to Adam about my plan for the night. I rummaged in my refrigerator and found a bottle of champagne, a wedge of ripe Brie, and dark purple grapes. From the cupboard I pulled out Parmesan crisps, a can of macadamia nuts, and a tin of my butter pecan bars. My filled picnic basket called for a celebration, so I packed an overnight bag and tucked in a few romantic surprises—not exactly tame ones, if you get my drift.

I knocked on Adam's apartment door. No answer. Where was he? Was I too impulsive in booking the getaway without checking with him? Worried now, I pounded on the door. It finally opened to reveal a disheveled, rumpled, blurry-eyed Adam, whom I had evidently rousted from a catnap.

"Good thing you're rested up," I said. "You have a big night ahead of you." I pushed my way into his apartment. "Go take a shower, pack a bag, and put on something nice. I'm kidnapping you. No, I won't tell you where we're headed, and don't worry. Tat is covering for you."

Within fifteen minutes Adam emerged from the bedroom smelling clean and looking like a restored, albeit puzzled, man.

Chapter 35: The End of the Tunnel

I handed the cabdriver a slip of paper with the name of the hotel, put my finger to my lips, and with a wink I signaled for his silence. Adam riddled me with questions during the cab ride, but I sat as tight as a clam. He tried every angle to make me talk, including sulking. Although it's an effective technique, I remained impervious to his sad little attempt at pouting. He pinned me against the cab door and threatened to hold me captive until I told him what I was up to. I giggled and shoved him off me. Astrid's stubborn streak must have rubbed off on me. Wait a minute —I was stubborn before I met her.

Adam gave me a funny smile when the cab pulled up to the hotel. "Okay, now I know we're staying at the St. Francis, but what I really want to know is why," he said. "It isn't my birthday. Did you get a promotion? Out with it, lady."

"Nope. I'm not telling you just yet," I said as I paid the driver. "Patience, mister."

The hotel room overlooked Union Square, where March's setting sun made the sky a palate of rose and gold, and the city lights were winking in the dusk. The view was magical, as if designed by Walt Disney. I dimmed the room's lights and set out our small repast. We settled into two squishy overstuffed chairs, and I lifted my glass of champagne in a toast. Adam touched his glass to mine with a gentle clink. "The opening is sold out," I said. We missed our dinner reservation.

It wasn't what you may think. We talked for hours about the grand opening and how far we had come since the day we had first walked into the beat-up bar. With a jolt, I remembered I had failed to call Astrid to let her know the opening was sold out. While Adam made the call, I kicked off my shoes, stretched out on the bed, and tried to look alluring. The bed was soft as a dream. With his back to me while looking out the window, Adam gave Astrid the news. With the months of sleep deprivation, half a bottle of champagne, and a nosh of cheese and grapes in my stomach, I fell fast asleep while he was on the phone. There went our romantic evening of celebration. I think I even snored. How sexy.

Cottonmouth and a headache woke me in the morning. My contact lenses were suction-cupped to my eyeballs from sleeping in them, and I was still wearing my dress. Adam was asleep next to me, but he had had the wits to strip down to boxer shorts. I watched him sleep and would have paid a million dollars for a glass of water, two aspirin, and my toothbrush.

With the stealth of a snake I slithered out of bed to brush my teeth and run a comb through my tousled hair. Peeling off my wrinkled dress, I wrapped myself in one of the hotel robes. I made a mental note to steal it; it was like folding myself inside a marshmallow. Calling room service from the bathroom phone, I ordered coffee, juice, and eggs Benedict to be delivered in an hour. Adam was propped against the headboard when I returned to the room. He patted the mattress and crooked his finger at me. I knew what that meant.

I crawled across the bed and sat next to him cross-legged. He grabbed my hand and gazed at me with a look so tender it made my heart flutter. He said, "You know you're in love when you think your girlfriend's snoring is sexy."

Oh, great. I did snore. Wait a minute. I did a double take. We hadn't spoken the "love" word yet. We loved each other; that was apparent. We just hadn't said it. What were we waiting for? I said, "You know you're in love when you think your boyfriend's nose whistling when he sleeps is sexy." Adam smashed me back on the bed and covered me with his body. Thank the Lord, or maybe my fairy godmother, saying "I love you" didn't break the magic spell.

We leisurely made love while waiting for room service. The carnal celebration, delayed because of my sleep-deprived coma the night before, was sweeter than what I had anticipated. Afterward, I couldn't believe the hunky man I had plastered on the pages of his website was dozing right next to me. Not long ago, I considered myself unlovable. I was still a bit vulnerable and have some self-doubts, yet I felt comfortable with the person I was. I was capable of love and open to being loved. I wished my mom were alive so I could tell her I was in love. I would leave out the lovemaking details, but Astrid would be tickled when I told her we uttered those three little words.

Room service knocked, and Adam darted to the bathroom to find a robe while I marshmallowed into mine again and answered the door. I wondered if the room smelled of sex. If it did, room service guys were probably accustomed to it. He rolled in a cart, uncovered the plates, and set our breakfast on the table after I cleared the rubble from our celebration feast. With practice, he turned a blind eye to the aftermath of lovemaking. Flustered, I signed the bill, and he left.

When I closed the door behind him, I realized I had forgotten to leave a tip. He acted perturbed when I caught him in the hall until he figured out I had called him back to rectify my error. As I added a tip to the bill, I glanced down to see that my open robe revealed too much skin. I snatched the collar closed around my throat. Later I kicked myself, because the hotel had already included gratuity on the bill I had signed.

While the eggs Benedict didn't match Adam's, the sauce was lemony, and the eggs were poached the way I liked.

Crispy hash browns with bacon and bell pepper sat next to a selection of strawberries, kiwi, and melon. The coffee was full-bodied and blistering hot. A grapefruit tree must grow outside the kitchen door; the juice tasted that fresh. If our spa appointments weren't in an hour's time, I would have called downstairs for another order, for we had eaten poorly during the months of renovation.

Our appointments at the spa were for facials, a couple's massage, and manicures. I scheduled eyebrow waxes, too, but Adam canceled his and said, "My eyebrows are fine, thank you very much." Again, the expense was out of my budget, but we needed the pampering and restoration.

With my face smashed into the massage table, I unintelligibly told Adam that we needed to book the same spa package for Tat. He somehow understood what I said and muffled his agreement. Tat deserved the pampering as much as we did. Did Tat have a woman in his life? Why didn't I ask that before? I lifted my head and asked Adam if he knew. He said, "How did you not know that he's been dating Paige from Paige Design for months?"

I was an unobservant idiot. Of course they should be together, what with her bohemian aura and his gentle yet artistic soul. Before we left the spa, I made dual appointments for the works under the name of Frank Simpson.

A morning at the spa leaves you relaxed. You also look as though you were caught in the eye of a mild hurricane, if such a thing exists. My hair was a mess, my skin was blotchy from the facial, and my body had turned to Jell-O, but I didn't care. Adam had told me he loved me. Back in the room, we showered together and made love again under the warm water.

Chapter 35: The End of the Tunnel

Adam watched football while I dressed. Did I don a chic outfit for a day of shopping or a visit to the museum? Nope. I put on overalls and work boots. Work was waiting for us at Mac's with the much-anticipated grand opening two weeks away. (Just so you don't think less of me, I didn't steal the hotel robe.)

At the end of the day, I called Astrid to let her know Adam said he loved me. "Took him long enough," she said. "He told me he loved you the night I met him. What is wrong with that boy? I thought he was smart. By the way, isn't hotel sex the best?"

How the hell did she know we stayed at a hotel? I bet Tat ratted us out.

Chapter 36: The Opening

Friends may come, friends may go,
Friends may peter out, oh you know.
But we'll be friends through thick and thin,
So long as this bar doesn't run out of gin.

— Traditional English toast

The finishing touches on Mac's Place were almost complete, and a flurry of activity made the room buzz. Adam hired a crew to clear out the construction dust, wash the windows, clean the bathrooms, and wax the floors. The suppliers delivered the produce, meat, liquor, beer, and wine. The menus arrived from the printer one day ahead of schedule. Adam and Tat did a final round of interviews for the waiters, bartenders, and kitchen staff, or, as Adam called them, his miniature *brigade de cuisine*. We let the media in for a sneak peek in exchange for their promise of coverage. We were ready for the great unveiling.

The soft opening with our friends and the construction team was a crazy party. The crew got crocked and gave "MP" beer an enthusiastic, albeit drunk, two thumbs-up. Our friends got a little hammered, too. We had a few problems, such as a supplier who didn't show up with Adam's order of halibut, and an incompetent busboy. Adam resolved the issue by firing them both.

Nervous energy with minuscule productivity made me walk on the balls of my feet the day of the grand opening. Frenetic best describes my behavior, but Adam and Tat were unruffled. Their movements in the kitchen were fluid and graceful. Adam sent me home after I interrupted them with the same question three times because I hadn't listened to their answer. He said I was more of a hindrance than help, and his team would finish the last details. Wounded, but thankful, my dismissal gave me time to relax, shower, and dress for the evening.

Instead of standing in the shower, I allowed myself the luxury of a tub soak. I lounged in blissful lavender-scented bubbles. Preoccupied by the preparations for the opening, I suddenly realized I hadn't decided what to wear. Bubble-bath aborted, I wrapped myself in a towel and stared into the abyss of my closet. *What to wear?* I cursed Adam for having it easy. All he needed was a clean chef's coat at the ready. I rejected jeans, khakis, skirts, sweaters, and silk blouses. I was afraid my only choice would be my bra and underwear. *That* would make a statement, wouldn't it?

And then I knew what to wear . . . my dress from Paris. A little dressy for Mac's Place, but you can't go wrong with a classic black dress. It would be agony standing in stiletto heels all night, but I was willing to make the sacrifice for the team. It's all about how you look, right?

I picked up Astrid an hour before the grand opening, because Adam and the crew didn't want me to arrive any earlier, even though I had offered to do so. She was radiant in a simple skirt and floral blouse with a teal scarf tied in a jaunty bow at her neck. Unlike me, she thought about what to wear ahead of time.

Mac's Place shimmered in anticipation of its debut. The wood of the bar glowed in the soft lighting, and the flowers' aroma hinted of summer. The dilapidated pub Tat had found months before was now restored and refreshed, and it looked loved. It reminded me of the pubs I had fallen in love with in London, with the added element of sophistication.

We had created a masterpiece—a place where you want to linger.

I settled Astrid in a chair and brought her a glass of wine. A hundred guests were about to descend on us, yet the air was calm. The waitstaff loitered, and to pass the time they wiped silverware that didn't need polishing. Many had helped to prepare for the event, and all I was left to do was to wring my hands.

With the musician already playing, we opened the doors. The room was packed in minutes. Folks lingered at the bar, explored the restaurant, and talked about its history. Many of them knew each other. I guess the young professional community was tighter than I realized. The two women on whom I had eavesdropped in the bus were leaning against the bar. I made my way across the room and confessed I had listened to their conversation during their commute home.

"I remember you," the blonde girl said. "You stared at us and had a funny smile." *Damn.* Once again, I vowed to be more discreet when people-watching.

I fielded questions from the media, and I helped to pull together group-shots when the photographer from *San Francisco Vibrations* magazine circulated. He wanted a photo of Adam, Tat, and Astrid in front of Mac's Place. I interrupted Astrid and Olivia's animated conversation when I collected Astrid for the photo. I suspected I was the topic of discussion. Astrid confirmed this when I led her over to the photographer. "Olivia said you have natural talent in public relations." It floored me. My role model and mentor's comment flattered me beyond belief. Elated, I ignored Adam's grumbling about leaving the kitchen for the photo.

The musician ended his set and asked the guests to find their tables. The conversations remained animated. Adam and Tat served a sampler of many items from the regular menu. The blend of flavors was odd, but somehow it worked. I remembered that, with the hubbub of the day, my food intake consisted of a piece of toast for breakfast, so I cleaned my plate and eyed Astrid's leftovers. Without a word, she traded my empty plate for hers. I loved that woman for good reason.

The room gave Adam and Tat a standing ovation when they came out of the kitchen. Blushing, they motioned for everyone to sit and made the rounds of the room. My chest swelled with pride, and I flashed back to the first time I had hoped the white-coated chef would stop at my table. He came over and planted a firm kiss on my lips while I swooned. He hugged his mom, who started bawling.

The crowd filed downstairs after dinner for the music. We had booked a four-member band that played music from the British Invasion, and they rocked the house. Astrid removed her hearing aids and beamed from a front-row table while sipping her whiskey on the rocks. Dancers packed every spare inch of the room. My eyes met Adam's, and I knew what he was thinking. We needed to make space for a dance floor, given that live music moves you to express your joy through dance. Adam wove across the room, doing an awkward go-go dance and wearing a dastardly grin. I covered my eyes, hoping he would go away, but he pulled me close, and we danced to the Kinks' "You Really Got Me." I was incredibly, positively, magnificently turned on. Those Brits knew how to write a lyric.

Phenomenal reviews ran in the newspaper. A month later, the two-page spread in *San Francisco Vibrations* had about twenty photographs. The magazine's cover was none other than the photo of Adam, Tat and Astrid in front of Mac's Place. I was in the photo, too, but you could barely make me out. I was peering through the front window, bearing an unflattering toothy grin.

Part IV: The Last Story

Chapter 37: The Call

Death leaves a heartache no one can heal.
Love leaves a memory no one can steal.

— From a headstone in Ireland

The summer after the grand opening of Mac's Place, I got the call I had been dreading. Astrid had passed away with grace during the night. She was 89 years old. I grabbed a taxi and asked the driver to hurry. Racing to the nursing home wouldn't change anything, but I hoped that the faster I arrived, the sooner the pain of the knife piercing my heart would ease. For my protective coat of indifference was long gone. No pill on the market could relieve the sorrow that brought me to my knees.

The staff at the nursing home greeted me at the door with hugs. Their eyes were red from crying. Death is common in their line of work, but it doesn't make it easier to handle. Those in helping occupations have enormous hearts. Astrid lived in the home for years, and the staff loved her like family. From the doctors to the orderlies, in one way or another, she touched the life of each staff member. To comfort me, each relayed a story about Astrid. Some were poignant, others comical, but the stories showed how much they cared about her.

"That's my Astrid," I said with a chuckle.

I hated to break the news to Adam and Tat, who were as fond of Astrid as I was, or maybe more so. No, that was not possible. Astrid was my best friend, sister, mother, and grandmother rolled into one. She was more than that. She was also my cheerleader, guardian angel, therapist, and coach. Relaying the news to Adam and Tat over the phone would be heartless, as they would need a comforting hug.

I hopped in a cab and headed to Mac's Place, which was not yet open for the dinner crowd. With a shaking hand I led Adam to a seat at the bar. He saw I was shattered and knew to wait until I gained control over my voice and emotions so I could speak. I dislodged the lump in my throat and said, "Astrid is gone." He lowered his head, and his tears formed pools on the bar.

Tat caught a glimpse of us through the kitchen door window and knew something serious had happened. He banged the door open and braced himself at the bar. In a strangled voice I explained that Astrid had died during the night. He poured a shot of tequila, slammed it, and turned his back to us. His body was wracked by silent sobs. I watched while Adam and Tat's hearts were ripped out, but I could do nothing to stop the pain. Adam and I went to Tat's side of the bar, and we tried to find comfort in an awkward three-way hug.

Adam made phone calls to cancel the night's reservations, giving the terse explanation of "family emergency." Though Astrid wasn't related to us by blood, she was our family. The next round of calls he made was to the staff. He gently explained that Astrid had passed away and he was giving them the night off. He poured Tat another shot of tequila and filled two glasses with whiskey for us. We toasted our good fortune that we were privileged to know one tough old cookie.

Over the course of an hour, the staff filtered into Mac's Place. They had the night off but couldn't stay away. Astrid touched their lives, and they needed to be with each other in the place she helped create. The dishwasher fought back tears as he said, "Astrid gave me a generous bonus and made me promise to not say a word to Adam about it. She threatened to hit me with her handbag if I did."

"Impossible," Adam said. "She didn't have access to the Mac's Place bank account."

The dishwasher explained that she had written him a personal check, but not from the restaurant's account. The other employees shared similar stories about Astrid handing them bonus checks. One could make her college tuition payment, another bought an engagement ring, others took trips or paid delinquent bills. Tat, with a stammer, confessed that she had given him a check before Mac's Placed opened and said, "Buy an acoustic guitar, and quit playing that racket you call music." She was a one-woman lifesaver.

Astrid's body was flown to Garden Valley to be buried alongside her parents, husband, and daughter. San Francisco was her home, but her roots were deep in Minnesota. I called Olivia to tell her the news. Her tears broke my heart all over again. "Take as much time off as you want," she said. "I know what Astrid meant to you."

I made a reservation at the sole hotel in Garden Valley and booked my flights. I called Mildred and said, "Astrid was my closest friend, and I would like to come to her funeral."

"Oh honey," she said. "I know who you are. You were a devoted friend to my beloved sister. When are you coming? Astrid's room is ready for you."

I canceled my hotel reservation and packed my bags. On an impulse, I threw in a copy of my unfinished manuscript. What better place to write Astrid's story than from the home where she grew up? Adam and Tat would join me later for the funeral.

Chapter 38: Garden Valley Hospitality

There is peace and rest in comfort and sorrow.

— Søren Kierkegaard

I had learned from Astrid that Mildred was a spinster, but she doted on her gaggle of nieces and nephews. Mildred had lived with her parents in their dotage and was their keeper until heaven called them home. The other siblings had long since moved away, and by default Mildred inherited the house. The family sold off most of the surrounding farmland over the years, but Mildred farmed three acres with the help of hired hands. She was proud of the collection of ribbons she had won at the county fair for the vegetables the farm produced. Without children of her own, she tended to the oversight of each acre like an affectionate mother.

A dog bounded to my taxi when we pulled into the driveway. She was a mutt with a heavy dose of Australian shepherd blood. She did a Tasmanian devil dance at my feet and plopped down with her tongue and tail wagging. I fell in love with her, and, by the way she gazed up at me, I knew the feeling was mutual.

The farmhouse and bucolic setting were out of the pages of *Rebecca of Sunnybrook Farm*. The sun snuck under the front porch overhang and made the bottom of the Swedish-blue door glow. White wicker furniture gathered on the porch, as if in a silent prayer meeting. The trees were celebrating the glorious spring day by wearing their pink bonnets while bees hummed a summer tune in their ear. The daffodils had lifted their frilly yellow petticoats over their heads and were doing the can-can in the breeze. A picket fence surrounded a vegetable garden on the side of the house, sweet pea vines in full bloom embracing its slats.

A cedar shingled chicken coop with old paned windows housed eight or so French hens. Attached to the coop was a chicken wire run where the birds pecked and scratched in the sun. The contraption had wheels so the coop could be moved around the yard, depending on the season and the weather. It looked cozy. A cocky rooster circled the coop as though he were the Lord of the Manor who had lost his key to the front door. Crisp white sheets on the clothesline flapped in the breeze. *Wow. People still do that?* If someone wanted a description of a perfect Midwest farmhouse, you wouldn't need to say a word. You'd merely drive to the front of Mildred's house and say, "There it is."

Mildred flew down the front porch steps and embraced me. "Astrid described you to a tee, Meredith. She was right; you look like a movie star." Her comment stunned me, because Astrid had never said one word to me about my appearance. "I see you met my dog Rosie. Don't let her con you out of treats; she's masterful at feigning deprivation. Rosie is a descendant of the puppy Astrid rescued from a ditch when she was a little girl. Someone dumped a gunnysack full of pups, and one survived. Astrid named the dog Violet, because wild violets grew on the side of the culvert where she found her. All of Rosie's female canine relatives are named after flowers. Let's get you up to the house so you can get settled."

Forty years my senior, Mildred lifted my suitcase as though the bag weighed nothing and headed for the house. We trooped up to the second floor with Rosie ahead of us taking the steps two at a time. In Astrid's old room, a faded patchwork quilt topped the bed, a chipped bowl and pitcher were on the dresser, and an antique table served as the nightstand. A rag rug was right where you would drop your feet when rising from bed on a frigid winter morning. The room was like stepping into a Norman Rockwell painting.

Rosie stared up at me with doe-brown eyes, and her tail thumped, thumped, thumped against the floor. "Make yourself at home, and join me downstairs after you freshen up," Mildred said warmly. "You must be weary from your journey. A cup of tea and a lemon crisp cookie is just what you need. Be sure to keep an eye on that dog. She'll jump on the bed when you turn your back on her."

I sat down on the floor with Rosie for an earnest conversation. I said I was happy to meet the distant granddaughter of Astrid's childhood dog. When I buried my face in her neck for a hug, I caught a whiff of skunk. A bird's nest worth of twigs was tangled in her fringed tail. Rosie knit her tan eyebrows when I said she needed a bath. She understood English, as if she were a human in a dog suit.

I washed my hands, combed my hair and, before heading downstairs, peeked back into my room. As Mildred had predicted, Rosie was asleep on the bed with her head on the pillow. She jumped off in guilt when she heard me and followed me downstairs with her tail drooped in remorse over her transgression.

The house was a beehive of activity. Flowers needed to be arranged, tablecloths had to be ironed, and silver candlesticks begged to be polished. Visitors and family flowed in and out like the tide. Rosie's tail returned to perpetual wagging while she said hello to everyone. Like Astrid after the death of her daughter and husband, I had become numb. Handing me silver polish, Mildred said, "Now that you've finished your tea, make yourself useful, Meredith." I snapped out of my dazed state and found a silver bowl to polish. The busy house provided therapeutic comfort. I wondered which one of the teenage girls bouncing around the house was the smart-ass great-niece Astrid likened me to when we first met.

During my week at Mildred's house helping to prepare for the funeral, the phone never stopped ringing, and I believe I met every person who lived in Garden Valley. Minnesotans must consider it mandatory that, when someone dies, the bereaved house must be kept busy. The tradition must also include delivery of mass quantities of creamy casserole dinners.

The pastor stopped by each day. We engaged in long conversations about God, mortality, morality, redemption, and love. We also engaged in a long discourse on the nuances of pilsner over pale ale. I would attend church if I could find a pastor with this one's gentle way and love of beer. The funeral director was an old family friend, and he discussed the arrangements with the family in the front parlor behind closed doors. Mildred emerged with the others after an hour, and she was dabbing her eyes. New tears stung mine as I hurried to hug her.

Rosie never left my side. I found comfort in her following me everywhere. She leaned against me when I stood at the counter and rested her chin on my knee when I sat. If I left the room without her seeing me leave, she searched the house and greeted me when she found me, as though she was sure I had been abducted. I asked Mildred why Rosie followed me. "I can't explain it," she said. "Usually she sticks to me like lint. Maybe she senses your sorrow."

Rosie insisted on sleeping next to my bed. One night she couldn't stand it any longer, and my sleep was interrupted when the fifty-pound dog landed on my chest and shoved a wet nose into my ear. I pushed her to the foot of the bed, where her bulk sprawled a third of the length. Rather than curling up in a fetal position, I made my toes flat like the tips of screwdrivers and pried my feet under her. Rosie grunted, but, unlike the fair maiden in *The Princess and Pea*, she found the lumps quite comfortable. My feet cramped up, so I opted for a restless night in a fetal position.

I was foolish to think there would be time to work on my novel; the house was a circus. During a momentary lull in visitors and chores, I carried my manuscript to the picnic table on the front lawn to reread my work in progress. Away from the story for months, the words seemed new to me. Given my raw emotions, reading it without crying was impossible. With the read-through complete, I picked up the pen and it hovered over a notepad while I waited for inspiration. I decided to write about the time Astrid had rescued the puppy from the drainage ditch, and the mysterious writer's vortex sucked me in. The voice didn't whisper—she shouted—and I had to write fast. When she raced ahead of me, I scribbled one-word reminders in the notepad's margin.

Right when the flow of words started to slow down, Mildred joined me at the table and said, "You're in for a treat. It is *kroppkaka* night. Be prepared to help, because it's a group effort." Having no idea what she was talking about, I pressed her for an explanation. She shrugged and said, "You'll find out. Be in the kitchen at four o'clock." I continued to work on Astrid's novel until it was time to report for duty.

The women of the family, wearing hand-smocked aprons, were already gathered in the kitchen when I arrived. Mildred handed me an apron. While she tied the strings for me, she said, "*Kroppkaka* are traditional Swedish dumplings made with potatoes, eggs, and flour, and the centers are filled with bits of fried salt pork. The dumplings are boiled and eaten with a splash of cream poured on top, salt and pepper, and dotted with butter. Some eat *kroppkaka* with lingonberry jam or white sauce seasoned with allspice, but I don't care for it that way. Swedes concocted the dish during the harsh Swedish winters. Potatoes are harvested late in the summer and stored in the root cellar. Toward winter's end, the only food remaining in the larder might be potatoes and salt pork. The poor souls had to invent something to eat using those two ingredients."

Walking to the pantry, she turned over her shoulder and said, "Brace yourself, Meredith. Making *kroppkaka* is hard work, but completely worth it."

Some of the women peeled mountains of potatoes. Mildred directed me to help the salt pork crew. I grabbed a knife and cut the meat in small cubes. I didn't know anything about salt pork, but Adam probably knew what to do with it. While the potatoes cooked in bubbling pots, we fried the salt pork until it turned crisp and the color of toffee. I snuck a taste. The meat was chewy and delectable, like bacon without the smoky flavor.

We mashed the potatoes and added flour and eggs. I asked to read the recipe. "The recipe isn't written honey," Mildred said. "We make it by feel. The starch and water content vary a great deal, depending on the potato's age and the nutrients in the soil. You never know how many cups of flour and eggs you'll need. We keep adding them until the dough is good and stiff."

We took turns blending the flour and eggs into the potatoes. During my stab at it, the wooden spoon snapped in two, and Mildred proclaimed the dough ready. We dusted cutting boards with flour and formed golf-ball-sized dumplings with a teaspoon or so of the salt pork neatly tucked inside. Mildred slapped my hand when I grabbed another sample of the pork. I couldn't help myself.

We dropped the potato dumplings in large pots of boiling water. While they cooked, we set the table and cleaned the kitchen, which looked as though we had detonated a bomb in a flour mill.

"I love *kroppkaka* for supper," Mildred said, "but my favorite way is to eat the leftovers for breakfast. You fry half-inch slabs of the dumplings in butter until golden brown."

"I'm looking forward to dinner and breakfast tomorrow morning," I said.

She snorted. "We call it *supper* around here. Dinner is at noon." I stood corrected.

Expecting a bland, leaden, glutinous lump of flour and potato for supper, it surprised me that *kroppkaka* were flavorful and almost fluffy. For the millionth time I wished Adam were with me. At supper, Mildred asked what I was working on at the picnic table. Since saying the words "I am a writer" made me uncomfortable, as though I had foisted myself uninvited into the ranks of the greats, I hesitated before answering her. I stared at my hands until she lifted my chin and said, "Well?"

Swallowing the fear, I finally said, "I'm writing a novel with Astrid as the main character. I'm not a good writer, but I work on the manuscript when I have the chance. I wish I knew more details about her life."

Mildred chuckled. "You're right. Astrid was quite the character. I'm sure the book is wonderful." Without a word she left the supper table and returned with two hatboxes. "Here's more material for you, honey." The letters Astrid had sent Mildred over the years spilled over the rims of the boxes when I opened the lids.

Chapter 38: Garden Valley Hospitality

I slid the letter out of the envelope that had fallen on my lap and began to read. *"Dearest Mildred, I have devastating news. I had another miscarriage . . ."*

I couldn't read another word for the tears in my eyes. I gently folded the letter and returned it to the hatbox. Reading Astrid's words would require strength and solitude. *She didn't tell me she had miscarriages. I wonder why she didn't. Did the death of her daughter overshadow all other pain?*

Adam and Tat flew in the day before the funeral. The farmhouse had room for them, provided they didn't mind sleeping on the parlor floor under handmade quilts. In the straight-laced Midwest community, Tat was an enigma. If I had told the townsfolk that Tat parked his spaceship among Mildred's tomato plants, they would have believed me. Everyone was polite but covertly stared with their mouths hanging open in an unbecoming manner. He didn't seem to notice.

Adam and Tat declared a one-night moratorium on casserole dish suppers made by the neighbors and made dinner for us. They raided Mildred's vegetable garden and then headed for the market on borrowed bicycles. I wish I could have seen the faces of the folks in town who hadn't yet met or heard about Tat.

Mildred was concerned when Adam banned her from the kitchen while they cooked. I assured her that Adam and Tat not only were superb chefs but also knew how to operate a pot scrubber and dishrag.

A relatively small group gathered at the supper table that night. The teenage nieces and nephews had gone to the movies, and other family members were visiting friends. Twelve of us convened at the table . . . I said we were a relatively small group, not a tiny one.

The meal Adam and Tat had created was fantastic, as I knew it would be. It was fit for a king, and even more so for us weary mourners. The conversation was light at first as we savored each bite. They had broiled rib eyes from grass-fed beef and topped the steaks with a slab of bleu cheese coated with toasted pine nuts. The crispy shoestring french fries dusted with coarse sea salt, vinegar powder and minced chives were worthy of applause. From Mildred's prolific garden, they had tossed a vegetable medley with fresh dill weed. Tat brought out strawberry shortcake topped with a cloud of whipped cream sweetened with honey.

Reenergized by food and lubricated by wine, the conversation had become boisterous. Stories about Astrid, the farm, and the old days abounded. Astrid would have loved the party, but I shook off the thought as it made me sad.

We washed the supper dishes, and the group assembled in the front parlor. Mildred brought Tat a vintage red stool that looked like a prop from the *I Love Lucy* show, and he grabbed his guitar from the corner of the room. Having once again grossly underestimated Tat's talent, I swallowed a lump when he sang Cole Porter's "Ev'ry Time We Say Goodbye." Then he crooned "'Til There Was You" and "Goodnight My Someone" from *The Music Man,* which he followed up with Gershwin's "Someone to Watch Over Me." *How did he know my favorite songs?* He needed to put punk rock behind him; his calling was in the gentler side of music.

At midnight we hugged goodnight, knowing the next day was sure to be grueling. While the guests took turns brushing their teeth in the bathroom, Adam and I were lingering on the stairs for a private kiss when we noticed

Chapter 38: Garden Valley Hospitality

Mildred and Tat engaged in a quiet conversation at the end of the hallway. What were they talking about?

Chapter 39: The Funeral

When you are sorrowful look again in your heart, and you shall see that in truth you are weeping for that which has been your delight.

— Kahlil Gibran

I woke at first light, which is unusual for a city girl like me. I would usually sleep in until nine o'clock on the weekends, so something must have stirred me. I padded to the window and parted the lace curtains just as the rooster was ruffling his feathers and announcing to the world that it was time to get up.

Below me, Mildred was tending her vegetable patch, wearing a straw hat and gardening clogs. I yanked on jeans, a sweatshirt, and sneakers and joined her. Rosie was at my heels. The morning was cool around the edges, but I knew it would work itself into a glorious day. I interrupted Mildred's thoughts when I said, "Good morning."

With a start, she turned to me and said, "Oh good. I need the help getting this done before the funeral. The green beans need picking, and the weeds are choking the strawberries. Grab gloves, and here's a basket for the beans. Pick the long beans for tomorrow's supper and set aside the ones the size of your pinkie. I pickle the small ones with dill, red pepper flakes, and several cloves of garlic. Also, check the tomato plants for hornworms, pluck the bastards off, and give them a good squash. I don't use pesticides . . . I was an organic gardener before you city slickers decided it was chic."

Chapter 39: The Funeral

We worked side-by-side for half an hour without speaking, yet our silent companionship was restorative. My mom enjoyed working in the minuscule backyard of the house where I grew up. She often asked me to join her while she planted flowers and mulched the soil, but I never did. In Mildred's garden, however, I fell into a trance. I worked with the rising sun on my back and had to ditch my sweatshirt. I loved the dew on the leaves, the worms that squiggled when unearthed, and the abundance offered by the bean vines. The soil smelled fertile. I watched robins do shots at the birdbath while others used it as a Jacuzzi. A randy mourning dove chased a poor gal around and wasn't picking up on her body language that she wasn't interested in romance. I understood then why my mom loved working in her garden. The promise of what will appear from the tender shoots and the gratification of a freshly tilled and weed-free garden row is satisfying.

My mind was free to wander while I worked. I solved the world's problems while hunting for "pinkie-sized" beans in the rash-inducing vines. I then moved into oblivion when I weeded the rows of strawberries. The task helped to rest my tired brain. I enjoyed reviewing my progress; the result of my work was tangible.

I told Mildred I regretted not capturing before and after pictures on a camera. "Don't worry," she said. "Come back next week. The weeds will be back too, so bring your camera." I swore I could hear the ghost of crotchety Astrid in her sister's voice. It made me ecstatic.

Up until that point, my green thumb was a sick shade of chartreuse from killing houseplants with kindness or neglect. I overwatered the plants or failed to pay attention to them for weeks. Giving me a houseplant was the equivalent of sentencing the poor thing to death row, so I abandoned the endeavor of growing plants in my apartment and resorted to fake ones. My morning jaunt with Mildred in the vegetable patch, however, made me yearn for a garden—especially since my apartment in San Francisco was surrounded by about sixteen gazillion cubic feet of brick, asphalt and concrete.

Rosie sniffed gopher holes and left wet, dirty kisses on my face. Mildred scolded her for stepping on the strawberry plants, but she wagged her tail and trampled some more. The dog enjoyed the morning in the garden as much as I did. Along with a garden in the city, I wanted to bring Rosie home with me, but that would be unfair to her. She would get depressed, being cooped up in my apartment all day after her free range on the farm. Who knows? Maybe she would enjoy the elevated status of pampered city dog over her life as a lowly farmhand. But it was silly to consider stealing Rosie, because my apartment building had a no-pets policy, and Mildred would never part with her.

We finished weeding. My T-shirt was sweat-stained, and my face was smudged with dirt, but Mildred was spotless. From our harvest, Mildred and I made spinach, chive, tomato, and zucchini omelets. Before folding the eggs over, I grated white cheddar cheese on top of the veggies. The bacon was turning crispy when the rest of the household stirred. Adam and Tat shuffled out of the parlor with disheveled hair and baggy jammies. They looked like twelve-year-old boys who had stayed up all night at a sleepover. My heart melted.

The homespun breakfast fortified us for the emotional day, and strong coffee swept the cobwebs from our heads. The bathrooms were overtaxed with showers and shaving, so I boiled water for sponge baths when the water heater was drained. While doing the breakfast dishes, something caught my eye out the kitchen window. I just about choked when I saw Tat, buck-naked, washing himself off with icy water from the garden hose. His back was to me, which gave me a view of a snow-white butt and broad back covered with intricate tattoos. He scrubbed his body and hair with a bar of soap and shook off the excess water like a dog. With a towel around his middle, he lathered up and shaved. I'll wager that the enterprise left more than a few bloody nicks in its aftermath. He wet his toothbrush with the hose and brushed his teeth. It made me want to take an invigorating bath in the yard.

Tat came into the kitchen, and I said, "Good thing Mildred didn't see you."

He chuckled and said, "She suggested it. Best wash-up I've ever had."

When he returned to the kitchen after dressing for the funeral, I reeled. He wore an impeccably tailored suit, a crisp white shirt with French cuffs, and an electric-blue Jerry Garcia tie.

"Tat, you cut a dashing figure," I said. "I wish Astrid could have seen you dressed in that suit."

"But she did. I wore this getup whenever I took her out to dinner. She approved. She bought it for me."

All were dressed for the funeral in their Sunday best, but resolving the transportation situation was tricky. We had plenty of cars, but who would ride in which was a brief dilemma. After stutters and starts, we loaded up to head for the church. I glanced out the car window before we pulled out of the driveway. Rosie was staring at me with doleful eyes. I opened the door, and she hopped in, leaving a trail of muddy paw-prints on my clean skirt. I hugged her doggie, skunk-smelling neck and slammed the door shut. Mildred,

Tat, Adam, and I chattered as though we were on our way to a party, not a funeral. The air was almost festive.

Rosie waited outside the church during the service. Adam, Tat, and I sat in the fourth pew, leaving the first three for the family. Mildred left her seat and gathered us up. "What are you doing way back here?" she asked. "Sit with us. You're our adopted family members, for Pete's sake."

When we moved to the front pew, I scanned the church just as Olivia and Adam's parents were walking in. Adam and I rushed to greet them. "We decided at the last minute that we wouldn't be able live with ourselves if we missed Astrid's funeral," Adam's dad said. "She was like no other, and so important to you two. Important to us as well. We had to be here."

Compared to Penelope's dreadful funeral, Astrid's was like a gala ball. The music was uplifting, the eulogy inspiring, the service unforgettable. The pastor mentioned me as a savior during Astrid's last years. *Me, a savior? I don't think so. It was she who saved me, and for that I will be forever grateful.*

The service ended with a bagpiper playing "Amazing Grace." Rosie danced circles at my feet when I left the comfort of the music and the calm of the sanctuary. That was nice.

The congregation passed under the shade of an ancient oak tree while crossing the church lawn to the cemetery. I could almost see a young Astrid and Sven sitting on a blanket under that tree, tongue-tied and on the brink of love. What a charming picture it painted on my distraught, tired heart. It gave me peace.

We said our goodbyes to Astrid at the poignant graveside service. I slipped my arm around Mildred's waist. The gesture was meant to comfort, but with the way she squeezed me back, I believe I received more comfort than I gave. Rosie leaned against us.

Tat ended the service by singing "Somewhere Over the Rainbow" from *The Wizard of Oz.* To this day, the song gives me chills. If you listen intently to the lyrics, you'll know what I mean. The words are sad, but soothing. *Sleep well, my dear friend Astrid.* I knew we would meet again, but how bittersweet the moment. One by one, the funeral attendees hugged Tat or shook his hand when he finished singing before moving on to hug Mildred. Astrid's friends were no longer afraid of Tat. They recognized that he was at heart a gentle giant who clearly loved Astrid. It dawned on me that Mildred must have asked Tat to sing at the funeral when they were whispering together in the hallway the night before. I'm sure he was honored.

Chapter 40: The Celebration

Food is the most primitive form of comfort.
— Sheila Graham

Adam and Tat dashed to the airport after the service to get back to Mac's Place to prepare for the next day's dinner crowd, while the rest of us returned to the farmhouse for the Swedish version of an Irish wake. The children played in the yard while the adults visited, reminisced, and pored over photo albums scattered around the house. The party was upbeat, but now and then you would see a quiet hug or a tear dabbed with a hankie.

The kitchen and dining room tables groaned in unison over the amount of food covering their expanse. Although I hated the reason for the gathering, I was happy to be part of one of the famous potluck suppers Astrid had told me about. The food was abundant, made from scratch, and smelled delectable. The tables were crowded with bowls of potato salad, creamed corn, yellow pea soup, and plates of stinky pickled herring. Meatloaf and fried chicken sat beside tuna noodle casseroles, and, of course, someone brought Swedish meatballs.

I was completely put off by the plate of *lutefisk*, which is dried cod that has been soaked in a water and lye solution, which makes the fish gelatinous. That is my least favorite texture in the world of food. Equally disgusting were the slices of headcheese, raw onion, and peppercorns swimming in a pool of vinegar. Astrid had told me that head cheese, a Swedish cold cut, is made by boiling the head of a pig for hours and then putting the meat into a mold to chill over night. Something releases from the skull of the pig and makes the mold set up like Jell-O laced with pork. *Gross.*

Baskets piled high with homemade breads and rolls were set near a bowl of lingonberry jam. Ice-cold milk was in a frosty ceramic pitcher, and another was filled with lemonade with mint and thin slices of lemon floating on the top. Coffee flowed, and aquavit was hauled out. The dessert table was piled with apple, pecan and berry pies and coconut, devil's food and pound cakes. Plate after plate was filled with towers of cookies, fudge, and brownies. Minnesotans must have coined the phrase "comfort food."

Once everyone made the rounds of the potluck table, I grabbed a plate of my own. The contents of one of the casserole dishes were a mystery to me. I detected creamy white noodles peeking out from under a brown sauce with bits of hamburger and mushrooms. It smelled like home. Mildred joined me at the table to clear away empty dishes. I asked her if she happened to know what the mystery casserole was. "Of course, dear," she said. "It's Astrid's famous beef stroganoff. I made it this morning while you dressed for the funeral."

I set down my half-filled plate, lowered my head to my chest, and wept. For the love of God, would I ever stop crying? Alarmed, Mildred swept to my side, and Rosie was right behind her. Mildred patted my back and said, "Astrid shared her secret recipe with me years ago, and I kept it safe from our prying neighbors. In one of her last letters she asked me to give it to you when she died. She said the recipe is important to you but didn't say why. You were a dear friend to her, and I'm pleased for you to have her recipe. Thank you for being kind to my sister."

She dug into her apron pocket and pulled out a yellowed, tattered recipe card. I recognized Astrid's handwriting. Her hand had become shaky, but her distinctive style was the same. Blinking back tears, I said, “This is the most precious gift I’ve ever received. I’ll treasure her recipe, and her secret is safe with me. I am truly honored.”

Mildred dissolved into giggles. I blinked some more. What was so hilarious? She clutched her side as if it hurt and wiped not tears of sorrow but tears of mirth from her eyes. I waited until she caught her breath to tell me what she found so funny.

“My sweet girl, the recipe Astrid guarded with vigilance for years was one she adapted from the back of the Campbell’s Cream of Mushroom Soup can.”

My mouth dropped open.

“Close your mouth, dear. You’ll catch flies.” She went on to explain that no one knew Astrid’s stroganoff was made with canned soup because the women in the county would never dream of making dinner from a can. “I didn’t know she made it with the help of a can until the day she left for San Francisco. Once I dried my tears that day, I read the recipe and had the best laugh of my life.”

My tears vanished, and Mildred and I cackled. The guests must have thought we had dipped into the aquavit. We were as sober as Mormons but tipsy with laughter. As we composed ourselves, Mildred spied an empty dish to clear and made her way to the kitchen.

I scooped a giant spoonful of beef stroganoff on my plate and searched for a quiet corner to enjoy my first taste of Astrid’s delicacy. I wanted to be alone with it. Rosie followed, but that was okay; she was delightful company. No one was on the front porch, so I plunked down on a wicker chair. I shoveled a forkful of stroganoff into my mouth and just about choked.

It was my mom’s recipe.

I managed to swallow and laughed again. That time, I laughed at myself. I had searched the world for a fancy beef stroganoff recipe with complicated directions and fine ingredients, while the secret had been in my pantry all along. Canned soup was a staple on my shelf for those late nights when cooking sounded like a horrible occupation. I had spent thousands of dollars on restaurant meals in search of Mom's recipe. Rather than a fancy sauce and culinary school worthy techniques, her recipe included seven ingredients, and one was from a can.

That old adage is true—the simple things in life are the best.

Thank you, Mom, and thank you, Astrid.

Chapter 41: Life After Astrid

One reason a dog can be such a comfort when you're feeling blue is that he doesn't try to find out why.

— Author unknown

My vacation time was exhausted, and endless deadlines loomed at work. I left Garden Valley the day after Astrid's funeral, but I hated to go. I would miss everyone and the unhurried pace of farm life. As I was packing, Mildred said, "If you don't visit often, Rosie and I will be angry with you."

My apartment was cold and empty when I arrived. Astrid didn't live with me, but it felt as though she had moved out while I was away. To distract myself from the ache in my heart, I cleaned my apartment, which was cluttered and overloaded with as much junk as my brain. My pantry looked as though I had unloaded my groceries by standing back ten feet and hurling the food onto the shelves. On a roll, I organized the closets and cupboards too, because nothing is more satisfying than opening a junk drawer and finding what you're after. My apartment and spirits were lighter when I finished the job in the wee hours of the morning. As William F. Buckley said, "Industry is the enemy of melancholy." *Amen to that, Mr. Buckley.*

The following week, my spirits sank again. I missed Astrid and longed for a cozy chat with her. Calling Mildred daily helped, but I still suffered from a tender hole in my heart. Memories of Astrid would come to mind like a freight train and lay me low. Falling asleep at night was difficult, and depression was closing in. Worried, I saw a doctor, and he prescribed what I called "my happy pills." The pills diluted my anxiety and made it possible for me to sleep, but my new worry was about becoming a drug addict.

I passed an alleyway while scurrying home from work in a San Francisco summer downpour and saw a shadow of brown fur. Thinking I saw a rat, I shuddered and quickened my pace. I walked three yards before I realized that what I had seen was larger than a rat. I retraced my steps and peeked around the corner. A toffee-colored miniature Dachshund was cowering next to a dumpster. He gazed up at me with forlorn brown eyes when I approached him. I stretched out my hand for him to smell, and when he didn't snap at me, I patted his head, and his tail wagged in a blur. I studied his name tag. It had no address or phone number, only his name . . . William. The night wasn't cold, but he was wet and shivering. Leaving him in the alley was unthinkable.

I tucked him under my raincoat so he would go unnoticed when I snuck him into my building. William strutted around my living room as if he owned the place. I shed my coat, which smelled of wet dog, and tossed it onto the dry cleaning pile. William and I stared at each other, wondering what to do next. His shivering hadn't let up, so I filled the kitchen sink with warm water and gave him a bubble bath. He cooperated, but his woeful eyes made it clear what he thought of the bath idea. Sure enough, he raced around my apartment like a dog possessed after I had dried him off. Laughing at him only made him run faster. He was thrilled to be out of the cold and cleaned up, and he was ready for dinner.

That presented a problem. I didn't have any dog food.

I scrambled an egg, thinking the protein would be good for him. Who knows when he had last eaten a decent meal? William downed his dinner in three bites and pranced at my feet as if to say, "Is that it?" I made him another egg, and while I was at it I made one for my own dinner. Then I slathered a toasted bagel with cream cheese and topped it with a slice of ham and the egg. William watched every move and made it clear he loved bagels too. I shook my head and said, "Nothin' doin', buddy."

I called Adam to tell him I had a new man in my life. "He has puppy-dog eyes, loves food as much I do, and stands a towering ten inches tall."

"I'll come over and beat the interloper to a pulp after I close Reverie for the night," Adam said.

At the dining room table, Adam and I debated what to do with the dog and settled on starting with posting flyers around the neighborhood. William hopped up on my lap and fell into an exhausted sleep while I typed the flyer. Next we checked the lost dog postings in the newspaper, but no Dachshund was mentioned anywhere. Why wasn't William's owner searching for him? The poor dog was homeless. Adam tacked up the flyers on his walk home, and we hoped his owner would notice them in the morning.

'William' is such a formal name for a dog that looked as though God had forgotten to read the instruction manual when assembling him. Either that, or God is a comedian. Clearly, whoever named him William wanted to bestow the poor dog with a little dignity. Adam, wanting William to embrace his Germanic heritage, called him Wilhelm. I called him Bill.

William's legs were too short for his tube-shaped body, and his feet were shaped like paddles. With hind legs longer than his front legs, he looked as though he was always walking downhill. With his pointy nose, wiry whiskers, and receding chin, no wonder I mistook him for a rat when I saw him in the alley. His ears made great spinnaker sails when fully perked at the mention of his name.

I made a nest for William next to my bed and tucked him in. He thought that was a ridiculous idea and hopped up to join me, burrowed under the covers, and curled into a ball. My bed must have looked more inviting than his.

In the morning I called the dog pound, placed an ad in the paper, posted more flyers, and bought dog food and chew toys. Thank goodness it was a weekend, because leaving a strange dog alone in my apartment while at work wasn't an option. By Sunday night I hadn't heard from his owners, and I asked Adam to watch him for me on Monday while I was at work. I began to think I inherited a dog, and I didn't mind.

I called my landlord and pled my case. He agreed I could keep the dog if he didn't bark and I paid him $150 a month in extortion—I mean, extra—rent. I bought a leash and a name tag engraved with my phone number. William officially became my roommate, and I hoped he would prove to be better than my college roommates.

I called Mildred and said, "I found a boyfriend for Rosie. He's short, dark, and handsome, and they would make a cute odd couple." I hired a young man to walk William twice a day. William didn't mind being left home alone, as it allowed him plenty of uninterrupted time to nap.

Sleeping was William's second favorite activity in life. The first was eating. William would sell his soul to the devil if he had a dog biscuit tucked in his cape pocket. Adam called him "a food whore" for good reason. The Navy would be smart to commission a research study on William's "foodar," for it would advance their radar and sonar technology; that dog could detect the sound of a food wrapper twenty miles away. For someone so short, he packed it in. Did I make it clear he lived for food? We had that in common.

Small dogs didn't thrill me, but William was different. He didn't yap, he was good company, and he adored me. The little guy had enough personality for three dogs twice his size. I swear he even had a sense of humor.

A mouse set up housekeeping in my closet and shredded a package of toilet paper for a nest, which drove William nuts. The scent was ambrosia to his nose, even after I had cleaned up the mess. Whining, he ran from the closet door, to my feet, and back again a dozen times, as if saying, "Come quick! A mouse is in the house." His face also said, "Shit, I wish I could talk. I need to tell her about that mouse!"

Since his short legs couldn't carry him far when he ran away from home, I was convinced that his former owner lived in my neighborhood. I peeked over my shoulder when I walked him to see if anyone was chasing after us to claim him. To play it safe, I often walked William in a park six blocks away. I suggested to the dog walker that he put William in a disguise whenever they went outside. The look the guy gave me said he thought I was nuts, but I was half-serious.

William loved to curl up on my lap, but only on *his* terms. If I picked him up when he wasn't in the mood, he made it clear I infringed on his personal space, and he would jump down. However, when he wanted to sit on my lap for a snooze, he made himself weigh about fifty pounds and turned into a limp noodle if I needed to get up. He liked to perch on the sofa armrest so he could survey the apartment. I owned a living gargoyle—it is likely that he sat on the arm of the sofa to stay out of harm's way. He was probably tired of getting squashed when someone flopped on the couch without seeing him.

Chapter 41: Life After Astrid

William was a wimp when it came to cold weather and rain. With a sleek coat and no body fat he wasn't protected from the elements by natural insulation. If the ground was wet, he picked up his paws and frowned at me, as if I had just forced him to step into something nasty. If I didn't time his potty breaks between rain showers, he refused to go. He considered himself a delicate flower that shouldn't be forced to endure the injustice of wet weather. He crossed his legs and held it until he either sensed, or smelled, that the rain had stopped. Prancing at the door, he let me know he needed to take care of business.

Conversely, when the sun streamed in my windows, he followed its path to bathe in the warmth. I joined him a time or two, and the sunbath was lovely.

It dawned on me one day that, since William's arrival on the scene, I had forgotten to take my "happy pills." He was no Astrid, but he was equally opinionated and knew how to make me laugh. In that way he helped to fill the void in my life her death had caused. Whenever the dark cloak of depression would begin to wrap around my shoulders, he either acted like a clown or wanted to crawl onto my lap for a cuddle. I tossed the happy pills down the toilet and considered myself cured. Doctors should prescribe a dog, not medication, when their patients are battling demons.

Not only did I love William for his companionship and sweet spirit, but also he made healing from Astrid's death a lot easier. He helped me know I should cherish the time I had spent with her rather than merely mourn her passing. I now smile every time I think of her instead of getting weepy.

Chapter 42: Profound Impact

The moment you have in your heart this extraordinary thing called love and feel the depth, the delight, the ecstasy of it, you will discover that for you the world is transformed.

— J. Krishnamurti

I mentioned earlier that Adam and Astrid's meeting with the lawyer about the purchase of Mac's Place had a profound impact on my life. Well, here it is.

Mildred asked me to come to Garden Valley for the reading of Astrid's will. To be more accurate, she commanded me to attend the meeting with the family lawyer. Unable to face it on my own, I ordered Adam to come with me. William made the plane trip with us in his dog crate under the seat. The flight schedule cut it close, but we grabbed a cab and raced into the meeting just ten minutes late. Panting and disheveled, we appeared to have jogged into town rather than come by plane.

The lawyer mumbled through the obligatory legalese before reading Astrid's will. She had left the bulk of her estate to her family. She also gave money to the nursing home to expand its library, as well as a generous gift to each of the employees of Reverie and Mac's Place. The will gave instructions to commission Tat's girlfriend to design a stained-glass window for the church. Astrid wanted the window dedicated to the memory of her husband and daughter. I knew Paige would be pleased to take on the task.

The last provision of her will stunned me. Astrid left her half of Mac's Place to me.

Chapter 42: Profound Impact

We stood to leave the lawyer's office, and Mildred said, "You kids need to talk, and you must be hungry. We ate already, but I packed a lunch for you. How about we drop you off at the church for a picnic and a chat? We'll take William to the house to meet Rosie. He must need to stretch his legs after his morning in that blasted crate."

The churchyard was an idyllic spot for a picnic and a serious conversation about Astrid leaving me her share of Mac's Place. I started to babble as soon as we piled out of the car. "Hush," Adam said. "We have plenty of time to talk about that later." He carried the basket to the shade of the oak tree where Astrid and Sven had had their awkward first picnic. We spread out the blanket and unpacked three bean salad, turkey sandwiches, watermelon, and gingersnap cookies. Mildred had also tucked in a Thermos of iced tea.

As I sank my teeth into my sandwich, Adam said, "Well, Astrid made us business partners. Will you be my partner in name as well and marry me?"

Gulp. I didn't expect that. Nor did he expect to be knocked over by a 130-pound woman.

I crushed him in a hug until he gently pushed me away. He fished into his pocket and pulled out a small box with a diamond-and-sapphire engagement ring and a thin gold band. *This and my heart ~ Sven* was engraved inside the wedding band. *How did Adam come by Astrid's ring?* I wondered.

He pulled a letter out of his pocket and said it was the last letter Astrid wrote to Mildred before she died. The letter, in part, read:

> *If that fool of a man Adam hasn't already asked her to marry him when I'm dead and*

> *gone, hand him my wedding ring and tell him to get on with it. If Adam and Meredith have had enough sense to get married without my nagging, string the ring on the chain with the locket Sven gave me when he proposed. She can wear it around her neck. She was like a daughter to me and I want her to have it. No sense wasting it by putting it in my grave.*

He told me that Mildred had given him the ring and letter the day he had arrived for Astrid's funeral. He had said, "Don't worry. I'm on it already. I've carried around an engagement ring for weeks, waiting to find the right place to ask Meredith to marry me."

Now he said to me, "I saw the oak tree in the churchyard at Astrid's funeral and knew the proposal needed to be made under its branches. I asked Mildred to make our basket lunch today and feigned innocence when she suggested we enjoy it at the church."

Yes, Mildred the Sneak had been in on it all along, with Astrid as co-conspirator from the grave.

Adam slid the diamond ring on my finger and gave me a kiss so tender my socks melted. He pulled a small card from under the box's silk lining and handed it to me. A note in Astrid's handwriting said:

> *For my adopted daughter on her wedding day. May your marriage be as happy as mine was. I love you. Astrid.*

Instead of our wedding plans, we talked about Astrid and the way she continued to guide our destinies. How I wished she could walk me down the aisle. As soon as I said those words, I knew Mildred was the one to do it.

While Adam reminisced on Astrid, I let my mind drift to the wedding invitation design.

Epilogue

All I really need is love, but a little chocolate now and then doesn't hurt!

— Charles M. Schulz

Because of Astrid, I found Mom's recipe, experienced heart-stopping love, and became a better person. My mom, Adam, Astrid, Mildred, and Tat are on the top of the list of the ones I love. The great many that follow can't be named in any particular order, as they jumble together like puppies at play. At the top of the nonhuman list are William and Rose.

The most difficult person I learned to love was someone who wasn't very nice. In fact, she was downright unpleasant to be around. That person was me.

Redemption came after self-realization. My wake-up call came in the form of poor decisions and lost opportunities. I realized I needed to make drastic changes in my behavior.

The best decision I made on the road to redemption was to throw myself in Astrid's path. She taught me to view myself through a different lens and not take myself so seriously. The most important gift she gave me was permission to forgive myself. Once I did, I opened my mind, body, and soul and became a compassionate and fallible person. Through that process, I found love. I also became someone my mother would be proud of. Redemption.

It might be coincidental that Astrid helped me find my mother's beef stroganoff recipe. My mom would have called it divine intervention. The recipe itself taught me a valuable lesson in that life isn't about the trappings, but about the simple things. Finding pleasure should be easy and free from entanglements. A life filled with should-haves and must-bes is burdensome. Simplicity in life gives the most pleasure, if you allow it to happen.

The following spring, Astrid's beer-loving pastor officiated our wedding, and the reception was on Mildred's farmhouse lawn. My friend Petunia flew in the day before the wedding and created my bouquet and flower arrangements from sweet peas and French lavender from Mildred's garden. Mildred walked me down the aisle. Olivia was my matron of honor. Adam's mom wore beige lace and cried through the entire ceremony. I tried to not be offended.

Tat did triple-duty that day. He was Adam's best man, and he made the dinner for our reception. You won't be surprised that he served beef stroganoff—yup, Mom's and Astrid's recipe. Tat then left the kitchen help to do the dishes while he played the Beatles' song "I Will" from *The White Album* for our first dance.

My new mother-in-law welcomed me into the family, but didn't fully embrace me to her bosom. Adam caught a bug on our honeymoon in Venice and spent three days in the bathroom after we arrived home. His mom came to the apartment to feed him thin broth and pamper him back to health while I went to work. On one of the days she stayed with him, she did our laundry. I found the gesture sweet until I saw that she had ironed Adam's shirts but had left mine in a wadded ball at the bottom of the laundry basket. Her passive-aggressive message was clear. "You are married to him, but he is still my property." Or maybe the message was, "You are lousy at ironing." Either way, it ticked me off.

Adam and I moved to a larger apartment and set up housekeeping. My kitchen had been inadequate for a professional chef, and his building didn't allow pets. A couple of years after we were married, Mildred called us with a proposition. We knew Astrid had left the building with the market and the apartments above to Mildred. The Korean man who lived in Astrid and Sven's old apartment and ran the market wanted to retire and break his lease on both. Mildred asked if we wanted the market . . . either to buy outright or to lease from her. Or, we could buy the entire building. We didn't need to think about it; we bought the building. Mom's house money helped us with the down payment. Unlike when he purchased Mac's Place, Adam agreed to use the money that way this time.

We moved into Sven and Astrid's apartment, converted the market into a gourmet kitchen store, and named it *The Chef Recommends*. Inside the market we installed a small bistro that served breakfast and lunch. I quit my job at the public relations firm to run the market full-time.

Our major focus is Reverie and Mac's Place, but the new endeavor does a brisk business, thanks to me. Okay, I'll admit Adam deserves a smidge of the credit too. Remember when I considered my degree in business to be benign? It isn't. You find it handy when you own a business. Adam does the product selection and food side, while I handle the marketing and manage the business affairs. Olivia is a regular customer and my best friend.

Adam wants to open a high-tech demonstration kitchen and offer cooking classes. He doesn't know this yet, but I talked to a local television station about giving him a cooking show and taping it at the kitchen once it is built. More than interested, the station manager asked their legal department to draw up a contract. I don't think Adam will agree, but we'll see. I want him on national television, too.

He would be a natural on a major network morning news program.

Tat no longer works for Adam. His departure was painful, but we are happy for him. He had switched from punk rock to acoustic and gained a following in the local music scene. His fans love his innovative interpretations of songs from standards to oldies to bluegrass, as well as the music he writes.

Over drinks one night, I convinced him to change his style. To be taken seriously in the music business, his look needed to match his sound. He agreed. My hairdresser gave him a new cut and color while I watched and sipped wine, and we shopped for new clothes. His new style is a cross between Bruce Springsteen and Neil Diamond. He spent thousands of dollars on plastic surgery to repair the holes in his ear lobes from the nasty gauge earrings. While he still didn't conform to conventional standards, he tidied up a bit and sanded down his rough edges. As I predicted, a record executive heard him play at a bar one night, and now Tat is either in the recording studio or on tour. We miss him, but he visits when he is in town for a gig.

My fraud allegation against the director of the non-profit agency led to her arrest and conviction. The investigation took years, because unraveling her web of deceit was difficult. The story was on the front page of the newspaper for days. The director had skimmed money from grants, falsified records, and destroyed the trust of her donor base. She had run a Ponzi scheme that didn't steal money from investors but bilked senior citizens of their financial assistance in their last days. The court found her morally bereft. The agency was forced to close, but reincarnated itself under new leadership. I now chair its board of directors, and it does meaningful work with measurable results. The press never caught wind of who alerted the Feds. Thankfully, my name never made the paper.

I tinker with my novel when I have the luxury of time. The force of the story sucks me in, to the detriment of more mundane matters such as bill paying, grocery shopping, and laundry. I still fantasize about being published. Even if nothing happens with the book, I am always happy to pull out Astrid's letters and my manuscript from my desk drawer and spend a lazy afternoon with her.

William is still with us, but his muzzle and paws are flecked with gray. He continues to be a character. He tried to not show it, but his heart was broken when Rosie cheated on him and produced a litter of puppies last summer. He forgave her when we brought home one of the pups; his tail wagged at warp speed at the sight of her. We named her Lavender . . . Astrid's and my favorite flower. I adore Lavender—or Lavie, as we call her—but raising a puppy in the city is hell. If you're brave enough to do it, I give you one important piece of advice. You must remove all shoes from your house. A puppy considers footwear fair game for teething material.

I continue to volunteer at the nursing home, where I read to a darling little old man. Unlike Astrid, he liked me from the start. He never married, but he was a brazen flirt and womanizer. He told me he left hundreds of broken hearts in his path. It didn't surprise me. I saw the photograph of him in his Navy officer's uniform; he had a Clark Gable swagger back then. A hole was left in my heart when Astrid died, but my little old man helps to fill the void with love.

When Adam and I can sneak away from San Francisco and our restaurants, we visit Mildred and the farm. She now takes yoga classes twice a week. The vision of her in downward facing dog pose staring at the crepe paper skin on her knees makes me chuckle.

On one of our visits I decided to make flower boxes for the railings of her front porch. I crafted the boxes out of golden knotty pine and painted the wood to match the front door. It dismayed me to see that the boxes had rotted through a year later. I didn't understand what happened. The ghost of Astrid was in the room when Mildred said, "Don't you know why people were buried in pine boxes in the old days?" I got her point.

Mildred visits us twice a year in return, and we go to the theater or ballet, take long walks through Golden Gate Park, and window-shop as though we carry rolls of money in our purses. She never lets Adam or me cook when she visits, and she makes beef stroganoff the night she arrives. She says our reprieve from cooking is payback for her use of our spare room. It's funny, but she leaves me to do the dishes after dinner while she watches her game show. I'll never complain, but she makes a mess of the kitchen when she cooks. How does she do that? She cooks for an hour, and I need two to clean up after her.

During Mildred's last visit, I told her I was going to redecorate the guest room and needed her help. I wanted to paint the room, buy all new furniture, and pick out fabrics for the bedding and curtains. She was excited about the project and demanded that we start on it right away.

The first store we went to was called *A Bun in the Oven.* "Oh, Meredith, dear," she said, "I don't think they sell bedroom furniture here. It sounds more like a bakery."

"It's a baby furniture store, Mildred," I said. "We're redoing the guest room as a nursery. I'm pregnant."